Praise for Kaitlin Bevis's
Daughters of Zeus . . .

"From the first paragraph, I was enthralled with this story. I read it all in one sitting and enjoyed every minute of it. What a great spin on a Greek myth! Move over, Rick Riordan!"
—Amazon Top Reviewer, Rita Webb, Author of *Daughter of the Goddess*

"I enjoyed Hades and Persephone's sweet romantic relationship. Persephone has her flaws, but she is likable and learns along the way. The author's writing is descriptive and entertaining. I am looking forward to the next book."
—Rebecca Foote @ Paranormal Muse

"Everyone needs to check this book out; I can't rave enough about it. Bevis is definitely a new talent to keep an eye out for. I give this 5/5."
—Sarah Brown @ Head Stuck in a Book

"I found this book to be a fun and fast-paced adventure through Greek mythology with a modern twist."
—Stephanie Ward @ A Dream Within a Dream

"*Persephone* is a fun, imaginative, smart retelling of my favorite myth, fusing modern culture with a rich world of magic. I had such a great time reading this."
—Amazon Top Reviewer, Molly Ringle, Author of *Persephone's Orchard*

"This story will completely suck you in. . . . This book is the first of a trilogy and I can't wait to see what's in store for these amazing characters.
—Amazon Top Reviewer, Melissa Groeling, Author of *Beauty Marks*

Books by Kaitlin Bevis

The Daughters of Zeus

Persephone

Daughter of Earth and Sky

The Iron Queen

Aphrodite

by

Kaitlin Bevis

ImaJinn Books

This is a work of fiction. Names, characters, places and incidents are either the products of the author's imagination or are used fictitiously. Any resemblance to actual persons (living or dead), events or locations is entirely coincidental.

ImaJinn Books
PO BOX 300921
Memphis, TN 38130
Print ISBN: 978-1-61194-781-6

ImaJinn Books is an Imprint of BelleBooks, Inc.

Copyright © 2016 by Kaitlin Bevis

Published in the United States of America.

All rights reserved. No part of this book may be reproduced in any form or by any electronic or mechanical means, including information storage and retrieval systems, without permission in writing from the publisher, except by a reviewer, who may quote brief passages in a review.

ImaJinn Books was founded by Linda Kichline.

We at ImaJinn Books enjoy hearing from readers. Visit our websites
ImaJinnBooks.com
BelleBooks.com
BellBridgeBooks.com

10 9 8 7 6 5 4 3 2 1

Cover design: Debra Dixon
Interior design: Hank Smith
Photo/Art credits:
Woman in water (manipulated) © Katalinks | Dreamstime.com
Shell texture (manipulated) © Mariia Pazhyna | Dreamstime.com

:Laqw:01:

Dedication

To my favorite **brother,** Tyler Bithell. Your encouragement and support means the world to me.

Chapter I

ONCE UPON A TIME, there was a woman made of stone. She was beautiful and perfect and strong. Blind to her beauty, Pygmalion took a chisel and reshaped her to better fit his own desires. Still, though her flesh softened and her shape altered, she remained strong and unchanged within.

Frustrated, the man appealed to the gods. "The women of Cyprus are all unsuited for a man of my station. Breathe life into this stone, and I shall build a great temple in your honor."

"The city of Cyprus is filled with women made of flesh and bone," the Goddess of Wisdom reasoned. "Perhaps the problem does not lie with them."

Artemis nodded. "Do not blame the prey when you are not worthy of the hunt."

"Never." Ares's eyes glittered with disdain.

But Pygmalion found a surprising ally in his quest. "Build me a temple that touches the sky, and the woman will be yours," decreed the God-King.

Pygmalion agreed, and when he set the last stone of the temple into place, Zeus breathed life into the statue, hollowing out her insides and removing every trace of who she once was to replace her very essence with what Pygmalion wished her to be.

According to the myth, the statue became a perfect wife. Beautiful, dedicated, and obedient to Pygmalion's every whim.

But I know better than anyone that perfection has a price.

A STRING OF YELLOW bile connected my chin to the rim of the toilet seat. I didn't have time for this. Eight minutes until the meeting, two more for Persephone to realize I wasn't simply running late, and *maybe* three before she came after me. Fifteen minutes in total if my luck held. I needed to get to work. "Get yourself together, Aphrodite."

Don't cry. Zeus's whisper reverberated in my skull. *Never cry.*

My stomach heaved, but I had nothing left. The hollowness in my gut burned around the edges. Leaning back, I drew my knees to my chest and wrapped my arms around them.

"Just a nightmare," I whispered, though the inadequate word made me sound like a scared little girl trembling over an imagined monster. Zeus was real. Real dead, yeah, but facts never mattered in the night when my carefully controlled thoughts broke free to wreak havoc on my sleeping mind. Alone in the dark, I knew what I'd never admit to myself awake. Zeus would never be dead. Not to me.

There's more than one way to achieve immortality. You don't actually have to be a god, or live forever, not if you can screw someone up so much they can't forget you no matter how hard they try. When you live in someone's fears, in someone's nightmares, you never die. Not really.

I pulled myself off the ground, acutely aware of the seconds ticking by. Glancing at the mirror, I realized there was no way I'd be able to get myself presentable in time. Even *I* needed a break from worshipping at the porcelain god to look presentable.

"Okay." I took a deep breath and cast a glamour. Piece by piece, I put myself together until the illusion of perfection settled over me like finely fitted armor.

Glamours allowed gods to change their appearance. The changes could be subtle, such as how I'd changed the color of my dress to bring out my eyes, or vast, such as Zeus disguising himself to look like some unfortunate woman's husband or household pet. I didn't do full-body glamours. But the little touches packed a punch. There's power in beauty. And I needed every advantage I could get.

The doorbell rang, and I swore under my breath. Persephone never asked to come in. She ported through the shields I kept around my tiny beach house like they were nothing. My mind ran through a mental list of everyone who knew where I lived as I stepped out of the bathroom.

Persephone.

Okay, short list. Who would be at my door at three in the morning?

"Who's there?" I called, closing the bedroom door to hide the tangled and twisted sheets. My hand trailed along the banister as I walked down the stairs. Thanks to a small, open floor plan and minimalist furniture, I could almost see every inch of the place. No one hid within these walls.

I hesitated when I reached the door, listening. Surf crashed against the sand, but no other sound penetrated the walls. A glance through the peephole only showed a shadowy figure with broad shoulders. "Who is it?"

"Me."

Ares. Gritting my teeth, I tossed my hair back and unlocked the door. Fiery eyes greeted me, igniting months of pent-up anger toward my . . . what? Ex? Did our brief fling last summer even qualify as a relationship? Hell if I knew.

"Aphrodite." He stepped forward, the motion seeming almost unintentional as his eyes drank me in. When he came up against my shield, he frowned.

My hand itched to slam the door in his face. Instead, I called up my most dazzling grin, dropped the shield, and threw myself into his arms. "Ares!" I made myself laugh—as if he hadn't broken my heart—when he picked me up and spun me around. "I haven't seen you in—"

The word *forever* caught in my throat. Gods can't lie. Like, it's physically impossible. But human sayings have a tendency to get stuck in my head. "Thirteen months."

"You counted?" A cocky grin lit up his face as he set me down and crossed over the threshold. "Got you something." He drew a long, thin brown paper bag from his coat and handed it to me.

I withdrew the picture book inside, smiling when I saw the cover. It was a children's book on mythology. Flipping through the pages, I saw tiny envelopes begging to be opened, three dimensional cut-outs, and a hodgepodge of items fastened to the page like a scrapbook. As a new goddess, some of the nuances of humanity eluded me. Reading their take on our history, particularly how they framed myths for their children, gave me some insight. It was amazing how much humans got wrong.

I flipped to a page that showed a young girl reaching down to pluck a flower from the edge of the riverbed, seemingly unaware of the frost creeping up the petals. The heading proclaimed the myth of Boreas and Orethyia as the origin of winter. I turned to another section and my gaze landed on an illustration of Eris, the Goddess of Discord, holding a golden apple between Hera, Athena, and Artemis. I frowned, reading the section title. "The Divine Beauty Contest."

Ares glanced over my shoulder, his breath familiar against my neck. "If you'd been around back then, you would have won that. Hands down."

Whatever Ares saw on my face made his grin falter. He backed away. "I would have called, or come by, or *something* after—" He shoved his hands into the pockets of his leather jacket. "I'm sorry. I was stuck in a jar. It's a long story, and we're already running late."

Late? My insides went cold, and I set the book down on the kitchen countertop. "She told you." Persephone might be a powerful patron, but I'd worried more than once that her naiveté would be my downfall.

"Poseidon got a lead on the missing demigods, so he pulled her into a meeting to talk strategy. Nothing they think I'd be any help with." He smirked, stepping into my small living room, dark eyes flitting over the slim furnishings. No one took Ares seriously, and he liked it that way. "Hades stepped out long enough to ask me to collect you." A flicker of concern lit up his eyes as he looked me over. "And I can sense that you have enough power to dreamwalk. So why did he send me?"

Dreamwalking didn't take much power. But the ability to *stay* asleep long enough to slip into a dreamscape helped. Persephone understood why peaceful sleeping was an issue for me, so we'd arranged to meet early. If I couldn't show, she'd 'port in to physically pull me into the dreamscape.

"Believe me, I'm asking myself the same question." I moved backward until I bumped against the couch. Sitting down, I crossed my legs and studied Ares.

His gaze lingered on my legs for a split second before he caught himself and met my eyes. "Have the nightmares gotten that bad?"

You don't get to ask about my nightmares. I flashed my teeth at him. After Zeus died, Ares, Adonis, Hephaestus, and I took off on a celebratory road trip, thinking Zeus would never trouble us again. Right up until I'd woken up screaming. "You're really not going to elaborate on how you managed to get stuck in a jar for over a year? Seriously?"

"No, I'm really not." His hands stayed in the pockets of his jacket as he leaned against the wall opposite me, putting as much space between us as the small room would physically allow. "Look, I get it. I'm the last person you want to talk to about this, but you need real help, Aphrodite. If *this* is the full extent of Persephone's solution, I mean, it's cute, but—"

"Cute?" I held up my hand. "Let me stop you right there. Our queen is not 'cute,' she's—"

Ares rolled his eyes. "That whole queen thing was never made official."

"We swore over our *powers!* How much more 'official' does it get?"

"She gave them back after she killed Zeus."

Not mine. When Zeus created me, he'd thrown in an extra special quirk, making me obedient to anyone in his bloodline who outranked me. Only Persephone outranked me now. But refusing to break the vow of fealty that gave Persephone control of my powers made obedience my choice rather than his. Ares might see the distinction as meaningless; after all, I was hers to command either way. But some days, the subtle distinctions between Zeus's choices and mine were all that kept me sane.

"She's strong." Ares held out his hands in appeasement. "I'm not contesting that."

I rolled my eyes and picked up my phone, making a show of looking at the time while he talked.

"But strength doesn't trump knowledge. I've been around a lot longer. I know a thing or two about—"

"And we're officially late." I tossed the phone toward him before he could elaborate. He didn't know anything about what I'd been through. If he did, that night would have ended a *lot* differently.

Ares caught the phone by reflex. "You can't afford to be seen as weak."

My nails bit into the palms of my hands. "I know."

"I don't think you do." He crossed the living room, pausing to set my phone down on the arm of my couch. "You bound yourself to Persephone. On one level, her claim to you may help, because no one is going to touch you unless they want to deal with her. But if they *do* want to get to her or send a message, then you're a good way to do it."

"I knew the risks when I swore to her."

"Did you? Because you made a statement that you didn't have to. You chose a side—"

"There are no sides anymore." Zeus's death might have set me free, but the circumstances of his demise created a major power vacuum and completely upset the hierarchy of gods, who were long accustomed to picking sides and petty squabbles anytime they got together. Right now, everyone had fallen into an uneasy truce. I knew Ares didn't expect it to last long, but I had hope. This was a new pantheon. There weren't as many of us left, and our issues were a bit more meaningful than beauty contests and scandalous gossip.

"In this moment, yes. But peace never lasts. Persephone might slip up or Poseidon could go off the rails—hell, he's halfway there already. But something is going to happen and we're going to be at each other's throats again. We all know it. Why do you think we all spent the last few thousand years in our separate corners, ignoring one another?"

"To make it easier for Zeus to pick you off?" I suggested, studying the half-moon indentions my nails left in my palms. Zeus had been systematically killing off his offspring and absorbing their powers, unbeknownst to the Pantheon. That was, until he abducted Demeter's daughter and Poseidon's son. Going after the children of realm-rulers was too great an offense to ignore, so the Pantheon came together and fought Zeus in a bitter battle, heavy with loss.

"You made a statement, Aphrodite. But the only advantage you've got to back it up is charm. That's not always going to be enough."

I could do shields, healing, glamours, and all the standard stuff as well, but most of the gods that were left had received something extra from both of their parents. I only had one—Zeus. "You mean the charm I used to *completely* incapacitate you?" I snorted. "I'd say it's enough."

Charm, or charisma, is like mind control. If used correctly, I can look any human, and most gods in the eyes and make them do whatever I want. Lucky me, since gods need worship to survive. Since I'd only been created a couple of years ago, I didn't exactly have a cult following to support my existence.

Ares shifted, visibly uncomfortable at the reminder. "I'm not one of the gods you should be worried about."

I frowned, trying to figure out who he thought I *should* worry about. Athena, probably, though she'd always been friendly enough to me. Poseidon maybe? Only an idiot would let their guard down around him. Still, I considered everyone else in the Pantheon to be a friend.

"Let me help you." Ares stepped forward, closing the space between us.

I narrowed my eyes. "What I need, you can't give me."

Ares gritted his teeth. "Fine. But for now, we need a convincing reason to explain why we're late, not to mention why we're showing up together."

He had a point. The other gods wouldn't actually ask, but I didn't want to start the rumor mill churning with the idea that either Ares or I were too weak to dreamwalk without assistance.

"Okay, so it's the middle of the day in Bangkok." Ares's face screwed up in thought. "If we 'port into a traffic jam there, then we *could* say that we got caught—"

"How did you even survive before me?" I slid my arms around him, shivering when my skin came into contact with his cold jacket.

"Oh." Ares said, catching on. He lowered his mouth to mine. "Yeah, that'll work, too."

His lips burned against mine, warm and eager. Familiar. The kiss deepened, then multiplied. Ten kisses as short as one, one as long as twenty, and the entire universe dissolved into Ares's touch. For one precious second, I felt like more than a tool. More than Zeus's abomination willed to life. Some*one*, not something.

But his kisses were lies. And they hurt more than any truth I'd ever faced. Memories sprang to my mind unbidden. The whisper of fabric, a gentle caress, his lips against mine. *What you're looking for,* he'd whispered, *I can't give you.*

My back hit the couch, pinning his arm beneath me.

"Are you ready?" he asked, breaking away.

"Yeah," I whispered, my voice hoarse with what? Pain? Wanting? Whatever this feeling was, I didn't like it. Or maybe I liked it too much.

Ares pressed two fingers to my forehead and pushed me into the dreamscape.

Chapter II

SAND PRESSED against my back, not quite as hot as Ares's arms, but close. He pushed off me in a hurry and scrambled to his feet with a curse.

"By the Styx, Ares, get some clothes on," Artemis snapped, but the laughter in her voice undermined her ire. "But that's one mystery solved. You owe me money, Heph. I told you he wasn't missing. Just holed up with some piece of—Aphrodite!"

"Hi, Artemis," I managed to say, though I couldn't see her around Ares.

Ares held out a hand to help me up, and I flashed him a grateful smile. Dreamscapes followed the same shifting laws dreams did. You couldn't see past what was directly in front of you. There was no periphery, no glances of something in the corner of your eye, no awareness of anything lurking off to the side. Artemis would have been able to see Ares's bare back, but not much else. Since clothes can be summoned instantly in dreams, there would be some natural assumptions made about my own state of dress prior to entering the dreamstate, not to mention *why* we were late.

"About time you two showed up." A cold shadow fell over us.

I craned my neck, squinting against the sunlight blazing around a Poseidon-shaped silhouette. Short, spiky, bleach-blond hair completed his surfer-boy image. He didn't look much older than twenty-five, and never would, unless he glamoured himself to look older. Gods didn't age past their prime. Not physically anyway.

"Well, look what the tide washed in." I flashed Poseidon my prettiest smile and dropped Ares's hand.

"Really?" Artemis protested. "With *Ares?* I know you're new, Aphrodite, but I thought you were smarter than this. Did no one warn you about him? Athena, weren't you supposed to be on that?"

"Come sit with me, Aphrodite," Athena directed from somewhere to my left. "We should talk."

"Are we late?" Ares moved aside so I could take in the group of gods gathered at a wicker beach table a few feet away.

"Just a few minutes," Hephaestus replied from his seat. He glanced past Ares to me. "Good to see you, Aphrodite."

Half of Hephaestus's face looked like an unrecognizable web of twitching scar tissue with skin hanging in odd places. One eye socket drooped, empty and melted. The other half of his face looked completely normal. Perfect, even. I forced myself to focus on his good side when I met his eye and smiled. "You, too. Sorry to keep you guys waiting. We were—"

"TMI." Persephone pushed past Poseidon and swept me into a hug that smelled of wildflowers and sunshine. Her hands felt cold against my back, and I jumped, surprised at the unexpected chill. Since when did the frickin' embodiment of spring feel cold? "We can all fill in the blanks. How are you? It's been so long."

"I saw you at the last meeting," I reminded her, pulling back.

"A *month* ago." The small, fluffy blonde looked far too young to be a goddess of any importance, but two years ago, Persephone went from a neophyte goddess to a super power in the Pantheon when she defeated Zeus. As the heir to both Demeter and Zeus, and the wife of Hades, Lord of the Underworld, she ruled three of the four realms with undisputed access to the fourth, thanks to an unlikely friendship with Poseidon's deceased son. No single deity had amassed so much power since the days of the Titans. "We should—"

"I hate to interrupt," Athena said from somewhere behind Persephone. "But I have a lecture to give in the morning, so if we could move along, that would be great."

"Right." Persephone pulled me toward the remainder of the once great pantheon and dropped into a seat next to Hades at the end of the table.

Ares sandwiched himself between Hephaestus and Artemis, who promptly smacked the back of his head. "She's *three* years old."

I rolled my eyes as I slid out the chair next to Athena's. Technically, Artemis wasn't wrong about my age. But when a god is created rather than born, they come into the world mature. Physically and otherwise.

"Poseidon, I believe you were next on the agenda?" Hades asked, getting us back on track.

I gave myself one second to admire Hades's perfectly chiseled features, the electric blue eyes blazing behind the midnight black hair hanging in his face, and the amazing body that went with it. Then I took a deep breath and did my best not to drool. Hades was the epitome of taken.

"Yeah, sorry about the disruption." Persephone smiled at Poseidon.

Poseidon's entire demeanor shifted when Persephone turned her attention to him. His chin lifted, and his gaze stayed riveted on her face, not even flicking down the rest of her. "No need for apologies." He gave a cordial nod. "But perhaps I owe Aphrodite one for the location." He focused on me. "I wasn't sure how you'd feel about returning here, but I've put so much energy into this dreamscape that constructing another would be inconvenient."

Where were we? I glanced around for a clue, but didn't see anything distinguishing this beach from any other. *Oh.* He could only mean one place. Cumberland Island. Zeus had abandoned me on this shoreline moments after my creation. I'd spent days terrified behind a shield until Persephone found me.

Poseidon's ocean eyes churned, the color fluctuating with the sea, shifting from blue to green to brown, with white waves cresting in miniature around his pupils. When I didn't voice any objections to the locale, he returned his attention to Persephone. "I've got a lead on the missing demigods."

That got everyone's attention, and for good reason. Demeter had been the one to notice the uptick in missing person reports matching the description of demigods. And description would be all she could go on, since most humans don't believe in gods anymore, much less that George down the street was actually half of one. Hell, George probably didn't even know these days. But to anyone in the know, demigods stood out like a sore thumb. All demigods shared similar coloring. The ichor in their blood turned them gold to the extreme: hair, skin, eyes, everything except their actual blood looked golden, which made no sense to me, but I hadn't been around during creation to add my two cents in, so whatever.

"You could have led with that," Artemis said, scooting forward in her seat.

"I only wanted to explain this once." Poseidon cut a glance toward Ares and me, but before either of us could say a word in our defense, his gaze returned to Persephone like a magnet.

"I noticed an anomaly within this cruise line." Poseidon summoned a stack of brochures and passed the ink-laden papers down the table.

"Fantasy Cruises?" I struggled to hold the advertisement steady enough to read against the whipping wind. "What—? Poseidon, I appreciate the insane amount of detail you put into these dreamscapes, but really, can you cut the setting down a notch?"

The wind died down to a gentle breeze. "They leave with more passengers than they return home with," Poseidon explained. "No one seems to notice, which, if you know anything about human recordkeeping, is unusual in and of itself."

That last bit was for Persephone's benefit, as the rest of us knew *everything* about human recordkeeping. One perk of being created as a deity instead of being born like Persephone, was coming into existence with the accumulated knowledge of the gods—unless they deliberately withheld it—over the entirety of creation. There were exceptions, of course. We weren't omniscient. Unless prophecy was involved, future and current events were beyond our scope. But when it came to random human crap, we knew almost everything.

"You think people were charmed into forgetting them?" Artemis's dark eyes narrowed in concentration as she studied the brochure.

"Is that possible on this scale?" Persephone asked.

All eyes turned to me.

"I *might* be able to charm an entire ship into forgetting that I exist, but I mean, using enough power to pull off mass amnesia would be a stretch, even for me."

Poseidon summoned another group of papers and passed them down the table. "The memory loss regarding the person's existence doesn't last long—just the circumstances of their disappearance. Missing posters go up in a matter of days."

Athena handed me the sheets. I took one and passed the rest to Persephone, then studied the paper in front of me, which featured a smiling demigoddess named Otrera.

I swapped papers with Ares. Sure enough, his missing poster featured another demigod. Demigods weren't exactly common anymore. That this many would use the same cruise line seemed statistically impossible.

Poseidon rifled through more papers. "There are almost exactly as many missing demigods as missing passengers. I've sent spies on these ships, but they come back as clueless as the rest of the passengers. That means they were either charmed, or the passengers went missing in port. We need to get to the bottom of this. But to do that, we'll need someone with unrestricted access to both realms, who is too strong to be charmed."

In other words, he needed Persephone. But judging by the way her shoulders tensed, she didn't want to go.

Persephone gathered her wavy hair into a ponytail at the base of her neck. "I have no interest in pursuing an investigation in your realm at this time." She held the blond locks steady for a moment before dropping her hand with a sigh. The gesture made her look tired. I couldn't help wondering how things were going for her since Zeus's defeat.

"I'm aware of your reluctance to visit my realm. But we *need* to know what happened to the demigods." Poseidon's voice sounded gentle, as if he was trying to be nice, which somehow seemed even creepier than his usual lewd skeevyness. "You know I wouldn't be asking you to do this otherwise."

"She said no." Hades's voice left no room for argument. "Next option."

Persephone shot him a grateful smile, and I found myself struck at the contrast between the two of them. She seemed to radiate the very light he absorbed. When they were together, it almost hurt to look at them. I guess opposites *did* attract.

"Poseidon has a point," Athena interjected. "Persephone, I realize your plate is a bit full, what with three realms to run, but if you delegate *those* responsibilities, surely you'll have time—Something funny, Ares?"

Ares swallowed his snicker, looking chastened. "Actually, yeah. I'm imagining what Zeus or Demeter or any other realm ruler would have done to you if you'd suggested they take time from their rule for recon. I mean—" He paused, giving me a look so significant across the table that I sat up straighter. "Zeus used to send Hermes out for *everything*, including kidnapping his dates."

He had, hadn't he?

"Well, we all know how vested Zeus was in our survival," Athena said icily.

Persephone cleared her throat. "Hades, how many times have you set foot outside of your realm in the last millennia? Three?"

Hades nodded. "Sounds about right."

"How about you, Poseidon? Once? Twice?" Persephone arched an eyebrow at Athena. "You wanna give them a lesson on time management, too, or can we get back to the task at hand?"

Persephone had been under pressure to redistribute her power ever since she killed Zeus. Athena knew good and well *why* Persephone didn't want to visit Poseidon's realm, but implying Persephone wasn't competent enough to handle the responsibilities that came with her realms gave Athena the leverage she needed to keep applying that pressure.

"We are spread considerably thinner than we once were," Athena reminded Persephone. "We *all* need to take a more active role—"

"Why?" Hephaestus interrupted. "Since when do we care about demigods?"

"They're weaknesses. Our children can kill us," Poseidon argued. "So if someone is collecting them—"

"*Our* children?" Hephaestus glanced around the room. "I had a few spirits back in the day, but demigods? Never bothered. And as far as I know, most of you didn't either. Artemis? Hades? Persephone? Aphrodite? Any of you have children among the living?" He waited until we shook our heads before continuing, and I tried really hard not to notice that he hadn't included Ares among the childless. "Then they can't kill us."

"But Steele can," Athena said, referring to the only weapon in the world that could kill a god. "And despite your claim to have destroyed it all—"

"I did," Hephaestus insisted.

"—it's made a resurgence and been linked to the missing demigods. If something or someone out there is trying to collect our weaknesses, we need to know why." Athena's voice left no room for argument.

"Send me." Since I'd sworn fealty to Persephone, I could act as her proxy. Between gods, vows of fealty go much further than obedience or pledges of loyalty. Persephone could use me as an extension of her powers. She would never ask me. But I could volunteer.

"Aphrodite." Persephone's eyes widened. "No, you don't have to—"

"Thank you for the offer, Aphrodite, but this is a bit beyond you." Poseidon didn't even look at me. That would involve tearing his gaze from Persephone's face.

Hades narrowed his eyes, apparently as creeped out by Poseidon's intense focus on his wife as I was. "Unless someone else wants to volunteer, you're out of options."

Artemis studied me for a long moment before speaking. "Aphrodite has more charm than all of us combined, and, since she's sworn to Persephone, she can act on her behalf should matters move beyond Poseidon's realm. It's a perfect solution, right, Athena?"

Athena flashed her a tight-lipped smile. "Perfect is a strong word, but yes, I suppose it is the best alternative we can hope to come up with. Are you sure you're up to this, Aphrodite? You don't have much experience—"

"Neither does Persephone. And you were fine with sending her." I turned to Poseidon, raising my eyebrows. "May I have permission to travel in your realm?"

"It would seem I have no other options." Poseidon's smile didn't reach his eyes. "Your cruise departs in seventy-two hours." Tossing me a thick envelope, he added, "Don't be late."

Seventy-two hours, huh? That wasn't nearly enough time to shop.

Chapter III

THE HEAD CONCIERGE, Miguel, set my bags down on the marble floor of the entryway with a reverence generally reserved for holy artifacts. And let's face it, anything belonging to me was.

"Is this room more to your liking?" His pupils were wide under the influence of my charm.

Lemon-scented cleaning solution assaulted my nostrils as I glanced around the sun-filled room. The suite curved around the back of the ship. Taupe shades covered the floor-to-ceiling windows, which was just as well, since we were still in the port.

"There's a kitchenette through here with a fully stocked fridge." Miguel left the luggage at the door and walked around the bar. "Everything is complimentary, of course. If you need anything else, simply dial five on your phone and you'll reach your personal concierge. Life jackets"—he edged around the bar to open a door by the curved staircase—"are located in the half-bath." He motioned to a set of white cabinets. "Along with a safe, bathrobes, and towels."

I nodded, stepping out onto the balcony to take in the wicker lounge chairs, whirlpool, and dinner table. My view of the buildings crowding the Miami port tunnel would soon give way to endless ocean. I glanced down, enchanted by the way the steel-blue waves rippled against the ship like silk.

"You'll need these." He placed two plastic cards on the bar. "Your room keys act as a credit card for any on-board spending. All charges will be billed to the room. You'll also require the key anytime you wish to leave the ship. Should you need me, anytime, please let me know."

"Actually . . . wait." I rushed back into the room and pulled at my smallest suitcase, jerking to stop when the plush carpet rendered the wheels inefficient. "I guess here is fine." I grunted, unzipping the front pocket to reach one of the bright-yellow folders I'd tucked inside. Inside it, I'd put pictures of all the demigods who'd vanished off this ship within the last year. Holding the file out to Miguel, I asked, "Do you recognize any of these people?"

He flipped through the missing flyers, his expression morphing from eager to devastated with each sheet. "No." Miguel's shoulders sagged. "Is there *any* other way I can help you?"

"Could you show them to the rest of the crew?" Grinning at him to show that I wasn't upset, I waited until the disappointed steward met my eyes again. Then I eased off the charm a touch. Charm could be tricky. I couldn't have my new personal assistant throwing himself off the boat in a fit of despair, now could I? "If anyone recognizes them, bring them to me."

"Of course." He waited, his dark eyes adoring. "How else can I please you?"

I considered. If a swipe of the room key monitored every purchase, arrival, and departure, then maybe I could pinpoint exactly when the demigods went missing. "Would you be able to access the records from previous cruises?"

His dark hair fell into his eyes as he nodded again. "I can look them up by name or booking number. Would that be helpful?"

"Why, yes, it would." Looking at the records *after* everyone checked in would be more efficient. After all, identifying the demigods *about* to go missing was the first step in my plan.

I thought back to the picture Miguel took of me before I boarded the ship. "My picture is linked to my account, right?" If those pictures were in the system, a simple search would tell me how many demigods were on the ship. Then I'd know who to keep my eyes on.

"It is. We have to make sure the picture on the card matches the person holding it before they make any purchases or leave the vessel."

"Perfect. What time do you get off?"

"Eleven-thirty."

"I'll see you then."

He hurried out of the room. When the door closed, I kicked off my heels, enjoying the feel of the thick white carpet beneath my aching feet before climbing upstairs, dragging my smallest suitcase with me. The wheels thudded up each step as I yanked the heavy bag behind me. Even in February, Miami felt muggy. All I wanted to do was take a shower and change into something cool.

"Not too bad," I murmured, looking around the bedroom. It actually reminded me of the cookie-cutter beach house I'd charmed my way into back in Pebble Beach. Two white chairs and a small, glass-topped table were set up in front of the half-wall that allowed an unobstructed view of the living area below. A smaller windowed wall leading out to a tiny balcony stood adjacent to the staircase.

I grunted as I heaved my suitcase onto the king-sized bed with enough force to send a ripple of movement along the length of the white comforter. But I barely got the thing unzipped before I heard voices outside my room.

"I'm telling you, this is *my* room."

"No, sir." Miguel's heavily accented voice sounded out of breath, as if he'd just run a marathon. "This room belongs to a young woman, I—"

"Open. The. Door."

The lock clicked and I made my way to the staircase, determined to charm whoever came in the room into moving on.

Below me, the door swung open, slamming into the wall. The blue paintings shuddered, but held, and delicate clinking sounds came from the chandelier. A familiar demigod stepped over the threshold.

"Adonis," I breathed.

"Ask them to swear fealty to me." The memory of Zeus's voice echoed through my mind.

Adonis had been there, along with Ares, Hephaestus, and Persephone's priestess, Melissa. But only Adonis had been immune to my charm. He'd seen the way my body moved of its own accord, forcing me to obey Zeus's command. I'd known what would come next, but I was powerless to stop it. Zeus had planned to use me to force Ares and Hephaestus to swear over all their power until they turned to dust. Suicide by devotion. Then he'd planned to make me kill Adonis and Melissa for him. Not because they were a threat, but because killing them would hurt me. And then maybe, if I was very, very lucky, Zeus would have let me die instead of forcing me to live on as his puppet.

Behind Adonis, Miguel babbled apologies while making wild motions to indicate how Adonis had forced himself into the room. Neither one of us paid any attention to him.

"Aphrodite?" He looked dazed at the sight of me.

Memories bombarded me.

Words rose in me, filled my mouth, and pushed against my lips. Swallowing, I forced them down, but they tore at my throat. A strangled, keening wail filled the room, sounding so alien, so desperate and helpless, that, at first, I didn't place it as mine. I wouldn't do this to them. Zeus would kill them in an instant. I wouldn't—couldn't—Stop!

My lips parted of their own volition, and I clapped my hand over my mouth. Zeus crossed his arms, looking bored. I couldn't resist forever, and he knew it. Every fiber in my being pulled at me to obey his command.

I looked away from Zeus, but found I couldn't face the blind devotion in Ares's and Hephaestus's eyes. There was nothing left of them. All they wanted to do was please me. This was wrong. My vision blurred, and I blinked away the tears, looking to Adonis instead. His bravery and strength was telegraphed in his stiff posture and the trust in the eyes he kept glued to my face.

A small smile formed on his face, cool and confident. Just wait, *it seemed to say.* We'll get out of this.

And we had. All because of him.

"Is he traveling with you?" Miguel wedged Adonis's suitcase between the door and the frame. He looked ready to throw Adonis out of the room if I said no.

"You can go," I told Miguel, infusing enough charm behind the words to make sure he did as I asked.

"What—" Adonis asked when the door closed behind Miguel. "How— Why are you here?"

Oh, gods. I recovered from my shock enough to realize what Adonis being here *meant*. "You need to leave." I rushed down the stairs, nearly tripping in my haste to reach him before the cruise left shore. "Adonis you need to *go*. It's not—"

"This is *my* room," he argued, snapping out of his daze enough to grow defensive. "Bought and paid for. I don't know what you're—"

"—*safe*. You can't be on this ship." I reached for his bag as I grabbed his arm, propelling him toward the door. That I'd charmed my way into his room seemed too great a coincidence to process right now. For now, I just thanked the Primordials that I'd discovered him on board before it was too late. "Come on, I'll walk you back to the dock."

"What do you mean, it's not safe? He wrenched his arm free and grabbed his bag from me. "What is going on?"

"Demigods are going missing." I filled him in as best I could, stealing anxious glances toward the balcony to make sure the ship hadn't yet set sail. "It's not safe for you to be here."

Adonis swore, his eyes going to the chandelier as he digested what I told him. "I can't just leave," he said finally. "I'm here for work. It's this big event. We've got shoots scheduled at each of the ports and—"

"Any other demigods?" Demigods, particularly those in possession of charm, gravitated to fields like modeling, performing, or politics. What better way to get multiple demigods in one place than by targeting their most probable career paths? I made a mental note to check if the other cruises were geared toward any demigod-heavy fields.

"What?" Adonis shook his head. "None from my agency. Across the whole convention, maybe three or four." He swore again. "I've got to warn them."

Having three or four demigods on one ship was far too unlikely to be written off as coincidence. They were probably all targets. But if he told them, if they behaved differently because of what they knew, I might lose my chance to figure out who or what was taking them. "Let me handle that. In the meantime," I pushed him toward the door, "why don't we find your boss, and I don't know, maybe charm him into thinking you stayed on board the whole time? Do you want a raise? I think I can work in a raise. Let's just—"

He didn't budge. "What's your plan?"

"Right now? To get you off this boat." I clenched my jaw, wishing Adonis were a normal demigod I could just charm into leaving. But Adonis was special. Thanks to centuries of inbreeding, Adonis was not only immune to anyone else's charm, he seemed to have control over his own. The inbreeding bit isn't as gross as it sounds. Before Zeus died, he'd experimented with turning demigods to gods. Adonis's parents were both Zeus's offspring. As

Aphrodite

were their parents before that, and their parents before that. Making Zeus Adonis's grandfather, great-grandfather, great-great grandfather, and so on, on both sides.

Okay, maybe that is as gross as it sounds, but gods don't have the same incest taboo as humans. We don't pass on genetic material, just power.

Adonis leaned against the door. "I spent enough time with you last year to know that you're not infallible, Aphrodite. None of you gods are, no matter what you think." He pushed away from the door. "Demigods are going missing; *I'm* a demigod. So are my little sisters—"

"You have sisters?"

Adonis gave me a look that warned me that topic was closed. "What are you planning to *do* here? You're not wearing a glamour; why? Anyone who knows *anything* is going to look at you and see goddess. Is that part of your plan? Is the Pantheon using you as a distraction? Someone that random power signatures can be attributed to while Persephone or one of the gods works in the background?"

"How about I explain on the way." I pulled open the door, but Adonis shut it, keeping his arm pushed against it for good measure. With a frustrated sigh, I whirled on him, talking fast so he'd *leave* already. "I can't hide that there's a god on board, even with a glamour, because the power that it takes to maintain a glamour is something we can sense. Almost no one has heard of me. I figure it's better to let who or whatever is behind this notice me so they can write me off. Let them assume that I'm *not* one of the very few gods who could withstand the level of charm it takes to pull off what they're doing."

Adonis fell silent while he considered that, taking an infuriatingly long time to do so. "Okay, but what if instead of blending in, you used a glamour to look like us. Demigods can't normally control their powers, so any stray power could be explained away if you looked like one of us." The more he talked, the more excited he seemed to get about his idea. "There's this demigoddess I know—Elise. She was supposed to come to the convention, but she landed this skincare gig at the last minute. We could say it fell through. You could look like her and get taken *with* us. You'll get to learn everything that's going on and if you need to, you can teleport back to the rest of the gods to bring in the cavalry."

I rubbed my temples, trying to think of the fastest way off the ship. We'd have to go to the main deck, right? "That's . . . an elaborate plan."

"Thanks. So . . . ?"

I tugged at the door again to no avail. "I could look like her, but I couldn't claim to *be* her. I can't lie, remember? So what if someone asks her a question that I *can't* answer? Don't you think I'd actually draw *more* attention to myself if I tried and failed to impersonate a demigod?"

"But you've lost the element of surprise," he protested. "So whatever is behind this is going to see you coming. What about the demigods that have already gone missing? By being so obvious, you might actually be putting them in danger. And then there are the demigods still on board. Did you even consider them?"

There wasn't a good way to tell him this wasn't a rescue mission. I wasn't supposed to stop the demigods from going missing. Just observe, report, and let the realm rulers figure out what they wanted to do with the information.

As it turned out, I didn't need to say anything. Adonis studied me for a long moment, his mouth dropping open as he figured out what I wouldn't say. "We're expendable to you, aren't we? You don't actually care that we're going missing. You just want to make sure whatever happens to us isn't a threat to you."

"Adonis . . ." I dropped my eyes, unwilling to meet his gaze.

"And you wonder why they all hate you." His gold eyes locked to mine, smoldering with rage. "The few mortals who even know gods exist."

No, we all knew. We'd never had to wonder. The boat bobbed on the waves as we left the port. I focused on the movement, the swaying chandelier, the subtle sound of the ocean beyond the glass walls, uncomfortable with the turn this conversation had taken.

Adonis clenched his fists. "You're callous, and selfish, and—"

Okay, enough. Calming ocean crap could only drown out so many insults. "You do realize you're not speaking to a collective here, right? Just me."

"What, like you're any different?" Adonis shook his head in disgust. "You've known for over a *year* Zeus wasn't the one causing demigods to go missing. Why didn't you warn me?"

"They aren't dead." Hades would have seen them in the Underworld.

"So what?" Adonis crossed his arms, then dropped them as if he'd realized he'd mirrored my pose. "You guys assumed 'not dead' equaled fine?"

"Zeus said he didn't touch the demigods, but that doesn't mean he wasn't behind them going missing. And the disappearances seemed to stop when he died. If I'd known you were still in danger, Adonis, I would have warned you."

"You would?"

"Of course." I'd throw myself into the hottest pits of Tartarus before I let Adonis get hurt. He'd trusted me. Even knowing Zeus could have made me kill him with a word, he'd put his faith in me. That meant more to me than he'd ever know. I grabbed his hands. "I'm warning you *now*, aren't I? You're my friend. You're not expen—"

"We are not friends," Adonis exploded.

My breath caught. Adonis's faith in me had kept me going through one of the *worst* moments of my life. Adonis's strength held me together when giving in felt like the only option. He hadn't just stopped me from doing something I'd spend the rest of my life regretting, he saved my life. I wouldn't still *exist* if it wasn't for him. But now, he was looking at me as if he'd rather I didn't.

"You really don't get it, do you?" His golden eyes raked over my face, full of anger and disgust. "What is it you're expecting here, Aphrodite? Gratitude? You think you can just tell me my entire *species* is being rounded up, never to be heard from again, and expect me to leave? To fall over my feet, grateful you deigned to warn me? Hell, no. I'm not going anywhere." He snatched his bag and headed toward the stairs. "If anyone should leave, it should be you. I can't be charmed into forgetting anything. Do your god thing and put a trace on me. Assuming 'not dead' doesn't equal catatonic, I'll fill you in on all the details when you find me."

Still stunned, I shook my head. "I'm not using you as bait."

"I'm a hell of a lot more motivated to get to the bottom of this than you," he argued. "Go do whatever it is that you do. I'll make sure my people stay safe."

"I can't track you." There were gods that could trace power signatures from across the globe, but I wasn't one of them. "But if you insist on staying . . ."

"I do."

"Then I guess I'll be needing a new room." I turned to go get my bags, unwilling to let him see how much his words had hurt.

"There are no other rooms." Adonis sounded tired. "They offered me this upgrade because mine was double-booked. Then they tried to kick me off the boat entirely because of you."

What, was he expecting an apology? I forced a smile to my face. "Somehow, I don't think I'll have trouble finding a place to sleep."

"Because you're going to charm someone out of their suite? No."

I raised my eyebrows at that. "And who exactly is going to stop me?"

Adonis looked like he wanted to protest, but then his shoulders slumped. "You know what?" He grabbed his bag and headed toward the stairs. "I don't care what you do. I've got to get ready for orientation. You can get your stuff out of here when I leave."

Awkward silence filled the room as Adonis lugged his suitcase upstairs. I kept my gaze fastened on the white carpet, feeling ashamed, defensive, and stunned all at once. Maybe I *should* have worried more about the other demigods. But it wasn't as if I *wanted* any harm to come to them. I wasn't a monster. Just not all that compassionate.

Persephone would care.

Yeah, well, Persephone was perfect and she had the power to do something about the missing demigods. I'd had my own stuff to deal with since Zeus died. So what if I'd assumed gods more capable than me were investigating the disappearances. I wasn't wrong. As soon as something popped up that I could help with, I'd jumped in, hadn't I? So why did I feel like that wasn't enough, all of a sudden?

What do I care what some half-breed thinks of me? I tossed my hair, trying to collect myself. To ignore how hurt he'd made me feel. Whatever. He'd made my job easier. Now all I needed to do was watch him, see what happened, then report to Poseidon.

Screw Adonis.

Chapter IV

WHEN ADONIS LEFT for orientation, I followed. So maybe I couldn't charm him into leaving, and I lacked the physical strength to drag him off the boat. That didn't mean I couldn't charm a few passengers into helping me out. I'd get a certain satisfaction in watching him be dragged off the ship.

Right up until I had to report to Persephone and Poseidon that I'd made a scene using charm.

Shoulders slumping, I realized that there was nothing I could do to remove Adonis without putting my mission in jeopardy. So I might as well use him. Chances were good that the other demigod models would be at this orientation as well. I needed to get a look at the potential targets.

I caught up to Adonis on the staircase. He tensed, but he didn't slow down or acknowledge my presence. By the time we reached the promenade deck, I had a pretty good idea where we were headed. When Adonis made a beeline for the main auditorium, I slowed.

"You know, if I had a gorgeous goddess following me, I'd slow down." An unfamiliar demigod stood beside the silver set of double doors. He looked taller than Adonis, but way more muscular.

"Tantalus." The muscular demigod offered me his hand, then shifted, grabbing me before I walked into the "Private Function" sign mounted on a gold pole. "Watch out."

Letting out an embarrassed laugh, I stumbled into Tantalus. I shouldn't be so hard on myself; I've only been walking for three years. It takes practice. "Thanks."

"Here for the convention?" Tantalus kept his hands on my shoulders and didn't move away from me or out of the way of the door.

"Um . . . actually . . ." I trailed off, stepping away from him and through the double doors into the darkened auditorium. I could charm him into not telling anyone about my investigation. I could even charm him into reporting to me if he saw anything suspicious. But in a room like this, there was no telling how far even a whisper could carry, not to mention who or what else would see the power signature from my charm. I searched for another reason for being here, but drew a blank. "I wanted to go on a cruise?"

I scoped out the rest of the room, taking a moment to get my bearings. Booths dotted the room, arranged in semicircles so everyone seated could see the stage, but no one sat. Sitting would indicate a time commitment no one seemed to want to give.

Stopping at the edge of the auditorium, I leaned against the back wall, soundproofing fuzzies tickling my bare arms. Deep in the crowd, Adonis stood out like a golden beacon, somehow managing to almost glow despite the dim lighting. He was engaged in an animated discussion with a woman who looked far too plain to belong to a modeling convention.

Tantalus followed me with a smirk and leaned against the wall beside me, hand planted right next to my head. "I'd buy that, if I ran into you on deck."

I smiled, looking him over. "Maybe I'm just enjoying the view."

Tantalus stepped in front of me, holding out his hands as if he were the gods' gift to man. Which, technically speaking. . . . "Well, look no further, sweetheart."

A violent shudder wrenched through me at the term of endearment. I wrapped my arms around myself as if I'd shivered.

"Cold?" His eyes roamed over me. "If you want, we can ditch this and go someplace warmer." The leer in his voice left little doubt that he meant his bed.

I considered his proposition. Well, not *that* angle of his proposition. I preferred men who worshipped me, not themselves. But Tantalus wouldn't question me following him around. He'd actually welcome the attention. And I wouldn't be heartbroken if something happened to him. That made him good bait. "What room are you staying in?"

He rattled off the room number. "It's one of the nicest on the ship. I could show you."

Adonis touched my arm, and I started in surprise. I hadn't noticed him coming this way at all.

"Can I have a word?" Adonis's question may have been directed at me, but his gaze never left Tantalus.

Tantalus shrugged, moving back almost enough for me to avoid brushing against him as I edged away from the wall. "She's all yours." His tone made the unspoken words "for now" as loud as if he'd shouted them.

I let Adonis escort me farther into the auditorium, but turned and waved a few fingers at Tantalus as we walked away.

"Stop that." Adonis whirled on me, gold eyes flashing.

"Why?" I tilted my head, and a lock of red hair fell over my shoulder. "Worried the evil goddess is going to hurt your friend? Oh wow, he's still looking at us." I waved, flashing Tantalus a flirtatious smile. "Don't worry, I don't think he'll mind my company."

Adonis gave me a flat look. "Are you serious?"

I kept my smile pleasant. "As a heart attack." Which, all things considered, wasn't terribly serious to gods, but I liked the phrase. "I can get all the information I need watching him, without the annoying attitude."

Adonis opened his mouth to protest, but I held up a hand to cut him off. "I'm not going to chase after you, Adonis. Not in your wildest dreams. And if you're expecting me to apologize or beg for your understanding, you are sadly misinformed. Because of our history, I told you why I was here and offered to get you somewhere safe. But that was just a courtesy."

Adonis snorted. "A courtesy?"

"You aren't entitled to a rescue mission just by virtue of being a demigod," I reminded him. "People go missing all the time without divine intervention. When's the last time you personally made any effort to find out why?"

He clenched his jaw, but didn't reply.

"I have no plans to hurt your friend," I assured him. "Or take advantage of him, or whatever it is you think we 'monsters' do, but—"

"It's not him I'm worried about."

And what did he mean by that? The crowded room burst into applause before I could respond.

"Ladies and gentlemen," called out yet another demigod who'd waltzed out on to the stage. "Welcome to Model Madness."

"Three or four demigods across the entire convention?" I challenged, while the demigod launched into a speech. Something about work, fun, and charity. I couldn't decide if he wanted to sell me something or get me *really* pumped up about being here.

Adonis shrugged. "Counting them. Tantalus works for another agency. Narcissus," he motioned to the demigod on stage, "runs my agency and the convention. And I already told you about Elise backing out at the last minute." He shrugged again. "There could be more I don't know about, but I doubt it. We're kind of a community."

Yeah, I'd already learned that much from Persephone's head priest, Orpheus. The demigods of today were so lucky. Back when Olympus stood, they didn't have Internet access to track one another down and form support groups.

"Adonis!" A tall, leggy, demigoddess broke free from the crowd and flung herself into his arms.

Adonis embraced her, but the movement seemed more out of reflex than affection. "Elise? I thought you got a deal with—"

"I changed my mind." She met Adonis's eyes with a look that made me think she was talking about something more than a career choice.

"That's . . . great?" Adonis's smile looked hesitant.

Elise gave Adonis a quizzical look, then started in surprise when she noticed me. "You're a—"

"Hi." I held out a hand. "I'm—"

"You know what? I don't want to know." She turned her attention back to Adonis, dismissing me as though I was beneath her notice.

My mouth hung open. Had that just happened? I was a *goddess*. I didn't get dismissed. I dismissed people. Gritting my teeth, I focused my attention on the stage as the crowd erupted into another round of applause. I could have spat something witty and snarky right back at her, but arguments with mortals were beneath me. She wasn't worth my time.

You keep telling yourself that, Aphrodite. Delusions are fun. If only insulting other people was as easy as insulting myself. Scowling, I studied the demigoddess out of the corner of my eye. Female demigods were rare. Divine genetics triggered the "Y" chromosome more often than not. Good thing, given how much stronger demigoddesses were.

Hercules got all his press for killing monsters in what looked like clever ways. But in reality, his charm drove those creatures to their death. They knew he wanted them dead, so they complied. People remembered the monsters. They forgot that his charm also drove his wife to kill her children and herself. In the end, he got so out of control that Zeus had activated the ichor in Hercules's blood to transform the hero into a god.

But compared to Helen of Troy, Hercules was small potatoes. Hercules's charm killed a few monsters; Helen's destroyed an entire civilization. I needed to learn this girl's lineage. She might not have any powers at all, but if she did, they'd be exponentially stronger than a male demigod's of the same bloodline.

Narcissus's golden eyes landed on me and widened. As soon as he wrapped up his speech, he hopped down from the stage, making a beeline for our weird trio.

"Please be with my agency," Narcissus begged when he arrived. "To stand out in *this* crowd is an accomplishment."

Adonis and Elise gave Narcissus a flat look.

"I mean," he said, backtracking. "Oh come on, look at her. You're all stars, anybody can see that, but you have to admit, she burns a bit brighter. E—" He snapped his fingers. "Get over here."

For a second, I thought he meant Elise. Then a beautiful woman with wide, intelligent eyes hurried across the auditorium after Narcissus, dodging tables and lingering models with a nymph-like grace. "E" whipped out a tablet and held a pen at the ready.

Narcissus looked me over. "Is she with you, Donnie?"

Was I? I raised an eyebrow and looked to Adonis.

He glanced between me and Elise, then let out a long-suffering sigh. "Yeah," he decided. "She's with me."

"With you?" Elise sputtered. "What do you mean *with* you?"

"Can we talk about this later?" Adonis asked in an undertone.

"Um. No." Elise's gold eyes flared and she drew her hands to her hips. "Narcissus, I apologize for being so unprofessional, but we were actually talking when you—"

"It's fine." Narcissus said with a dismissive wave of his hand. "You two can go."

"Adonis?" Elise tilted her head.

Adonis gritted his teeth, looking between Elise and me. "This isn't what it looks like, and I'd love to explain. Later maybe. But right now—"

"You ever consider a career in modeling?" Narcissus asked me, oblivious to the drama playing out between the two models. "Your kind needs all the exposure you can get, right?"

"Um . . ." My kind, huh? Modeling wasn't an uncommon cover career for a god struggling to find worship. We needed the worship, and we couldn't lie, which made pursuing acting or most other careers that threw you into the limelight difficult. But I had charm. I could get all the worship I needed simply walking through a crowded room.

"Aw, come on. A pretty girl like you?" Narcissus raised his eyebrows at me. "Sure you have. E, draw up the paperwork."

"Draw up the paperwork?" E had, at least, noticed I hadn't agreed.

"She's not here for—" Adonis protested, but Narcissus cut him off.

"Don't want me eating up all your girlfriend's time?" Narcissus ignored Elise's offended squeak at the word girlfriend. "I get ya. I wouldn't want to let her leave my sight either if I were you. I can work her into your shoots, if you want. I mean, geeze, look at you two." His golden eyes darted between us. "Step out of your heels, darlin'."

"What?" I gave Adonis a confused look, but even he looked taken aback at Narcissus's request.

Adonis shrugged, so I obliged. There weren't many models left in the room, but the few who remained did a double take when they saw me step out of my shoes.

"Stand closer."

Adonis and I moved until we were standing side by side. Beneath my feet, the carpet felt compressed and moist. Like the thin fabric was sweating.

"Perfect, E, look. They fit together like a fuckin' puzzle."

"They fit together." Her eyes darted up from her tablet every so often, as if she was trying not to look occupied by something on her screen. Was she playing a game? Why bother hiding it from her boss? Throughout this entire conversation, Narcissus hadn't so much as looked at her.

Narcissus studied us for a moment, his fingers hooked on the belt loops of his khakis. "I'd buy whatever you two were selling. Hell, yeah."

"Are you kidding me?" Elise stared at Narcissus as if he'd gone mad.

Okay, enough. I stepped back into my shoes and moved away from Adonis. "I'd only be in Adonis's shoots?" That would give me better access than I could hope to achieve without using charm.

"Of course."

"I'm willing to consider that."

"E, send her the paperwork. Adonis's suite, I presume."

Adonis opened his mouth, then closed his lips in a tight line, nodding.

"She's *staying* in your room?" Elise demanded.

"Elise . . ."

"Forget it." Elise shook her head and walked off.

Adonis watched her go, equal parts relief and regret evident in his expression.

I cleared my throat, drawing Narcissus's attention back to me. "I'm not signing anything." Gods can't lie, and who knew what this guy would try to work into his contract.

" 'Course not." He winked at me. "And even if you did, I somehow doubt you have a proper paper trail. But while your word alone is good enough for me, we shoot advertisements and no company is going to pay for photos without a written release. If I can't sell you, there's no reason to take your picture. How about I sign the paperwork for you later, and work out all those pesky details?"

"Mmm . . . still not going to allow you to put my name on something I don't understand. Walk me through the contract over dinner?" I needed to know who he'd spoken with to arrange the convention. Did someone suggest the cruise to him, or did he come up with the idea on his own? Where did he advertise Model Madness?

More likely than not, the information would be useless. Melissa and I had managed to hunt down Adonis last year using nothing more than social media. Thanks to their distinctive features, demigods weren't difficult to track down if anyone really wanted to find them. But still, there might be a chance I'd glean some detail important to my investigation.

"I'd be delighted. Tomorrow at seven? I'll drop the contract off in your room in a few hours. You can look everything over, come up with any questions you like. In fact—" Narcissus paused, considering. "Why don't you do a shoot with Adonis tomorrow to see if the job is to your liking?"

I glanced at Adonis. He rolled his eyes, but didn't object.

I forced a smile to my face. "Why not?"

Chapter V

ADONIS KEPT AN arm in front of the elevator door until we were both inside. But not in a polite, "here, let me get that for you" way. No, he *held* the door back as if the heavy contraption could spring free and crush him at any moment. Once we were both clear of the track, he drew his hand inside in a flash and hit the button for our deck, his shoulders relaxing when the elevator rose without incident.

"Okay ... why?" I motioned to his arm, then waved at the elevator door.

"I saw this movie once ..." Adonis shuddered, moving his hands toward his neck before jerking them down as if he hadn't realized they were in motion. "Elevators make me nervous, that's all."

"Must have been one hell of a movie." I studied my distorted reflection in the silver door, unsure how I felt about the way my body stretched and contorted depending on how I moved. "Do you want me to set the record straight with your girlfriend?"

"Ex-girlfriend," Adonis corrected as the elevator slowed to a stop. "And talking to her won't help. She's not upset because she thinks I'm with someone else; we both moved on a while ago."

"Didn't seem like it to me."

"No, it's not—" Adonis swallowed hard and held the elevator door back until we were both free of the metal confines of the apparent death trap. "She's like me."

I frowned. "Like you?"

"Whatever I am? She's the same. I met her parents. They're both demigods."

I felt the hair rise on the back of my neck. A demigoddess with Adonis's weird lineage would have an insane amount of charm, and she'd be completely immune to mine. Could she be responsible for charming everyone on the other boats? No one knew the true extent of Zeus's stupid science projects.

Adonis fell into step beside me as we headed down the hall. "That's why we broke things off. I couldn't get past what Demeter said, about Zeus having a female version of me out there that I'd ..." He trailed off, rubbing the back of his neck. "You know, be 'compelled' to breed with." Adonis's expression twisted, as if he'd tasted something foul. "So you can see how rooming with a goddess, after I dumped her because I didn't want anything to do with gods, might set her off." He frowned searching his pockets as we approached the door to the suite. "Where did—Right. They never gave me a key."

"Here, I've got mine." I slid my key card into the lock slit.

"Thanks." Adonis walked past me into the room. "Helluva day, huh?"

"For you, too?" I laughed, stepping out of my shoes. "There's an extra key on the counter. You can have that one."

"I appreciate it, but I'll need to get my own if I want to get on and off this ship when we reach a port," Adonis reminded me. He moved to the fridge, opened the door, and stared inside it for a moment, as if the contents might have shifted while we were gone. After a long minute, he asked, "You thirsty?" When I nodded, Adonis grabbed two water bottles out of our fridge and tossed one to me.

I caught the bottle and sank onto the white couch, letting my shoulders unknot as I leaned back. Sitting down instead of investigating seemed wrong, inefficient, but I couldn't think of anything else I could look into before Miguel gave me access to the computers. "I'll have Miguel take care of it."

The cushion dipped when Adonis sat on the opposite end of the couch, propping his feet up on the wicker table. He looked so dejected about his run-in with Elise that I took pity on him.

"You can do better."

"Huh?" He didn't even lift his head off the couch when he looked at me, leaving one cheek pressed against the thready fabric.

I shrugged. "Just saying. You could do better than Elise."

"Thanks?" He leaned forward, hunching over so his elbows rested on his knees. "I know she didn't come off great, but she's not that bad. I actually—" He shook his head. "Doesn't matter. After I found out what . . . I couldn't—Ah, never mind." He leaned back against the couch, staring up at the ceiling. "I'm not making any sense."

"You are, though." I took a sip of my water. "Being a living science experiment sucks, believe me, I understand. Even the most innocuous choices can feel . . ." I trailed off, unable to think of a strong enough word to capture what Zeus had done to us. Different methods, same result. We were both built to his specifications.

"Programmed?" Adonis offered, catching my eye.

"Exactly." My throat went dry. He *got* it. He got me. I swallowed hard, dropping my gaze from his, feeling flushed.

Adonis opened his mouth as if he was about to say something but a knock at the door cut him off.

When he rose from the couch, I waved a hand, motioning for him to stop. "I'll get it." I doubted anyone who bothered knocking intended to whisk Adonis away into missing demigod land, but why take the chance?

"Miguel," I exclaimed when I opened the door. "Just the man I wanted to see."

Miguel stared at me with adoration and handed me a manila envelope. "This was to be delivered to Mr. Eros's other room. It was marked urgent, so I went ahead and—"

"Mr. Eros?"

Miguel looked pointedly over my shoulder at Adonis and I blinked. Right. Last names. Humans had them. "Thank you." I passed the envelope to Adonis. "Could you do us a favor? Adonis here needs a room key . . ."

It didn't take long for Miguel to get everything settled. When he left, promising to return with Adonis's room card before the night was over, Adonis thanked him, closed the door, and ripped open the envelope. "Contract," he announced. "I'm gonna head upstairs and read this over."

"Why?" The contract was for me, after all.

He turned the contract around, signature page on top. For a moment, I could only focus on the beautiful, calligraphy-styled signature of Narcissus's name. Wow, Narcissus had gorgeous handwriting. Then the third signature line registered. Adonis's contract must have changed to accommodate mine.

"I need to make sure my shoots didn't change too much." Adonis handed me a second copy of the contract before heading up the curved staircase. "Looks like your trial shoot is early tomorrow. See you in the morning."

The morning? "Aren't you going to dinner?"

Adonis reached the top of the staircase and shook his head. "I'll call room service in a bit. Did you need anything up here before I get settled in?"

I nodded and grabbed my stuff from upstairs, taking the hint that I'd be sleeping on the couch. Not that it mattered. Gods don't need sleep. We're capable of it, of course, like eating, but it's not necessary for survival.

When I returned to the couch, I paused to grab a notebook and a pen from my luggage. For something written in legal-speak, the contract seemed remarkably straightforward. I still took my time going over the paperwork, but either Narcissus was much more honest than he came across, or he was smart enough not to piss off a goddess.

Afternoon transitioned to evening with clouds rolling in with such subtlety, I didn't notice how dark the room had grown until I found myself squinting at the notebook. The waves grew rough, sending the ship rocking back and forth in a way that made me glad I was immune to motion sickness.

Lightning flashed on the horizon, drawing me to the balcony like a moth to a flame. I pressed my hand to the sliding door as a crack of thunder reverberated through the thin glass. Then, without further thought, I opened the door and stepped out into the storm.

Chapter VI

RAIN SPLASHED against my upturned face as I stepped onto the narrow strip of balcony that wasn't covered by the roof of the deck above. Laughing, I spun around, arms spread. Lightning flashed and thunder rumbled, but I didn't care. I raised my voice, shouting back at the storm with wordless joy, and grinned, knowing that if it was raining where they were, Hephaestus and Ares would be doing the same thing.

"What are you doing?" Adonis's voice brought me to an abrupt halt. He stood just inside the suite. The balcony had more length than width, so he couldn't be more than a lounge chair and a half away from me. Still, the doorway magnified the distance between us. As if we stood in different worlds.

My world was more fun. "I'm celebrating." I spun around again, raindrops flinging off my skirt. "You'd know all about this if you'd come on that road trip for longer than a day and a half."

"Celebrating *what*?" Adonis's eyebrows were at it again, morphing his expression from wary to confused to incredulous. "And how? By pissing off the people in the next room?"

"Our room is shielded. No one can hear us." I leaned against the slick metal bars separating me from an eleven-deck drop into the choppy, cobalt waves. The boat lurched, plunging further into the storm.

"Would you—?" Adonis held out a hand, jolting forward in alarm.

"I'm not going to fall." I laughed. "And what do you mean 'what am I celebrating?' Are you kidding?" Lightning flickered over the sea. "This!" My outstretched hand gestured at the entire storm: the wall of thick, black clouds dominating the horizon, the storm-tossed waves, everything.

"This?" Adonis didn't seem to get it.

"Zeus's symbol. His . . . his identity." I tilted my head up, letting the rain drip down my body and drew in a deep breath. "Every storm, every flash of lightning. He took power in it." My face hurt from smiling so much. "But not anymore."

The thunder cracked in the sky, and I pushed off the rails and spun around, yelling again. "Because of us. We were a part of that." I couldn't contain the joy in my raised voice. "*We* defeated him."

Adonis leaned against the glass door, crossing his arms, his expression dubious. "Yeah, but didn't Persephone—?"

"We helped." Water gathered on the teak floor beneath my feet, cool, but still not as cold as the A/C in the suite. My mind flashed back to the road trip—the farther away we drove, the more real Zeus's death had become. "On the road trip, Ares"—I swallowed hard, unwilling to let my anger taint this amazing thing he'd done—"made us promise we'd never forget that Zeus might still be alive now, if not for us. That *we* did something good, no matter what else—" I kicked at the water beneath my feet, sending droplets back into the air with a blast of power, making them sparkle before they fell. "Every time there's a storm, we celebrate."

Adonis raised his eyebrows. "By getting soaked and screaming at the sky?"

"By dancing in the rain and shouting to the heavens," I amended, refusing to feel embarrassed. "We're gods. You're surprised we like ritual?"

Adonis shrugged. "Whatever floats your boat."

"Oh, punny." I snickered.

Adonis rolled his eyes, and stepped back.

"Oh, come on, wait," I called as he retreated into the room. "You should join me." Beads of rain dripped off my outstretched hand. "This is your celebration, too."

"Mine?" Adonis laughed. "All I did was knock you out. Not my proudest moment."

I drew in a surprised breath. Didn't he realize what he'd done? "Adonis, you saved our *lives*, and in doing so, you might have actually tipped the scales in Persephone's favor. If you remember, it was kind of a close fight."

Adonis looked down and rubbed the back of his neck. "I don't think—"

I crossed into the sheltered portion of the balcony to grab his hand, desperate to get him to understand how he'd changed my entire *existence*. He'd given me the strength to resist Zeus. Hell, he'd given me a *future*. Back when Zeus walked the earth, I'd known my days were numbered. But now? I could do anything.

"Battles like that . . ." My voice lowered. "They look like they come down to one person or one action in one big, flashy moment, but they don't. Major victories come in inches. Each action, each sacrifice, every small act of defiance adds up. Plus," I ducked my head, tucking a strand of wet hair behind my ear, "even if you don't want to take credit for what happened to Zeus, I'm alive because of you." Water droplets clung to my eyelashes when I looked up at him. "This is your victory, too. Celebrate. You've earned this."

An expression I couldn't read crossed Adonis's face. "Gods," he whispered, reaching for me as if entranced. "You are so—"

He broke off and stared at his hand as if it had betrayed him. "Uh, have fun." Adonis gave me a tight-lipped grin, and then stepped away, retreating into the room.

Shrugging off Adonis's dismissal, I returned to the edge of the balcony.

I was free. Zeus could never make me do anything again. *Except in my nightmares.*

"You can't hurt me." Opening my eyes, I blinked the rain out of them. "Do you hear that?" I demanded louder, infusing my voice with determination. The thunder rumbled, and I grinned to piss him off that much more. "I'm free!" Lightning flashed and I whooped, spinning around, flinging rain water off me.

"If we're going to do this—" Adonis reappeared at the sliding glass door and crossed the threshold, carrying his phone and a tray filled with shot glasses and two liquor bottles. "We're going to do this right. No one can hear us?"

I grinned and shook my head.

He set the tray down on a small wicker table between the two lounge chairs. "Can you?" He made a vague waving motion around the table.

"Oh, yeah, sure." I waited for him to press play on his phone, then cast a shield around the entire table, concentrating on keeping out water, not flesh or sound. Music filled the balcony.

"Thanks. Rum or tequila?"

"Rum."

He poured me a shot. "To winning."

I raised the glass to my lips. "To winning."

The thunder rumbled and we both yelled then took another shot. I spun around, grabbing Adonis's hands and taking him with me as I spun in circles, getting lost in the music and the rain.

An hour later, the storm raged on but our energy waned. Adonis dragged the two lounge chairs as close to the suite door as possible to protect them from any stray droplets, then tossed a couple of towels onto them.

I took the opportunity to flip on the light switch.

"*That's* better," Adonis cried as light illuminated the drenched balcony. He glanced toward the hot tub built into the corner. "Shall we?" he yelled, over a thunderclap.

"Maybe after the lightning stops." I laughed. I could survive a lightning strike, but Adonis might get crispy.

"Oh yeah. Good point." He collapsed into a lounge chair. "Okay then, your turn. You say 'Never have I ever' and—"

"And then say something I've never done." I'd gotten the gist of the game the first ten rounds, but Adonis still seemed flabbergasted I hadn't heard of this game before tonight, so he kept going over the rules.

"Yeah. And if I've done it—"

"You have to take a shot. Got it." I swiped a puddle off the watertight surface and maneuvered a towel beneath me before perching on the edge of my seat. "Never have I ever . . . lied."

"Aw, come on." Adonis was forced to take another drink straight from the bottle. We'd long since forgone the shot glasses in this game. "Well, *I've* never charmed my way out of a speeding ticket."

I swallowed a mouthful of rum as I tried to think of something else I'd never done before but was pretty sure he had.

Adonis smirked. "Come on, Aphrodite, you've only been alive two years. This shouldn't be hard."

"Three." But the man had a point. "I . . . never heard this song before today."

Adonis took a drink. "This is a great song. I've never stolen a car."

I scowled at him. I'd taken a shot almost every turn. "I've never hit a girl."

Adonis swore and took another drink. "I never apologized for that."

"I'll never ask you to." I laughed.

"I never . . ." His lips twisted in a knowing grin. "Shoplifted."

Okay, seriously? "You *are* cheating," I said, giving his shoulder a playful smack with the back of my hand. "You can't get all of your 'I nevers' from stuff you already know I've done thanks to Melissa's big mouth."

Adonis snickered. "Oh please, Miss 'I've never hit a girl?' Knowledge is ammunition, no matter the source." He tapped my bottle with his. "Drink up."

"Okay, okay." I took another shot and made a face. "Geeze, if I didn't know any better, I'd think you were *trying* to get me drunk."

"Oh, yeah, that's my endgame. You caught me." He dismissed my accusation with a snort. "Can you even get drunk?"

"Not with this." I swished the rum around in the bottle. "Gods can get drunk off divine drinks, but run-of-the-mill human stuff won't do the job."

"Oh, run of the mill, huh?" He shook his head. "Gods, talking to you is mind-bending. I've known my entire life that I'm a demigod. I mean, finding out I'm one of Zeus's crazy science experiments was news to me. But my day-to-day stuff is grounded in the normal. You don't even know where normal lives."

"Oh, I do," I joked. "Far beneath me."

"No, I'm serious. We've got to like . . . educate you or something. Everyone alive knows this song. Who knows what else you've missed? We could—" He broke off. "What are you doing?"

I bounced up and down, brimming with impatience. "I have a good one!"

"Go on then." He laughed.

"I never . . ." My voice sounded thick with self-satisfaction. "Kissed a demi-deity."

Adonis grinned. "I can fix that."

I waited a beat for him to remember his ex-girlfriend, whom he'd surely at least kissed. "Elise," I prodded when he leaned toward me.

"Holy—" Adonis exclaimed, lurching forward as if the memory had slugged him. "How did I—Augh. Fine," he groaned, taking a shot.

I laughed. "Maybe we should call it a night."

"Uh-uh, my turn." Adonis stood, taking the liquor with him. "Never have I ever"—he frowned as though articulating his thought took effort—"been arrested." His frown deepened. "I think."

"Okay, you've had enough." I rose to my feet, reaching for his bottle, but finding only air when Adonis held the tequila over his head.

Thunder rumbled, shaking the balcony. Adonis and I hollered back at it as the boat skipped over the choppy water. He lowered the bottle for a fraction of a second when he yelled, and I snatched the tequila from him, giggling at the startled look on his face.

"Give it back." Adonis reached for the bottle, but I danced backward, out of his reach, laughing.

"Make me."

He snickered and started to reply, then stopped, his mouth going slack as the ship emerged from the storm clouds, revealing a clear night sky. I turned to see what could possibly render the demigod speechless and gasped.

Quicksilver lined the midnight blue sea, shimmering like magic. The moon rose from the waves in a slow ascent, sending light scattering through the water in a way that could only be described as ethereal. We watched in utter silence as the light gathered into a ball of white-hot, molten silver and rose above the tide, casting a gleaming path in the water leading straight to us.

The ocean went dark as the ship plunged into another set of clouds. Spell broken, Adonis cleared his throat. "I've never seen anything like that."

"I wouldn't have either, if not for you." Swallowing hard, I set the tequila down on the deck and studied the way the moonlight hit his skin and the rain dripped off the contours of his face, committing every feature of the man who'd saved me to memory.

"What?" He shifted under the intensity of my gaze.

"I never thanked you," I realized.

Adonis looked down at me, his golden eyes darkening with an emotion I didn't recognize. "I'll never ask you to."

Somehow, we'd drawn closer together, pulled like the tide. We hovered there for a moment before his hands gripped the railing on either side of me. I tilted my face up to touch my lips to his. I'd intended to tease. A soft, simple kiss before ducking away with a breathy one-liner. Always leave them wanting more and whatnot.

I wasn't prepared for his reaction. His arms wrapped around me, pulling me against him. When his warm lips pressed against mine, they chased away all the cold rain dripping between us.

But there was no chance I'd allow myself to be outdone by a demigod. My hands grabbed at his shirt, pulling him to me with the same desperate fervor he'd used to pull me to him. Gathering the material, I yanked his shirt up. The soft fabric gave way to firm flesh.

He let me go to undo the buttons before they could break or strangle him. The shirt dropped to the soaking wet floor. Adonis lifted me up above the bars of the balcony and onto the flat railing. He kept one hand wrapped around me tight, solid and sure as he backed me against the railing off the ship. I bumped against my shield as his other hand slid across my skin, pushing my dress off my shoulders.

I wrapped my legs around him. As my dress rode up my thighs, my hands explored the paths the raindrops took down his golden flesh. There was no give to Adonis; he was all muscle. He tasted like salted lime and rain. His mouth moved away from mine and I cried out in objection, but then I felt his breath against my skin, kisses, featherlight, working their way down my throat to the hollow in my neck, burning away the cold.

A throat cleared. "Well, that escalated quickly. Playing fast and loose with the shields, eh, Aphrodite?"

Adonis jerked toward the voice. I slid off him, onto the flat railing of the ship. My shield was gone! Nothing but air separated me from the very long drop into the ocean. The boat bounced, hitting another set of choppy waves.

My tenuous position on the rail slipped into a vertigo-inducing nothingness as I fell.

Chapter VII

POSEIDON SWORE, throwing up a shield to steady me. I pushed off the barrier and swung back over the railing. When my feet touched the deck, I allowed myself to breathe again.

Adonis looked horrified. "Aphrodite, I am so sor—"

"I'm fine." Shaken, I bit my lip and tasted salt water. Why would my shield fail?

"Way to go, half-breed." Poseidon's eyes were as dark as the sea, and moonlight glittered off the waves within them as if in mockery of the moment Adonis and I shared. He stood in front of the white railing, the dark clouds creating a dramatic backdrop for the sea god. Raindrops glistened on his bare chest. He raked his hand through his hair, a surge of power drying the bleach-blond spikes as he extended the shield to keep the rain from dripping on him and disheveling his divine appearance.

Silence descended on the balcony. Either Adonis's playlist had ended or the phone sat outside the influence of Poseidon's shield. The whisper of the wind died down and the sound of waves slapping against the boat dimmed. Rain pattered against the shield, outlining the invisible barrier in a sheen of water droplets glittering in the floodlights.

But where was *my* shield? I searched for my power signature, but found nothing. Frowning, I recast the shield, then cried out, doubling over as pain flared through me.

Adonis whirled on Poseidon. "What did you do?" He put a hand on my back. "Aphrodite, are you okay?"

Poseidon held up his arms in mock surrender. "*Me*? I didn't—"

"Proximity." I waved off their concern. In Poseidon's domain, using my powers against him would cause an uncomfortable reverberation. Throwing up a barrier within his must have caused the same reaction.

"You didn't bring a token?" Poseidon frowned as he looked me over.

"Nope." A token was an object deities used to channel power from their native realms. Zeus hadn't granted me the ability to make one.

"What are you doing here?" Adonis turned his attention back to Poseidon.

"I needed a status update." Poseidon's eyes swept over me, slow and certain. The once-over felt invasive, but the detached look in his eyes made me wonder if his lingering gaze was more for show than genuine interest.

I moved to yank the sleeves of my dress up my arms, then stopped. Acting flustered would only give Poseidon more power, whereas if I played this right, I might be able to knock him off balance. Instead, I finger-combed my hair, affecting an air of casual annoyance. "Right this second? You couldn't have found a better time?"

Poseidon leered at me. "I could have waited, but I didn't figure you'd appreciate having an audience. If you're into that sort of thing, though, by all means." His hand waved in a regal "carry on" gesture.

Adonis grabbed his shirt from the deck, muttering obscenities under his breath.

"Your demigod can leave."

Adonis followed Poseidon's gaze to me, and for a moment, I wondered what I looked like. I was soaking wet, my clothes were disheveled, and gods only knew what my hair was doing. But Poseidon liked what he saw, if his lewd grin was any indication.

"Yeah." Adonis dragged the word out, his accent betraying his northern roots. He looked between Poseidon and me and yanked on his shirt, his shaking hands betraying him as he struggled with the buttons. "I'm not going anywhere."

Poseidon tilted his head toward Adonis. My stomach dropped when I saw the expression on the sea god's face. The ocean churned, causing waves to splash against the boat with enough force to send the ship lurching.

"Adonis." I moved between him and Poseidon. "It's okay. Go ahead." In the tense silence that followed, I mentally *begged* him to comply. The last thing I wanted was for Adonis to get himself hurt, or worse, killed, because of me.

Adonis clenched his jaw, took one more look at Poseidon, then stormed across the balcony, shoving a lounge chair out of his way as he crossed the threshold into the suite.

Poseidon waved, flashing Adonis a savage grin. "Have a good night."

"Enjoy that?" I asked after Adonis slammed the sliding glass door closed.

A light flipped on in the suite, followed seconds later by another light in the window upstairs. The balcony brightened a bit, illuminating the long wooden floor and gleaming silver bars separating me from the sea.

"Oh please, I just stopped you from making a huge mistake. That demigod"—Poseidon motioned toward the room—"is a professional victim. I've been keeping an eye on him ever since Demeter told me what he was. Do you know how much *time* he spends whining about how the gods have screwed with his family for generations?"

"He's not wrong." I gave Poseidon an annoyed look, crossing my arms. "What do you care, anyway?"

"Oh, I don't." Poseidon laughed, as though he'd said something funny. He meandered toward a lounge chair, taking in the empty shot glasses with amusement. "Do whatever you want with the demigod; just wait till he's not drunk. This"—he held up the near-empty bottle of tequila—"is almost as bad as charm."

It never even occurred to me that Adonis might be drunk enough to compromise his judgment. Still, of all the people to lecture me.... "Since when do *you* care about that kind of stuff anyway?" Poseidon was hardly the poster child for consensual sex.

His expression darkened, and he set the tequila on the small wooden table positioned between the lounge chairs with a thunk. "Things change. You can give me that status update any time now. I do have a realm to run, in case you've forgotten. My time is rather valuable."

"I should make you wait," I teased, forcing a lightness I didn't feel into my voice to disguise how unnerved I felt about being trapped within his shield. "It would serve you right after that stunt you just pulled."

It was like a switch flipped. Poseidon flashed me a cold smile. "You seem to have forgotten your place in the hierarchy." He moved toward me. "You're in *my* realm. Everything and everyone in it"—he gripped me by my shoulders, fingers digging into my flesh—"is mine. I brought you here for a reason. So when I ask for a status update, I expect you to drop whatever, or whoever, you're doing and give it to me. Savvy?"

Who the hell did he think he was, a Pirate of the Caribbean? I opened my mouth, ready to rip him a new one for the way his fingers bit into my flesh, but I stopped when I caught the scent of ambrosia on his breath. Was he drunk? A million myths featuring a pissed-off Poseidon swirled around in my mind, and my throat went dry when I remembered some of the things he'd done, even when he *was* clear-headed and rational: entire civilizations sucked beneath the waves, earthquakes shattering villages, Medusa. If he wasn't in control, I needed to tread carefully.

I swallowed hard, dropping my gaze from his swirling ocean eyes. "I'm sorry."

Poseidon let me go so fast I stumbled into the railing. "Good." He grinned at me as if nothing out of the ordinary had just happened and sat down on one of the lounge chairs. "So, what have you learned so far?"

I took a deep breath and sat on the chair opposite him, pulling up the sleeves of my dress with shaking hands. "I was waiting until Adonis turned in to do any serious investigating—"

"Yeah, I saw your idea of 'investigating.'" Poseidon gave me a wry look. "I've got a mystery you can solve later, if you're interested."

I rolled my eyes, but didn't rise to the bait. "I'll have more information in the morning. As far as I know, there are four demigods on the ship, but only three likely targets."

"Why not four?" He looked at the liquor bottles for a moment as if considering the contents, then shrugged and picked the tequila up, taking a cautious sip. "This is disgusting." He turned the drink over, dumping the alcohol onto the teak floor.

I felt a surge of power so strong my hair stood on end as the liquid in the bottle replenished. The fruity, too-sweet scent of ambrosia filled the air. My mouth dropped open. He'd summoned ambrosia? From nothing? What a waste of power. He took a gulp of the liquid, his eyes finding me over the bottle, gaze expectant. Right. Blinking, I forced my mind back to the discussion at hand. "Uh . . . Narcissus runs the modeling agency. Charming everyone into forgetting he came would be difficult, if not impossible, without leaving some major holes in their logic. Plus, his assistant follows him everywhere. I'll find out what room she's in tonight, but no doubt, she's close."

"Do you know where he may be now?"

I rattled off the room number Narcissus had included with his contact information when he sent the contract, then realized that wouldn't mean anything to Poseidon. "It's on the—" I waved my hand vaguely to the left. "Do you have a map of the ship?"

Poseidon summoned a map, pulling the small wooden table between us.

I studied the picture of the ship, trying to make sense of the decks and the room numbers. "Here," I said, pointing. "Also, his assistant might be a nymph. I couldn't tell, for sure, but she had that look about her."

"Okay." Poseidon nodded. "I agree. He's too high profile to go missing, but I'll keep an eye on him when I can. How about the other three?"

"There's Adonis, obviously." Shivering, I rang my damp curls out then stood, searching the balcony for a dry towel.

Poseidon's gaze followed me as I moved around. "Also not a likely target with you rooming with him."

"I can move to a different room." I located a sheltered shelf beneath the hot tub and knelt down to grab a bundle of dry, terry fabric before turning my attention back to Poseidon.

He shook his head. "You've been seen with him, so the damage is probably already done. Besides, I like you being here." Poseidon waved his arms, encompassing the balcony. "Easy access."

Forcing a smile to my face, I dropped back into my seat. "Tantalus, another demigod, is in this room." I pointed a spot on the map. "He's unattached. But his pictures won't be easy to explain away if—"

"Pictures?"

"They're all models," I explained, trying to rub some warmth into my arms with the towel. "It'll be hard to explain why demigods who were 'never on the ship' show up in pictures taken on the ship."

He shrugged. "They could be charmed into deleting them."

"A regular picture off a regular camera, sure." I flipped my hair down and rubbed the red locks vigorously with a new towel. Had I used glamour, this would have only taken seconds, but I didn't dare try to use any of my powers this close to Poseidon. That proximity thing hurt. "But they model for companies. There's an investment there that would be hard to shrug off, even with charm. So if the models are going to go missing, I imagine it will be before they end up in any shoots."

"Do you have their schedules?"

"I have Adonis's, but I can get the others."

"Who's the fourth demigod?" His eyes lingered on my legs as I dried them off.

"Elise. I don't know where she's rooming yet, but I'll find out tonight."

Poseidon raised an eyebrow at the obviously feminine name, and I nodded. "Yeah, there's more. Adonis told me her parents are both demigods."

"Interesting. So she's also immune to charm?" He took another swig from the bottle, finishing off the ambrosia.

"I've not tested it, but yeah, most likely. She'll be stronger than Adonis, right?" I dropped the towels onto the deck, warmer now that I wasn't dripping wet.

Poseidon raised his eyebrows. "If the pattern holds. Could she be behind all this?"

"Probably not," I admitted. The fact that she annoyed me didn't make Elise some kind of evil mastermind who needed to be eliminated. But a girl could dream, right? "Still, we don't know what she's capable of, so better safe than sorry."

"I'll look into her as well, so be sure to find out which room belongs to her." Poseidon stood, dropping the empty bottle to the chair, and kicked my towels out of the walkway.

I nodded, rising to follow him, curious to see if he'd teleport when he left or take a flying leap off the balcony. His waves could catch him. "Did the other cruises host conventions for demigod-heavy professions?"

"I can find out." A smile played on his face while he looked me up and down. "Anything else?"

The repetition of the question, combined with his lewd grin, made me nervous. I kept the wariness from my voice, schooling my expression to follow suit. "Not that I can think of at the moment."

Poseidon gave me an easy grin, moving closer to me. "See, that wasn't so hard. By the way . . ." His eyes flicked over me in a long once-over. "This is a good look for you. I know you're . . . frustrated I interrupted your fun." He reached for me, hand skimming down my arm. "I could help with that."

Resisting the urge to edge away and possibly offend the sea god, I chose my words with care. My powers were useless against him, and I didn't even have teleportation rights in this realm. I didn't see desire behind the predatory gleam in his eye at all, which somehow made him even creepier. He looked . . . empty.

My careful words fled as he pressed against me, and I stumbled back in an effort to get some distance between us. "Why? You're not even interested in me." *Stupid*, I berated myself, stepping away from Poseidon. This wasn't about attraction. I'd challenged him, insulted him, and belittled him. This was about power.

He closed the distance between us, pulling me to him. When he tugged at the zipper of my dress, the fumble in his fingers scared me almost as much as what he was doing. "You don't have to be interesting."

Fighting panic when my back hit the glass wall separating the balcony from the suite, I stammered the first excuse I could think of. "I, uh . . . Persephone and Hades wanted me to keep them posted. You know, dream-walk. Some other time?"

For one horrible second, I thought he wasn't going to back off, but their names had the desired effect. Poseidon dropped his arms to his sides. "As you wish. I'll swing by tomorrow with the information you asked for. Get me a copy of the schedules and those room numbers, and we'll see where things go from there."

I let out a breath I hadn't even realized I'd been holding. "I will."

"So with this Elise, there may be two demigods immune to much of what we can throw at them," Poseidon mused. "I imagine they were intended to be a mated pair." He walked to the edge of the balcony. When he reached the silver bars, he paused, glancing over his shoulder at me. "I think we've allowed Zeus's experiments to live long enough, don't you? If they're immune to charm, there's no telling what other oddities they have about them or what they may pass on. They're too dangerous."

My heart stuttered in my chest. "I don't think Persephone would like—"

"She's not in charge of this realm," Poseidon reminded me, flashing a vicious grin. "They're both here; that makes it my decision."

Sinking the ship would be so easy for him. "They could be useful." I leaned against the glass wall and studied my nails, trying to sound disinterested.

"Yeah, I'm sure you've found plenty of *uses* for the half-breeds." Poseidon turned his attention to the sea, his fingers gripping the silver bars tight enough to whiten his knuckles. "But there's too much we don't know. Why Zeus created them, for instance." Poseidon's thoughtful gaze latched on to something in the distance. "If Zeus wanted all the gods dead, why bother creating new ones in these demigods?" He shook his head. "I don't like it. They should die."

"Shouldn't we find out why . . . whoever is taking the demigods wants them?" Could Poseidon be behind their disappearances? They'd all vanished from his realm. But then, why ask Persephone to look into the problem? To avert suspicion, maybe? Or get her into his realm?

"Not if they can be used against us. For all we know, they can kill gods regardless of bloodline."

"That's a pretty big reach." I pretended to think over his concern, as if my opinion mattered to him one way or another. "But you could be onto something. We don't know what Adonis and his kind are capable of, but I'm in a pretty good position to learn." I infused a smile into my tone as I approached the sea god. "Why don't you give me a few days to find out more?" The boat would dock on the cruise line's private island in less than forty-eight hours. If I could get Adonis to land, he'd be safe in Persephone's realm.

"You'd like that." Poseidon studied the horizon, muscles tense. In the distance, stars blazed against the black backdrop of the night sky as the clouds receded into the distance. "But what would you be willing to do in exchange for such a favor?"

My mouth went dry. "Um—"

Without warning, Poseidon whirled and pulled me to him, covering my mouth with his in a forceful kiss. The ambrosia on his breath turned my stomach. His hands roamed over me, rough and demanding. I squirmed against the assault, trying to push away from him, but I couldn't break free.

The door to the balcony slammed open, startling Poseidon into releasing me. I moved away from him as fast as I could.

"You." Adonis moved beside me, glaring at Poseidon. "Need to leave. Now."

Oh, gods. Poseidon would kill him for interrupting. Still shaking, I tried to move, to put myself between them in the futile hope I could stop Adonis from getting hurt, but I couldn't make my muscles cooperate.

Poseidon didn't even acknowledge Adonis. He looked past him to me. "Well, Aphrodite? Is the price too high?"

I didn't have to ask what he meant. "Adonis, you should go," I croaked, feeling nauseated.

He glanced between me and Poseidon, then shook his head. "No."

"Adonis, go." My voice shook.

Adonis worked his jaw, and then let out a deep breath. He turned his back on Poseidon, looking me straight in the eyes. "Whatever he's got over you isn't worth it."

"I'm inclined to agree with him." Poseidon snickered. "Take a night, think it over, sweetheart."

I flinched at the word.

"If I'm still interested, I'll find you tomorrow. If not?" His gaze slid to Adonis. "Well, you'll figure it out." I felt a pulse of power wash through him.

"Poseidon, wait," I cried, jerking forward, my arms outstretched in a futile effort to stop whatever he planned to do next. He shot me a lewd grin, then vanished.

Chapter VIII

THE FEEL OF Poseidon's hands grabbing at me, his lips pressing against mine, his tongue snaking down my throat, coated me like a filthy residue. I wanted nothing more than to get it off.

"Aphrodite . . ." Adonis stared at the spot where Poseidon had been standing. "What the hell was that?"

I pushed past him to get into the room. Warmth pricked against my cheeks as my skin adjusted to the lack of wet wind zapping my body heat. Adonis must have turned off the air conditioner, because the room no longer competed for the title of coldest place on earth.

"I asked you a question." Adonis locked the sliding glass door with a click, and then moved from panel to panel, yanking the taupe shades down the floor-to-ceiling windows as if fabric could somehow create a barrier against Poseidon. Unfortunately, all it did was make the room feel smaller. "Time to think over what? What did you just agree to?"

"I haven't agreed to anything, yet." If my hands would stop shaking, I could unzip this stupid dress and change into something warm.

"*Yet?*" Adonis ran his fingers through his golden hair, his face pinched with concern. "Aphrodite, don't. I know he rules a realm and all that, but just because he's powerful, doesn't mean he's worth—"

"You think that I'd—" I stared at Adonis in disbelief. "For *power?* You think *that's* my price?"

"What else would you want from him?"

I stared at him for a solid minute, letting the words he'd just said hang between us.

"I'm sorry," Adonis said at last, shifting uncomfortably. "I didn't mean to imply—"

"That I'm a whore?" I snapped, all the anger and fear I'd felt on the balcony a moment ago latching on to a safe target. "Is that what you think of me? That I'll just have sex with anybody, no matter how much they make my skin crawl, as long as they offer me enough? That I'd be *willing* to—"

"You're the one who said 'yet.'" Adonis held his hands up in surrender. "Despite the fact that you're shaking. That nothing in your face, not an iota of your body language indicates you wanted *that*." He jabbed a finger out at the balcony. "Much less anything further. He's offering you something, or he's holding something over you. And I'm telling you, whatever it is, it's not worth it. If even half the myths I've read are true, he's bad news. We've got to get you out of here."

The heat of my anger dissipated, leaving me cold inside. My knees folded under me as I sat on the couch, hunching forward to cradle my head in my hands. "I can't leave."

"I know you want to find out what's happening to the demigods, but I can help you. "Adonis sat beside me. "I won't forget whatever happens. I can't be charmed, and I'm still willing to investigate for you. Put a glamour on me, and let whoever is behind this think I left the ship with you. You can meet me when we get back to Florida. I'll fill you in on everything I saw."

The chill from my soaking-wet dress bit into my skin too much to ignore. I pushed to my feet and fumbled for the zipper. "That isn't what I meant. I can't leave a ship in the middle of the ocean, any more than you can." My hands were shaking too much, my fingers too numb. I swore. "Do we have scissors?"

"What?" Adonis stood. "No. Here, let me." He cleared his throat, and once he finished unzipping the dress, he moved away from me. "You can't teleport?"

"No." I waited until Adonis walked to the kitchen, careful to keep his back to me, before shimmying out of my dress. Reaching into the suitcase, I pulled out a pair of yoga pants and an oversized gray shirt. *Socks!* My feet rejoiced when I slid the cotton fabric over my freezing-cold toes. I finger-combed my hair, and wandered into the kitchen. "Excuse me." Reaching past Adonis, I grabbed a bottle of water.

"Wait." He grabbed the bottle and put it back in the fridge. "Let's get something warm. I'll call" Adonis broke off, his gaze sweeping over me. "Uh, um. You know what, room service will take forever." He recovered. "Is coffee okay?" He rummaged through the drawer under the coffee maker. "We've also got tea and hot chocolate."

"Coffee's fine."

He nodded and frowned at the coffee maker, then started fiddling with it. "Can't Persephone teleport you out?"

"I'm not from this realm, so no." When my chest tightened, I forced myself to breathe. *You'll be fine.* I propped myself onto one of the barstools and leaned my elbows against the smooth counter, gazing across the wide expanse of living room, and focused on taking deep breaths.

The coffee maker clicked. Behind me, I heard Adonis draw two cups from the cabinet. "Can someone from this realm teleport you out?"

I shook my head. "*I* have to be from this realm or have permission from Poseidon to teleport." I turned to study Adonis. "Who'd you have in mind?" Poseidon was, to my knowledge, the only sea god left.

Adonis shrugged and turned to the coffee maker. The sound of liquid pouring into mugs filled my ears as the scent of hazelnut wafted into the air.

"Eh, well, if you turned me into a god in this realm, then I'd technically be from—"

"Turned you into a—" Incredulous, I spun on my seat to face him. "What the hell kind of idea is that?"

Adonis shrugged, looking embarrassed. "It's not something I *want*. I'm just problem solving. Throwing ideas out there."

I gaped at him. "What makes you think it's even possible?"

"Didn't Hercules get turned into a god?" Adonis passed me a cup of coffee, but I set the mug down on the countertop without taking a sip.

"For a little while. He died from lack of worship back when most of the other gods did, but—" I took a sip of my coffee, considering my words carefully. "It's not an easy process for either party." There was almost no power involved in apotheosis, the process by which a demigod was turned into a full deity. All it took was a spark to activate the ichor in a demigod's blood. "And there's a price."

"What kind of price?" Curiosity flickered in Adonis's eyes, but not hunger. My shoulders relaxed a bit when I realized he was legitimately curious about the process, not desperate to try it.

"Activating ichor doesn't automatically give a demigod enough power to survive as a deity." The ship hit another set of choppy waves, and the crystals on the chandelier hanging over the living room chimed melodically. Lights from the crystals moved along the white walls. I swallowed hard, pushing aside the reminder that even within these walls, I was trapped in Poseidon's realm. "It, uh, it takes time to build up, and even more time for the demigod's body to change enough to handle divine powers. So for a few months, there's . . ." I hesitated, trying to think of the right word. "A connection? No, more like a transfer. If I turned you into a god right now, my power would flow to you, and I'd be all but human for a few months. Eventually, your body would stabilize and my power would flow back to me." The open-ended link between god and newly created deity was an odd one. Without enough power, gods should die. But the link allowed power to flow back and forth, enabling both parties to live through the process, provided there was enough worship to keep them both sustained. They were pretty much useless, in terms of being able to *do* anything with their power until the transformation completed, but they lived. "And no, this wouldn't be your realm. You'd be getting an upgrade, but you were still *born* in Demeter-land." Even I'd been created on land. The "being stranded in the ocean" bit happened afterward.

Someone knocked on the door. I grabbed Adonis's phone off the countertop and checked the time. "I'm late for a meeting."

"A meeting?" Adonis reached for his phone, fingers brushing against mine when he took the slim device back. "With who? And why?"

"Do you think my investigation is limited to following you around all day?" I asked with a lightness I didn't feel. I pulled open the door and smiled at Miguel. "Be right there."

"I'm going to shield the room," I told Adonis as I cast the shield, double-and triple-checking the barrier. This time, the frickin' thing held without any trouble. Go figure. "Stay put." As if he had a choice.

Chapter IX

"YOU CAN LOOK up passengers by last name, or account number." Miguel moved the cursor over the computer screen. He clicked on a tab, and a lengthy list of names and numbers sorted into columns filled the screen. "Or you can search by room number."

We sat at the guest services desk in the atrium, out of sight, thanks to a carefully crafted shield. Miguel had chosen the middle of the three computers, claiming the machine to be the fastest.

"Does it print?" I glanced above and below the desk's surface but didn't see a printer.

Miguel nodded. "It's hooked up to a printer in the office." He motioned to the glass door behind us marked "Staff Only."

Passengers walked across the marble floor in packs, each group going in a different direction with a sense of purpose. Piano music played over the speakers, the lilting melody of *Beyond the Sea* setting my foot tapping against the rolling chair I occupied as I waited for Miguel finish this unnecessary software tour and hand over the frickin' computer already.

"And you can see their transactions by clicking here," he continued, showing me the appropriate tab.

"The one labeled transactions?" I tried to keep the frustration out of my voice. So far, everything looked pretty self-explanatory. So if I could just take the keyboard . . . "I think I've got this, Miguel. You can go now. Thank you."

"Happy to help." Miguel grinned and made as if to leave, then hesitated.

"Yes?" I didn't glance up from typing Narcissus's first and last name.

"These people you search for, and the man you travel with . . ." Miguel trailed off, as if debating what to say next.

I looked up. "Adonis? What about him?"

"I know of their kind. They are not . . . trustworthy. Be careful."

I thanked him, shaking my head with a smile as I thought how odd it was that Miguel would recognize demigods—and fear them even—but he didn't realize when he was in the presence of a full-blooded deity. Then again, maybe he'd been on other ships with some of the missing demigods and had been charmed into forgetting them. The memory, or lack thereof, would definitely be unnerving.

Filing that thought for later, I settled into my seat and combed through pictures of all the passengers on the ship, making certain I'd met all the demigods on board.

I had. I recorded their room numbers and looked at their transactions, trying to pin a pattern to their day I could share with Poseidon. Then I turned my attention to past cruises, and began compiling a list of demigod passengers and cruise dates. "Oh, forget this," I muttered after studying another ship's worth of passengers. I could charm a team into doing this for me later. Instead, I keyed in the names of the demigods I knew for a fact were missing. I needed to pinpoint exactly when they went missing on their particular cruises and figure out if there was any connection.

The music lowered in deference to sleeping passengers as the night wore on, and a general hush fell over the ship, interrupted only every so often by a group of drunken revelers making their way from one club to another. But by the time I got around to typing the name of the last missing demigod—Otrera Ephesus—into the search engine, even those groups wandered by less often. Perusing her file, I discovered that Otrera had sailed with Fantasy Cruise Line just before she went missing on . . . this ship. Scribbling down the name of our ship, and the dates, I moved on to the other tab.

Otrera had boarded the ship the day the cruise set sail, debarked two days later on the small island the cruise line owned, then boarded later again that afternoon. She hadn't scanned in or out again the rest of the cruise. Clicking on the next tab, I searched through her transactions and found the last one to be a drink charge at three a.m., on the third night of the cruise, from the karaoke bar. Then nothing, no activity at all.

My eyes burned with fatigue as I thought over what I knew. The missing demigods hadn't always travelled this cruise's route, but all the ships passed through the same coordinates within twenty-four hours of the demigods' last transactions.

Staring at the spot on the map, I yawned. I saw nothing notable there, just more ocean. Actually . . . I leaned closer; measuring distance with my fingertips. What made the location notable was the lack of surroundings. The coordinates marked the cruise's farthest point from land.

I cradled my forehead in my hands, yawning again. "Time to take a break." I could make sense of all of this later. Time to get up, and gather the papers, and . . .

And . . .

A knock on the shield caught my attention and I raised my head. Ares stood on the other side, his hands pushed into the pockets of his leather jacket.

"What?" I dropped my shield in surprise. "How are you—Why—?"

"You're dreaming, love." His pupils were wide with charm as he stepped behind the desk.

"Stop," I whispered as Ares knelt before me, gazing up at me with those blank, adoring eyes.

I couldn't see Zeus, but he was there. He was always lurking somewhere in my dreams, waiting to twist them into nightmares. His breath stirred the hair on my neck. But I couldn't make myself turn to face him. Not with Ares in front of me, staring at me as if he'd been blind and I was his first glimpse of the sun.

"Swear fealty." The hateful words left my tongue, but the voice belonged to Zeus.

"I swear." As Ares spoke, he crumbled into dust and bones.

I screamed his name, wrenching myself out of the nightmare and into a dreamscape.

"Aphrodite!" Ares's arms closed around me.

I didn't question his presence, just buried my head in his shoulder. "I'm sorry, I'm sorry," I whimpered. "I'm so sorry." I clung to him, fighting the panic rising in my chest from the horrible nightmare-turned-memory. I couldn't save anyone. Someone would always find a way to use me against the people I cared about. Why did I volunteer to come here? What did I think I could accomplish? "I wouldn't have let you—I didn't *want*—"

He made soothing noises and stroked my hair, holding me until my babbling turned coherent then ceased all together. Eventually, I put myself together enough to recognize that his arms around me felt warm and firm and *real.*

"How are you here?" I pulled away from him, voice hoarse.

"You, uh." He glanced down. "You called me here."

Horrified, I closed my eyes against the memory of me screaming his name. There was no recovering from this. No pretending. "I didn't mean to."

He shrugged, pushing his hands into the pockets of his leather jacket. "I don't mind. Bad dream?"

"Doesn't matter." Scrubbing at my face, I tried to regain some semblance of composure. "I, um, I need to meet with Persephone. I shouldn't have—"

"You're allowed to have nightmares, Aphrodite. Hell, you're entitled." Ares drew back, studying me with concern. "A year ago, you never apologized for anything. Now, you're tripping over yourself trying to undo what I just saw? What happened to you?"

You left. I stared at him, trying to come up with something less needy, less desperate, less . . .

True.

Everyone had left after Zeus died. Persephone disappeared into her grief and the responsibilities of running three realms for months. Melissa went off to college. Everyone else went back to their own lives, but I didn't have one outside of Zeus. At first, that freedom felt exhilarating, full of potential. Then everything I was so certain I knew turned out to be wrong. Surviving hadn't even begun to prepare me for *living* with what I'd survived.

I gave up and threw his own words from the other night back at him. "I can't afford to be weak, remember?" Summoning a hair tie, I stepped back and pulled my hair into a loose ponytail.

"This isn't weak." Ares motioned around the blank dreamscape. "This is you, dealing. Hiding from the aftermath, avoiding meetings unless someone can physically pull you in, pretending what happened doesn't affect you at all, that's not—"

"Your problem." I tightened the ponytail. "And frankly, not your business. I'm not one of your soldiers, Ares."

A frown marred Ares's perfect features. "You brought me here."

"I didn't *want* to, it just happened," I snapped, unable to contain my temper. "I just"—my temper fizzled as a feeling of uncertainty crept up my spine—"dozed off, I guess."

"You guess?" Ares tilted his head, eyebrows raised in confusion. Gods didn't need sleep. When we choose to sleep, it's a conscious action. "Aphrodite, where are you right now?"

I closed my eyes and shifted the dreamscape, pulling in my awareness of the world outside of my sleeping form. The details filled in. The "C" shaped desk, the brightly lit lobby, me, with my head buried in my arms, snoozing away. "My shields are still up," I realized, relieved.

"Maybe the strain of being in another realm got to you." Ares walked behind me to see the screen of the computer. Jumbled letters and symbols filled the display, but the pictures came through without any problem. "It takes some getting used to. But still . . ."

"I'm also maintaining two shields," I argued. "And it's been a long day."

"Two?" Ares glanced around.

"One around Adonis's room."

"He's here?" Ares raised his eyebrows. "That changes things. We can't let Adonis disappear. Have you told Poseidon?"

I swallowed hard. "Yeah. He knows."

Ares opened his mouth, and then closed it, studying me hard.

Part of me wanted to tell him, but it wasn't as if there was anything he could do. He was a realm away. The only person who could actually *do* something about Poseidon was Persephone. And I wasn't going to put him on her plate. She'd flip out and the other gods would "misinterpret" whatever her reaction was as a play for Poseidon's realm. "I'll handle Poseidon," I assured Ares. Though how well I could do that remained to be seen.

"I know." When I looked up at Ares in surprise, a ghost of a smile crossed his face. "You stood up to Zeus under much worse odds. You're nobody's doormat, Aphrodite."

I drew in a sharp breath. "Thank you."

Ares's eyes burned into mine. "Anytime."

Chapter X

"APHRODITE, YOU made it." Persephone's arms wrapped around me in a tight hug when I entered her dreamscape.

"Persephone..." I pulled away to look down at the short goddess, smirking at her Sailor Moon nightshirt. "We talked about this. What happened to all the clothes I sent you?"

"They don't stay on."

I gave Persephone a knowing look. "That was kind of the point."

Persephone turned bright red. "No, I mean the—" She plucked at the collar of her shirt. "The straps kept falling, and it got all twisty while I slept, and..." She continued babbling, trying to correct her verbal blunder, but only succeeded at getting more flustered. "How's the cruise?" she asked, giving up.

"Eh, it's been interesting so far." I glanced around, surprised to find myself in a golden meadow. Splashes of colors from indistinct wildflowers bloomed along the landscape. The heady scent of flora hung in air thick with sunshine. A picnic blanket, decorated with rows of giant daisies, wrinkled beneath me every time I shifted my feet.

"Have a seat." Persephone released me and sat cross-legged on the blanket. "What have you figured out so far?"

I filled her in, leaving out the threatening bits with Poseidon.

"Wow, you've been busy." She grinned, gratitude shining in her expression. "Thanks again for looking into this. So who do you think is charming all the passengers? The demigoddess?"

"I don't know." I hesitated. "Do you think there could be another goddess out there like me? I mean, maybe the way I was created..."

Persephone narrowed her green eyes in thought. "I don't think that's likely. Zeus gave you *so* much charm, *and* he kept enough for himself to charm me. Even with the remains of a Titan supercharging your powers, or however that worked, do you think he could he have spared enough to make a whole 'nother god?" She plucked a flower from the ground, spinning the stem between her thumb and forefinger.

Zeus had created me using the remains of Uranus's dead body to act as my second parent and enhance my charm. Don't ask. It seriously just gets weirder.

"I could be wrong, though," Persephone backtracked. "I'm not exactly an expert."

With that inspiring bit of confidence from our fearless leader, I leaned back on my elbows, drinking in the bright sunshine, and floated another theory. "Any Titans break free from the Underworld?"

Persephone shook her head. "Not that I'm aware of. Did any of the Titans even have charm?"

"One of them had to." Gods passed on their powers in lieu of genetic material. New powers hadn't manifested since Chaos.

"Which one?" Persephone peeled a yellow petal off the flower. A strip of green stem followed in the petal's wake. "I can look into it, see if they're still secure in Tartarus."

"Probably Uranus given, you know, me. But almost no knowledge from The Before got passed down beyond the first generation." Knowledge is power, after all.

The first generation referred to Hades, Poseidon, Zeus, Demeter, Hestia, and Hera. The original siblings who kick-started human creation. They called everything before creation The Before because they were super creative like that.

Persephone frowned. "I'll find out. Honestly, I'd like to have a sit-down with a Titan or two anyway."

I jolted up in surprise. "With a Titan? *Why?*"

Persephone hesitated. "I'm having a hard time negotiating all this new power. It's too much, and I'm too new. Every time I get a handle on it, the rules change. Maybe they'll have some advice."

"Probably, but they have no reason to share it. They weren't exactly nice. And what do you mean, the rules change?" I eased back down on the blanket, resting on my elbows again, but instead of tilting my head up to the sun, I kept my gaze trained on her.

She shrugged, pulling another petal free from the flower. "When I first arrived in the Underworld and started training, the lessons were almost theoretic. I had pretty much no power to work with, so I learned how to teleport and charm and all that without any real fuel behind it. But everything changed when my name went public."

I nodded, familiar with the story. Most gods came into being fully grown and capable of using their powers, like me. But when gods want the experience of raising a child, they go through the whole baby-making process and start from scratch, creating deities like Persephone, who are born and age until maturity, coming into their powers bit by bit along the way. Their bodies can't *handle* the full scope of divinity before then. Persephone had only just begun coming into her powers when Hades had offered her refuge in the Underworld. But then she allowed a rock star she idolized, Orpheus, to take his wife back to the living realm, and he thanked her in a way other gods have

Aphrodite

killed for. He took his story public, telling the whole world about his adventures and the benevolent goddess, Persephone, who helped him save his wife. With the assistance of his concert venues, fans, and media connections, the story went viral. Worship fuels power, so the more people talked about Orpheus's crazy new cult, the more power Persephone gained. Since she couldn't handle power yet, Hades helped her channel the excess into her training, then siphoned whatever was left away so the energy wouldn't burn through her.

She sighed. "Now that I've actually come into my powers, this is a whole different game. Before, I needed to throw as much energy as I possibly could into every single thing I did, just to survive another day. Now I'm supposed to try to conserve it?"

"Worship doesn't last forever," I reminded her. "Conservation is how your mom and the others survived so long after the fall of Olympus."

"I know. I'm just having a hard time figuring out how to accomplish all the same stuff with a lighter touch. I practically have to relearn everything."

"You could pass some of your powers on."

She shook her head. "The only god I trust enough to give Zeus's realm to is you, but since you're sworn to me, that doesn't actually alleviate the pressure and—"

"It would be a political nightmare." Plus, I wasn't interested in running a realm. I had enough on my plate right now. "Athena's the oldest without a realm. She'd be the logical choice."

Persephone shook her head. "I don't trust her, she's too Machiavellian."

"It's not as if Zeus's realm has sentient life anymore. Who's she going to hurt?"

"I don't know. I just . . . don't trust her."

"There are other options."

"Yeah, but I'm not ready to create life right now." She rolled her eyes. "Mine is complicated enough as it is."

"Fair enough." I smiled and looked up at the bright blue sky. Later, when she wasn't so stressed, I'd help her fix this dreamscape up. Ambient sounds were nice. This place was too quiet, too Silent Spring-ish. If she added a breeze, maybe some birds chirping, leaves rustling in the wind, that sort of thing, this dreamscape would be all right. "With all the power you got from Zeus, Triton, and your mom, not to mention all the worship you get from gods, humans, and souls, you've got tons of time to figure it all out."

"Yeah, except . . ." She dropped the mutilated flower into her lap and brushed her hands against her white skirt. "I *can't* throw as much power into stuff as I used to or—" she broke off, swallowing hard.

"Or what?" I rolled onto my stomach, so I could see Persephone without craning my neck, and folded my hands beneath my chin, crossing my feet in the air behind me.

Fear flashed in her eyes. "*Stuff* happens."

Could she be more vague? I opened my mouth, ready to demand to know what *kind* of "stuff" happened, when the dreamscape shuddered, and I felt a pulling sensation. "Guess you're waking up. See you tonight? We can talk more, okay?"

"Wouldn't miss it." Persephone waved, and the dreamscape went black around her. I blinked, and found myself back at the customer service desk with a crick in my neck.

Yawning, I printed off the passenger list for this cruise, complete with thumbnail images. After I tracked down Miguel and charmed him and a healthy chunk of the crew into searching all the available records for demigods, I headed back to the elevators. The sheer amount of paper I carried could have accounted for an entire forest.

"Let me help you." Tantalus's voice came from somewhere to the left of the mountain of papers. I craned my neck and saw him reaching toward the stack.

"Have at it." I dumped the pile in his arms.

Tantalus grunted under the unexpected weight and followed me into the glass elevator. "Waking up, or heading to bed?"

I punched the button for my deck and watched as the atrium dropped away.

Tantalus raised his eyebrows when I didn't reply. "What is all this?"

"Paper."

He laughed. "No kidding, but what's it for?"

The elevator dinged and I stepped off. "This way." I dropped the shield around the room, unlocked the door, and flipped on the light.

Tantalus walked into the room, his head turning as he glanced around with unabashed interest. "So, wanna—"

"What the hell are you doing here?" Adonis's angry voice echoed from the staircase, where he stood casting a bleary-eyed glare down at Tantalus.

"Manual labor." I smiled at Tantalus. "You can put those down over there." I motioned to the countertop.

Adonis was there before Tantalus made it to the kitchen, relieving him of the papers and not so subtly herding him back out into the hall. "Thanks," he said, slamming the door behind Tantalus.

"Wow," I stared at the closed door. "You *really* don't like him."

"What tipped you off?" Adonis managed a tight smile then glanced at his watch. "You know what else I don't like?" He raised an eyebrow at me. "Being locked in my room all night with no way out. I'm running late, thanks to you."

"Late?" The sun wasn't up yet. "Late for what?"

"I need to head to the gym before the shoot. Look—" He rubbed at the back of his neck. "You don't have to come, but I can't get out of the room without your help, so if you could just—"

The shield. Right. "No, I'll go. Give me a minute to get ready."

Chapter XI

"YOU KNOW YOU don't have to actually do the workouts with me, right?" Adonis held out a water bottle as we exited the gym.

I took it and took a long drink. I'd kept up with him the entire time, but just barely. "I've never exercised before," I gasped. "I figured anything that works up that much of a sweat had to be fun."

"So, guess this means super speed, strength, and all that stuff is a myth." Adonis steered me down the hall.

"Not exactly. I"—I motioned up and down my body—"am a slightly more than perfect version of a human female, with my exact build at their absolute prime and in top health. Way back when humanity had no clue how their bodies worked, much less the knowledge or resources to take care of themselves, it made a pretty notable difference. Now—" I shrugged. "Not so much. Of course you'd outpace me. You're taller, you have a more muscular build, and you dedicate a ton of time keeping yourself in great shape. Plus, you're a demigod. That gives you a boost anyway."

A smile played on Adonis's lips. "Whatever. I outran a god today. I'm just gonna bask in that for a bit."

"Bask away." I waved my hands, as though granting him permission.

After we got cleaned up and ready, we made our way down to the conference rooms on the other side of the ship. Adonis kept up a steady stream of playful banter, but there was an undercurrent of aggravation to it. He didn't want me here. I couldn't blame him for not being thrilled with having a shadow at work. It couldn't have been fun to be locked in his room all night, or facing down angry sea deities on my behalf. Whatever alcohol-induced warmth existed between us last night had fled in the harsh light of day. But at least he was making an effort to be civil rather than openly hostile. Two steps forward, one step back.

As soon as he walked through the door of the conference room, a woman came at me with a make-up brush. "Oh, I don't need makeup," I said.

She smiled in a way that looked decidedly unfriendly, her teeth glittering against her dark skin. "You're the new girl, huh? The one added to the shoots *after* all the clothes and supplies were packed and loaded onto the ship, *completely* screwing up any semblance of order we might have experienced for the rest of the week?"

I flashed my teeth at her, taking in the small mirrored room as another woman directed Adonis to a chair next to Elise. "That's me."

At the sound of my voice, Elise opened her eyes. "Really?" she said, turning to Adonis. "Tell me you two aren't here for the deodorant shot."

"Nah, clothing," Adonis replied. "We're in conference room C."

"Well, princess," the makeup technician said, drawing my attention back to her, "you may not need makeup day-to-day, but if you don't want to look like a bleached-out spirit dragging Adonis off to the netherworld, then you're going to stand still and let us do our work." She looked me up and down, her eyes narrowing in appraisal. "Let's see what we've got in your size."

Over the next half hour, they poked, prodded, and painted me while I tried not to seethe at the insult.

Worse, they completely ignored me. The makeup artists chatted over my head about the shift in the schedule as they curled my eyelashes and filed my fingernails.

"I'm just saying, it's not his call," one said, spritzing my hair with something that smelled like citrus.

The other looked up from filing my nails. "Might as well be. Have you ever heard anyone say no to that man?"

"Are you talking about Narcissus?" I hadn't sensed any power coming from the demigod, but their description sounded an awful lot like charm.

"Don't move, dear." The stylist yanked at my hair, working the citrusy stuff into the curls.

"Forget about Narcissus." Elise studied me in the mirror. "Do you have *any* idea what you're walking into?"

"Adonis," someone called from the other conference room. "We're ready for you."

"You mean, am I ready to stand around and have my picture taken?" I craned my neck to keep Adonis in sight as they whisked him away.

"Stay *still.*" A woman with bobby pins sticking out of her mouth snapped, yanking my head back into place.

The woman with the makeup brush tilted my head toward her and the two kept *touching* me, crowding me, nudging me this way and that. I gritted my teeth, swallowing hard as familiar feelings uncoiled in my chest.

Anxiety. Fear. Panic.

But these were just humans, and I was a goddess. Getting worked up over this was about as ridiculous as running in fear from an ant wandering on my picnic blanket.

"Hey, Beth." Elise held out her hands. "She's brand new, remember?" Elise stood, checking herself out in the mirror.

"Right." Beth drew in a deep breath. "Sorry, it gets kind of chaotic around here. What's your name, doll?"

"Aphrodite," I managed.

That raised some eyebrows, but the women continued working.

"I'm Beth." The woman pointed the brush at herself, then at the woman on my other side. "Sarah. And that's Elise."

"They do amazing work," Elise said with a smile. "But . . . maybe they can take a second to walk you through what they're doing?" She gave the women a look, holding their gazes until they nodded. "Great." She smiled. "It's easy to forget how overwhelming it is to be new, but we've all been there. Now, Jane's in 'C, right?" She glanced at the makeup artist.

"Yeah," Sarah replied.

"She's very good." Elise stood still as her assistant pulled off her robe and quickly wrapped the demigoddess into a thick, terry towel. "Very professional. But things are kind of chaotic this morning. So when you go out there, she'll have a quick chat with you about what she expects. If you have any objections to being touched, or if there's anything you're not comfortable with, say so from the start. She's very respectful."

"Um, thanks?" I eyed the demigoddess in suspicion.

"You kind of looked terrified." Elise shrugged in response to my unasked question. "You might want to work on that. Good luck." She followed one of the assistants out of the room.

"Ready for wardrobe?" a woman with a clipboard demanded, pushing a rack of clothes into the tiny room.

Beth and Sarah did make the effort to talk me through a whirlwind of clothing changes until they deemed me styled and dressed to super-perfection. I wore a pair of jeans and a white camisole top with a plunging neckline. Clipboard-woman rattled off a series of instructions as she led me into the conference room, then nudged me toward Adonis while another set of random humans set to work checking the lighting.

I stumbled, and a shirtless Adonis, wearing very tight low-riding jeans, grabbed me, holding me steady. "Stand closer to me." He slipped an arm around my waist.

"Touch or no touch?" the fashion editor demanded.

"What?" I blinked, trying to get my bearings. We stood in front of a white screen, all the light focused on us. Darkness swallowed the rest of the room. People wearing black shirts milled about on the periphery with an air of organized chaos as they chatted into earpieces.

The man groaned. "She really is new."

"Touch is faster," Adonis explained. "They put you in the poses they want, but some models aren't comfortable with that, so they only get verbal instructions."

"Uh . . ." I didn't like the idea of being moved around like a puppet.

"It's a lot faster, and we're already behind schedule," Adonis grumbled.

"Yeah, okay. Whatever."

"All right, let's get some test shots," another woman wearing an earpiece called.

"Isn't this for a clothing line?" I remembered seeing the brand's stores at the mall covered in black and white photography and blasting loud music. "Shouldn't we be wearing some?"

Adonis lifted me into the air and spun me around. "Laugh," he instructed. When I complied, he added, "They find the more their models wear, the less they sell." Adonis sat me down, and hooked his thumbs through my belt loops, pulling me closer to him. "The pay sucks, but the exposure's great."

"Clearly." I stepped back, giving Adonis an appraising look. He and Poseidon could compete for the title of least-dressed.

Adonis burst out laughing. "Sorry, sorry," he called to the photographer, before resuming his serious expression.

The photographer flashed him a smile before launching into another set of bewildering instructions like "Act natural," and "Don't smile. Pout!"

"Can we fix that in proofs?" one technician—I'd lost track of who did what by now—asked. "Or should we get makeup to . . ."

"She looks familiar." I squinted into the darkness, ignoring the chatter around me as I tried to make out the photographer's features.

Adonis touched my chin, drawing my gaze back to him before the photographer could pounce on my slip-up. When he was moved to a position that put his back to the camera, he solved the mystery for me. "That's Jane. You probably saw me talking to her yesterday."

My mind flashed back to the plain woman he'd been speaking with at orientation. "*Oh.* I'd wondered what she was doing there." I smiled to myself, feeling foolish for not considering that everyone at orientation wouldn't necessarily be a model "Makes total sense to have her *behind* the camera."

Adonis struggled to maintain a "serious" expression as he pulled me to him. His hand skimmed my side as he lifted my camisole a tiny bit, as instructed. My breath caught. All I could think about were his lips burning away the rain and cold last night. The photographer's voice pierced the buzzing in my ears, and I followed her instructions without thought, putting a hand to Adonis's chest, and looking up at him. His heart pounded against my palm as he swallowed hard and tucked my hair behind my ear. His gentle fingers traced my jawline to my chin, lifting my face to his, kissing-close.

"Okay," Jane called after a moment. "Let's reset."

People poured out of the woodwork, moving around us to adjust the equipment. As they rearranged white boards and tall stands with umbrellas attached to them, the ambiance in the room shifted. I'd never thought of light as something with texture before, but as the shadows in the room shifted from soft to hard, I wondered if anything was safe from the manipulations of gods and men.

"It makes sense for her to be behind the camera?" Adonis demanded as soon as it was safe to talk. "What do you mean by *that?*"

I blinked, confused. "She's plain, is all."

"That woman," he inclined his head in the photographer's direction, "speaks three languages, gives half her paycheck to The Humane Society, and would skin someone alive if they messed with one of her models. She is *the* person I'd call if I ever needed to bury a body, and she's so frickin' smart, she could probably get away with it. And in one sentence, you've reduced her to nothing but her features."

"What else am I supposed to go on? I've seen her in a crowd, twice. It's not as if I knew her life story." She hadn't even introduced herself. "And for the record, I could literally compel a corpse to dig their own grave, shield the location, and charm whoever dared investigate you into thinking that they're a bunny rabbit. If you need to bury a body, call me."

"Oh my gods." Adonis threw up his hands in frustration. "Could you *be* more conceited?"

"Okay, ready," Jane called, cutting Adonis off as she strode over and situated Adonis and me in another half-embrace. I followed her instructions, putting a hand to Adonis's chest, and looking up at him.

"Why is that a bad thing?" I whispered as Jane walked back to her camera. "I honestly don't get how anyone manages to function in a society with such a complex and contradictory social code. You claim to value honesty, yet you thrive on lies. Calling a plain person plain is somehow an insult instead of a statement of fact, meanwhile—"

"That's not—"

"—the only acceptable form of validation is from *other* people giving you compliments. But then, you have to deny them," I said. That didn't seem right. "I'm not from your social structure, remember? Those rules don't apply to me. If you keep expecting me to act like I'm human, you're going to be disappointed. I can't lie. Not even in kindness."

Adonis rolled his eyes, but refrained from commenting while Jane lined up the next few shots. When Jane asked me to twine my arms around his neck, he hissed in my ear, his breath stirring my hair, "You say that as if you're *so* far above us. Like you're beyond caring about looks at all, but I've never seen you walk past a reflective surface without checking yourself out. I *have* seen that self-satisfied look on your face when you realize you're the first thing everyone notices in the room. Don't pretend you don't enjoy it. I don't know why you're so hung up on impressing people you so obviously think are beneath you, but—"

He broke off when two women wielding powder brushes came over and dabbed at our foreheads.

"You *really* have a low opinion of me, don't you?" I said once they'd moved away. Why did that keep surprising me? He'd flat-out told me he hated gods and implied I'd sleep with someone for power. His opinion of me *might* slip lower if I bathed in the blood of children every night, but it wouldn't have very far to fall. "I look amazing. Owning that, being proud of that, is not some kind of flaw I need to overcome."

"No," he agreed. "But acting like you're somehow superior—"

"I *am* superior." How did he not get this?

"That doesn't mean you have to act like it."

Persephone kept saying the exact same thing and it drove me nuts. "But *why*?" I couldn't keep the frustration out of my voice. "Why do you give people the power to define you like that? Why do I have to pretend to be less, just to make someone else more comfortable with—?"

Jane cleared her throat. "Looking a little tense, guys. Try to relax, please."

I fumed in silence as one of her assistants rearranged us in an awkward position where I had one hand on my right hip and the other in Adonis's left pocket. His pose echoed mine and I could feel the press of his fingers separated from my skin by only a thin bit of fabric. I forced a smile to my face that I didn't feel, and the second I was posed with my face away from the camera, I resumed speaking. "You saw Zeus toward the end. Did you happen to notice you were the same height?"

Adonis spoke without moving his lips. "So?"

"Mmm . . . same build, too." I ran a hand up Adonis's arm, squeezing when I reached the muscle per Jane's instructions. "So tell me, do you honestly think it's a coincidence that you and I—How did Narcissus put it?" My voice hardened. "Fit together like a frickin' puzzle.'"

"Zeus assembled me. Piece"—I walked my fingers up his chest—"by piece. He wanted me to fit to him like this." I pressed myself against Adonis. "I'm this coloring because he had a thing for redheads. I don't have a solitary feature he didn't put there for his own personal enjoyment. Every aspect of my being, every *piece* of me—" I broke off, diffusing the heat in my voice. "Sorry," I called to Jane, voice bright. "Like this?" I leaned against Adonis, pulling him into an embrace that shielded me from the bright lights.

"Let's get you to move behind him," Jane suggested. "Adonis, can you kneel down, and . . You got it." The photographer flashed us a thumbs-up. "Tilt your head a little—There ya go, look that way, don't smile. Adonis, put your hands over hers and look here . . . Perfect!"

"What you said earlier," I whispered in Adonis's ear. "About feeling programmed? You don't know the half of it. And I'll be damned if I ever give anyone that kind of power over me again."

Adonis couldn't reply, facing the camera like he was, but I saw his jaw twitch. After a moment went by without us arguing, the heat fueling my indignation cooled, leaving hollowness in my chest that ached around the edges with dual parts shame and anger. I hated the way he made me feel as if

I'd done something *wrong*. I was getting tired of defending myself.

"Hmm." Jane evaluated us for a moment. "Uh, new girl? That expression isn't working for me. Think lovely thoughts, and gaze off into the distance." She waved her hands. "Thataway."

Lovely thoughts? Where were we, Neverland? Still, I pasted a smile on my face and gazed off into the distance.

"Okay, a little more solemn."

The fashion editor darted into the light to reposition me, draping me around Adonis like an accessory, and requesting I hold the uncomfortable position. We couldn't talk with both of us facing the camera like this, so I was left with nothing to focus on but the thoughts I'd stirred up and the chaos of the shoot.

"Move that knee," an assistant told Adonis, making me jump.

I hated knowing that Zeus designed me. Sometimes, looking in the mirror and seeing his handiwork made me sick. I could change absolutely every aspect of the way I looked. Become someone else. But was that better?

"Get her lips more dewy."

A woman dabbed something cold and sticky on my lips, tilting my chin up to examine them in the light. "Okay."

I'd become some scared girl, hiding behind a glamour, living in fear of my true reflection. But I wasn't going to give Zeus that much power over me. Maybe he had designed me, but I was more than just his plaything.

"Adjust that light—There ya go."

Another makeup woman darted into the light and jabbed at me with a stiff brush.

More than some poseable doll.

The fashion editor ducked into the shot to poke and prod me into position when I didn't respond fast enough.

More than a puppet.

My chest constricted as a set of hands darted into the periphery of light, tugging at my shirt when a pose twisted the fabric the wrong way.

I was a *goddess*. Strong, and beautiful, and powerful, and no one could—

When I felt hands on my hips, subtly guiding me to the correct pose, I lost it. "Would you *stop* that?" I jerked away from the hands as I struggled to draw in a deep breath.

"Aphrodite—" Adonis stopped when he got a good look at my face. Whatever he saw there gave him pause. "Okay, let's take a break. Can you guys give us a minute?"

The woman with the earpiece rolled her eyes. "We don't have—"

"That actually wasn't a question." Adonis looked her full in the eyes. "We're taking a minute. Give us some space."

Charm. He must be using charm, but for some reason, I couldn't sense it. In fact . . . I couldn't sense any power coming from him at all. I could sense his baseline last night, but now I wasn't getting *anything*.

Sensing a power baseline was kind of like gauging someone's mood. There are all these visual cues when someone's angry; set shoulders, clenched jaw, narrowed eyes, whatever. But instead of individually noticing all the tells, the brain interprets a *feeling* of anger. The brain's funny like that sometimes. But sensing someone *using* their powers is about as obvious as hearing an angry person screaming.

So why hadn't I picked up anything? And why the hell couldn't I breathe? What was wrong with me? My heart raced and my head felt light. The shadows in the room felt weighted, as if they were pressing in around me, squeezing.

"This was a stupid idea." I gasped struggling to draw in a breath to calm my racing heart. "I'll watch the shoot from over there." I started to move away, but Adonis caught my arm, his grip more suggestion than actual pressure.

"This is my job, Aphrodite, I can't just—" He broke off, shaking his head. "Look, I know these shoots are overwhelming at first. I get it. But I promise, I can get you through today and then you can tell Narcissus you're not signing on. But if you don't finish today . . ."

I'd be screwing him over. "What do I do?"

Relief flooded Adonis's eyes. "You're paying way too much attention to everything around you. You're supposed to be looking at me, right? So focus on me. Can you do that?"

I drew in a long breath, forcing myself to calm down. "Yeah."

"Okay." He looked over my head for an instant, breaking the charm he held over the others. "I can carry her. Keep going." He reached for my hands. When I didn't jerk away or object, he tugged me toward him, motioning for the photographer to continue. "May I?"

I swallowed hard and nodded. Adonis moved my arms to his waist then cupped my face in his hands. "See, you've got this."

Chapter XII

"RIGHT THIS WAY, please." A man dressed in a crisp suit led us into the dining hall. The lights in the massive room reflected back from the windows with a dazzling glare.

"Are you seriously still trying to go through with this?" Adonis asked under his breath as the server ushered us to the U-shaped second floor.

We'd barely had enough time to rush back to the suite and get ready after the shoot, much less come up with a game plan for this meeting. "I didn't know there were so many people involved in a photo shoot. If I charm them all into ignoring I'm there, I'll leave a noticeable power signature for sure. I don't want to make it obvious there's someone on board with enough charm to remember if you guys go missing." My thoughts flickered back to the envelope full of schedules I'd stashed back in our room. Schedules I'd promised to give to Poseidon next time I saw him. My stomach twisted with the reminder I'd have to face the sea god again. "I think I'm going to have to stick with the modeling thing."

"But you *hated* it," Adonis protested, misinterpreting the fear on my face. "And you freaked out back there."

I thought back to my sudden inability to breathe. The way my heart raced, thudding uncomfortably against my constricted chest. "Yeah . . . I don't know what that was."

"A panic attack?" Adonis suggested.

I shook my head. "Gods don't get panic attacks." I thought back to my nightmares. "I mean, we can panic, and there can be physical side-effects, but nothing like *that*." I shuddered at the memory. "I don't know. I'll figure it out. But for now, there are only four more shoots, right?" The next one would happen tomorrow morning on the cruise line's private island. "Now that I know what to expect"—and I knew better than to let them pose me—"I think I can handle it."

"Yeah, well, I hope you're right." Adonis waved to Narcissus as we approached the table. "It's my career if you're wrong."

Yet, if I'd decided to turn down the modeling gigs, he'd get annoyed that I'd risk the whole plan by confirming I was strong enough to charm a room full of people. I *hated* Adonis's ability to make me question myself. No matter what I decided, he'd interpret my choice as selfish. He made me feel as if there was something wrong with me, and a part of me bought his vision. But then he turned around and acted as if he cared, that I mattered, and he'd do something so nice, I got whiplash.

Narcissus stood until I was seated. "I take it you've had time to go over the contract?"

I nodded. "We had a few concerns."

Narcissus motioned to his assistant, what was her name? E? What was "E" short for, anyway? She drew out a tablet, prepared to make notes, and gave us an expectant look.

"Have you had a chance to look over the menu?" a server in a white shirt with a black bow tie asked as he passed by the table.

"*We* have," Narcissus confirmed. "But did you two need more time?"

Adonis glanced at the menu. "I know what I want, thanks."

"And I'll figure it out before you get to me," I promised.

Once our orders were taken and our glasses filled, I let Adonis take the lead. This was his career, after all. Point by point, Adonis hammered through the legalese until he felt satisfied with the contract. While they talked, I studied the dining room. There were no traces of power coming from any of the passengers. Nor were there any shields or glamours, and no one else here looked the least bit divine.

Below us, not quite at the center of the room, but drawing my eye nonetheless, were Tantalus and Elise. They were sitting with Jane and two other women I recognized from the shoot. From this vantage point, I could see if anyone took an unusual interest in their table.

Heads turned toward the demigods on occasion, but that was to be expected. Demigods stood out. Every now and then, their bouts of laughter would rise over the din of conversation. They all seemed to be teasing each other, but based on their smiles, none of them minded.

The server took my plate of stuffed mushrooms away and put a new plate with a grilled lobster tail and mashed potatoes in front of me.

"Thank you," I murmured, when Adonis nudged me. I returned my gaze to the table full of laughter below.

"So we're in agreement?" Narcissus set his fork down on his empty plate.

Adonis glanced at me.

"I have some questions. Not about the contract, but about all this." I raised my arms, indicating the cruise ship. "Do you mind if I take up a bit more of your time?"

When Narcissus hesitated, I applied a light touch of charm, too small to stand out above the demigod's power signatures, but expertly applied. A wave of pain accompanied the power. *That* was new. Proximity? I resisted the urge to look around for Poseidon. Even if he was in this room, proximity would only matter if I was using the charm against—

I met Narcissus's eyes. "Tell me you're a demigod."

His brow furrowed in confusion. "I'm a demigod. I rather thought that was obvious."

Not Poseidon in a glamour then, because the sea god couldn't lie. Realm sickness, then? Was that a thing? The knowledge clicked into place in my mind, confirming that it was indeed a thing. Mild discomfort could be expected during prolonged visits to other realms. I ignored Adonis's quizzical look, pushed past the pain, and pasted a smile on my face. "Model Madness." Drawing a notebook from my bag and a pen, I forced myself to focus. "How did you come up with that?"

Narcissus laughed and relaxed into his seat like staying was his idea. "It is clever, isn't it? I'd love to take credit, but this is an annual event. We're in our twelfth year. Excuse me." He flagged down a waiter. "Could I see the dessert menu after all?"

"Certainly, sir."

I tapped my foot impatiently while we went around the table ordering desserts and coffees. When the waiter wandered off, I asked, "Is Model Madness always on a cruise ship?"

He nodded. "Always. It's been a huge success."

"Do you always choose this cruise line?" My pen hovered over the paper, ready.

He shook his head. "Which line we go with depends on who offers the best rates. This year, the best price happened to be Fantasy Cruises. It's almost always Fantasy or Fascination."

That . . . wasn't as promising as I'd hoped. *What did you expect? Some super obvious, malicious motive?* Well maybe not *obvious,* but a hint of a direction to look in would have been nice.

I spent the next half hour questioning Narcissus between bites of cheesecake. My notebook filled with the names of every single person he'd interacted with while booking the cruise. I'd have to look up the past promotions for Fascination Cruise Lines and make certain Fantasy had actually offered Narcissus the best rate. All the same, prices wouldn't be difficult to manipulate with enough charm. While someone on this list *might* be behind the missing demigods, I'd be hard-pressed to find out for sure unless they were on the boat, too.

"That was . . . fun?" Adonis's voice sounded droll as we exited the dining room after Adonis finished signing the contract. People gathered in clumps around the elevators, their conversations ebbing and flowing with the chimes of opening doors.

I laughed. "That was tedious and boring as hell. Where are we headed next?"

Adonis shrugged. "The room." I must have looked disappointed, because he added, "Elise and Tantalus said something earlier about heading to one of the clubs after dinner, but I don't know if—"

"Perfect." I beamed. "You go with them, and I'll hang back and keep an eye on you. I think I've been too close to you. Maybe if someone has the opportunity to approach you . . ."

He grimaced. "So I get to be bait. Fun."

"Adonis." On impulse, I grabbed his arm. He turned, subtly shifting us out of the flow of traffic. "Look, I know you don't think that highly of me—"

The demigod rolled his eyes. "It's not—"

I cut off his false platitudes. "And I know we disagree on"—I paused as a group of teenagers walked by, close enough for one of them to brush against my arm on their way to the staircase—"pretty much everything. But big picture? That stuff doesn't matter enough to me to just stand idly by while you get hurt. I know you don't think of us as friends, but that doesn't mean I won't do everything I can to keep you safe."

Adonis sucked in a surprised breath. "Aphrodite . . ." Something akin to regret flashed in his eyes. "You don't owe me *anything*." He slid his hand through his hair, glancing around the lobby, then lowered his voice. "We should—"

"Adonis!" Elise spotted us as she emerged from the dining room, her face brightening. "You coming tonight?" She hesitated when her eyes landed on me, hurt flashing across her features for an instant before she buried it. "Bring your friend?" The unspoken "if you must," couldn't have been easy for her to leave off.

"We'll be right there," Adonis called.

After we dropped my bag off in the room, I followed the golden-haired demi-deities to the club. Music, dancing, men. Just the distraction I needed. The clubs on the ship were small enough to keep an eye on Adonis and the other demigods without too much effort, and I'd *have* to have fun to blend in. It would be obvious I was watching the demigods, otherwise.

Loud, pulsing music pounded through me as we walked through the door. Strobe lights flickered in the ceiling from faux diamonds the size of my fist. Adonis and Elise wandered off in one direction, and I let the crowd pull me in the other. I moved to the music, letting the pulse of the beat distract me, but not so much that I lost track of Adonis. He looked like a ray of light piercing through the crowd. Normal light. Not the pink, green, and blue spotlights sweeping the floor between diamond flickers. He found Tantalus, and the two struck up a conversation with one of Jane's friends.

Elise shoved Tantalus away from her with a friendly smile. Adonis moved his hands as he talked, and I felt a pang in my chest when I realized how relaxed he looked talking to them. His entire demeanor seemed so different from when he talked to me. Well, except for last night, when he'd gotten drunk.

A smile played on my lips and I tossed my hair over my shoulder. Sitting around and feeling sorry for myself was *not* my M.O. I just had, like, realm sickness, or something. But enough was enough. Time to stop moping and enjoy myself.

Elise glanced over at me, and her lips tightened in a thin line. When she broke away from the other demigods and headed my way, I ordered a Kiss on the Lips and wished for ambrosia.

"Can I sit here?" When I nodded, Elise flashed me a cautious grin and sat on a stool, motioning for the bartender. "How was your shoot?"

"Brutal."

She laughed. "Sorry, I couldn't believe Narcissus threw you into a gig like that. Everyone felt really bad after your freak-out."

My freak-out? Wow.

"I don't think any of them realized that when Narcissus had said he'd discovered a fabulous new face, that he meant new-new, you know, not just new to this con. Anyway, some of the other girls and I wanted to invite you to breakfast tomorrow, before we dock, to kind of give you a crash course. Are you interested?"

"Uh, sure." I blinked at her in confusion. "Why are you being so nice?"

"I was rude yesterday." She ducked her head, toying with a napkin. "My issues with Adonis are with Adonis. You don't have anything to do with them, so there's no reason I should take them out on you. I'm sorry."

I took a sip of my drink, which tasted delicious, by the way. Who knew adding peach schnapps and grenadine to pureed mango would pack such a flavorful punch? I put my glass down and looked at Elise. "I figured the attitude had more to do with what I am rather than who I'm with."

"Oh, that was a factor." She flashed me a sideways grin. "But hating someone outright because of *what* they are is a slippery slope, don't you think? If I'm going to hate you, it'll be after you've earned it."

I returned her smile. "I can respect that."

She tucked a strand of hair behind her ear. "There are ... questions I have to ask you." Her flush deepened. "I *have* to. I couldn't live with myself if I didn't."

I sighed, twisting the stem of my glass back and forth between my fingers. "I'm not charming Adonis."

"Oh, I know. We're both immune to charm."

I'd suspected as much, but it was still surprising to have it confirmed. "So what's your question?"

She took a deep breath. "Are you blackmailing him? Holding his family hostage, coercing him in any way, forcing—"

"I wouldn't do that." I drained my drink, resisting the urge to roll my eyes.

She took a moment to process that, propping her elbows on the bar and stirring her hot pink drink with one of those itty-bitty, useless, red straws. "So you're not threatening him, his family, or anyone he cares about?"

"No."

"Say the words," she insisted. When I did, she frowned. "Then what the hell is going on?" Her voice rose in frustration and she took a breath, as though forcing herself to calm down. "I'm sorry," she said after a moment, raking her gold hair back with well-manicured nails. "I just—Why are you here? And why are you here with him?"

"Maybe I just wanted to go on a cruise," I suggested, flagging down the bartender when he turned our way. His gaze flicked over me, then he raised an expectant brow. "Yeah, I'll have what she's having," I told him.

"On the house," he said, delivering the drink a moment later. He managed to tear his eyes off me long enough to notice another patron, and moved regretfully away.

I waited until I was sure he was out of hearing range before turning back to Elise. "We're not all monsters, you know."

"I do know that, actually, but he doesn't." Multicolored lights glittered in her eyes, making her look close to tears. "He *hates* gods. He left me because he didn't want anything to do with the divine game board, didn't want to be some god's pawn. And now I'm supposed to believe he's forgotten all of that and gotten cozy with one of the players?"

"It's not your—"

"Before you write me off," she interjected, locking her gaze to mine, "before you try any of that condescending, divine doublespeak, I want you to consider something." She waited until she had my full attention before continuing. "You are sharing a room with my ex. You wander around the ship joined at the hip. I see the way you watch him, hear the way your voice dips when you say his name. I liked him." Pain flashed in her eyes. "Do you think it's easy for me to ask you anything? Do you think I would bother if I wasn't terrified?"

She had a point. "No."

"Then, please, don't hedge." She broke off when the bartender passed by and waited a beat before continuing. "You're not with him." She eyed me for a moment, and I realized she wanted me to confirm that.

"Not like that."

Elise let out a relieved breath, her eyes trained on the crowd. "Then why are you on the ship at all? Is something dangerous going on, because when your kind get involved, people die."

I hesitated, not sure what to share. But just then, Tantalus headed to our section of the bar, sparing me from making a decision.

"Well if it isn't the two most beautiful women in the room." Tantalus plopped down on the barstool next to Elise. "And me, right between you." He flashed us a grin. "A guy could get ideas."

"Ugh, you're incorrigible." Elise rolled her eyes in disgust and slid off the stool.

"Ah, well." Tantalus propped his elbows behind him on the bar. "That one," he pointed at me, "owes me a drink anyway, right, sweetheart?"

I had questions for Tantalus as well, so I pasted a smile on my face. "I suppose it's the least I could do after your help last night." I patted the seat beside me.

"Yeah, good luck with that." Elise moved back. "I'll catch up with you tomorrow." She met my eyes. "I'll give you some tips. Introduce you around. I'm sure Adonis did his best, but men miss stuff. They don't always tell you everything you need to know."

The question in her voice sounded subtle, but I read her worry, loud and clear. She knew something was going on and didn't trust Adonis to tell her. "You're *absolutely* right. Can't wait to chat again."

She swallowed hard, face paling. But she forced a smile on her face, flipped her hair, and with a wave, turned to forge her way through the crowd. I had a feeling Adonis would have some explaining to do when she caught up with him.

My eyes flicked over to Tantalus before I turned to the bartender. "Two shots of whatever's in those blinky glasses over there." I motioned down the bar where a set of shot glasses flashed in time to the strobe lights.

"You got it."

I downed the drink then grabbed Tantalus's hand. "Dance with me?"

"Hell, yeah." Tantalus put his empty glass down and pulled me to him.

Mid-dance, I heard that oh-so-grating throat-clearing behind me. *Oh, crap.*

"Can I cut in?" Poseidon asked in a dry voice. He, for once, wore a shirt. Though the garish Hawaiian print kind of made me wish he hadn't bothered.

Tantalus rolled his eyes and looked over as if he was about to make some sort of sarcastic comment, then blanched when he saw Poseidon. "You're a—"

The sea god narrowed his eyes and the waves within them churned with a frightening intensity. "Get lost, demigod."

Tantalus took off.

"Shall we?" Poseidon held out his hand.

Aphrodite

Chapter XIII

I SCOWLED AT Poseidon, allowing my irritation to overpower my fear. If I let myself think about being cornered by him on the balcony last night, I would lose it. "I'm sensing a pattern here. It's kind of pathetic."

"You wish." He pulled me close, passing me through the shield surrounding him. "I'm here for a status update. You can resume"—he snorted—"whatever *that* was when I leave."

I pushed away from him. "*That* was dancing."

"Dancing?" Poseidon laughed, the sickening sweet scent of ambrosia bathing my face. "No, that was sex with clothes on."

"Did you not know that's an option?" I teased, pulling away from him. "I guess now I know why seeing you fully dressed is so rare."

"Why mess with perfection?" The pulsing lights dimmed within our shield to a soft, flickering glow. I could still see the rest of the club, but my view looked filtered, as if I was peering through a frosted window. Even the music faded to a softer volume. Despite myself, I felt impressed. Shields usually functioned as an all-or-nothing deal. Tempering the effectiveness of a shield, such as blocking only some sight, some sound, and so on, took a level of control that took centuries to master.

"To see how far it can fall, apparently." I wrinkled my nose and plucked at the sleeve of his shirt, eying the retina-burning, orange Hawaiian print with distaste. "They have stores aboard this ship, you know. I'm sure we could find you something a little less . . ." I couldn't even find an adjective bad enough to describe his current wardrobe. "Tragic."

"And I'm supposed to trust your judgment?" He smirked. "You really have a thing for demigods, huh?" Poseidon pulled me back to him, moving against me in rhythm to the music. "I thought you agreed to look into this to help protect us, not feed your half-breed fetish."

I wrinkled my nose. "If I give you a status update, will you leave?"

"Maybe." He summoned a glass of ambrosia. "Want one?"

I stared at him in disbelief. Last night, I'd been too shaken to think about the cost of summoning something from nothing. He'd just thrown away all my hard work, tiptoeing around, using only a light level of charm, trying to avoid notice. If anything, Poseidon was making me look stronger than I was, since *he* stayed hidden behind a shield the whole time he was on board.

"No, thank you." With effort, I kept my anger out of my voice. I didn't want to set him off again. Instead, I tried to ignore the way he pressed against me, and filled him in on what I'd learned last night, about the timetable and the ship's coordinates when the demigods would most likely go missing. "The next time the demigods will definitely all be together is for a modeling shoot on the cruise line's private island tomorrow morning. I've got the room numbers and schedules you asked for. I left them upstairs, along with my notes, on the table on the balcony."

Poseidon nodded. "I got them. I went by your suite first. You weren't around, so I tracked your glamour. It wasn't easy, given how little power you're using to . . . what? Change the color of your dress?"

"Wrinkles. My clothes didn't do well in the suitcase. I'm trying to avoid much notice."

Poseidon's lingering once-over seemed to indicate I was doing a poor job. "I'm surprised you're not using something a bit more extensive. Going unnoticed is easier when you're not so noticeable."

"Says the guy who just appeared in the center of a crowded room." Ocean-eyes and all. "I can't hide that I'm a god from anything that can read power signatures, but I don't have to confirm that I'm strong enough to bother with."

"I doubt whatever is behind this is on board yet. I haven't sensed a single signature that didn't belong to you or a demigod." Poseidon's breath in my ear gave me goose bumps. "Given any thought to my offer?"

"Yeah." I fought back a wave of nausea. "I'm not interested."

He blinked, startled. "You'd throw your demigod away?"

Taking advantage of his surprise, I pulled myself free from his grip. "If you think he's a threat, nothing I do will convince you otherwise. Though good luck explaining why you felt the need to sink a known ally of the *entire* pantheon to Persephone and the others." I stepped away, or tried to. The shield didn't allow me go farther than an arm's length from the sea god. Instead of allowing fear to break my composure, I studied Poseidon for a long moment, trying to see past how angry and scared he made me.

He shifted under the intensity of my gaze. "What?"

"We're not so different, you and I."

He snorted. "You flatter yourself."

"We've both been broken," I kept my eyes locked on his, "and pieced back together. I know what it is to hurt, and—"

"Oh, this is rich." Poseidon rolled his eyes, but I didn't miss the flicker of pain in them. "Words of wisdom from the infant goddess."

I took a tentative step forward. "I know what it's like to feel as if you're stuck in a role that's not worth fighting anymore, but everything is different now. You can change. I did. It's a new pantheon, and—"

"You think you changed?" The filtered lights made the sea god look as if he moved in stop-motion. "Why? Because you rebelled against Zeus?"

"He created me to be loyal to him." When my back hit the shield, I gritted my teeth and fought back a wave of panic. "So . . . yeah. I'd say I've got some experience with change."

"No, he created you to be *obedient* to him." When I tilted my head in confusion, smugness permeated the sea god's voice. "You never wondered why he didn't bother to make you *want* to obey?"

Where was Poseidon going with this? "Because he didn't *care* what I wanted? Why bother with the extra effort of—"

"What? You think that it would be *more* work to ensure you didn't spend every waking moment of your life trying to find a way around how he made you?" He smirked and shook his head as though astounded by my stupidity. "He didn't have to bother with giving you a personality, Aphrodite. You were disposable; he could have made you an empty shell. Do you actually think the personality you received was an accident?"

"*Stop* it."

"He liked a challenge." The colored strobe lights glittered against Poseidon's teeth. "Even when he had a sure thing. Unquestioning compliance would have bored Zeus, and you—"

"Stop!"

Poseidon gripped my arm so hard I saw stars. "You're nothing but Zeus's plaything. You haven't changed, Aphrodite." He gave me a rough shake and I cried out in pain. "You did exactly what you were designed to. He just never anticipated losing. And, don't flatter yourself—you had nothing to do with that, either. He lost because he didn't see Demeter's sacrifice coming."

"I said *stop*." I tried to pull my arm free, my shriek surprising even me. It wasn't until clarity dawned in Poseidon's expression that I realized his speech had been almost imperceptibly slurred. He let me go so fast I stumbled into the shield surrounding us.

"Wait." Poseidon reached for me, his hands out in a "calm down" gesture, befuddlement written across his face.

"*Don't*." I backpedaled to the side and away from him in a futile attempt to find a weak spot in his shield. My breath came in sharp gasps. "You're—" I tried to say "wrong," but the word wouldn't form. No, no! I wouldn't believe him. I tried again. "Everything you just said is—You're just—"

Poseidon lowered the shield and I fell backward, crashing to the floor.

"You're scum!" I scrambled to my feet, cradling my arm. The people near me stopped dancing. "Nothing but slime." I turned and stumbled out of the club, shoving past everyone until I could break into a run. When I reached the door to my suite, I stopped, realizing I didn't have a key.

"Come on!" I slammed against the door over and over again. Poseidon was wrong. He'd never been in my head. He didn't know what fighting every instinct Zeus gave me *felt* like, day in and day out.

But wasn't I still letting Zeus define me? I let the things he'd done control my reactions. He pushed left, so I moved right. In the end, everything I did still led back to him.

"No!"

"Aphrodite?" A hand touched my shoulder.

I jumped with a scream, backing into the door with enough force to hurt. When I registered Adonis standing there, I went limp against the wood, hand to my chest, struggling to draw breath into my lungs. "Don't *do* that."

"Are you okay?" Adonis's gaze latched on to my arm, which was fast turning into a mottled purple mess, and he drew in a surprised breath between his teeth. "Did Poseidon do that? Why isn't it healing?"

"I can't—" I gasped again. "I can't breathe."

"Here." Adonis unlocked the door and reached for me, but I jerked away from him.

"Don't." I stumbled into the room. "Oh, gods, he's right," I admitted, voice breaking. I stepped out of my shoes, moving on autopilot into the dark room, stopping when I reached the half-wall separating the kitchen and dining room. "He's absolutely right. He could have *made* me love him."

"What? Aphrodite, what happened back there? What did Poseidon do?" Adonis flipped a switch and light flooded the suite. "Did he—"

"Zeus could have *made* me love him." The flat of my hands pressed against the countertop. I stood hunched over, elbows locked, hair falling in my face as I stared down at the matte, white surface, breathing hard. "He could have just made me."

"That would have been horrible." The confusion in Adonis's voice would have been comic under different circumstances. "But I don't see what—"

"I could have been *happy*." A sob worked up my throat, but of course, I couldn't cry. "I wouldn't have known any better. Do you know how much easier that would have—" Adonis put a hand on my shoulder and something in me snapped. "Don't *touch* me!" I pushed off the counter as I spun to face him.

Adonis backed off, hands in the air. "Okay. I'm—"

"Do you actually think you're better than he is? Than any of them?" All my anger and confusion and fear focused on a safe target. I couldn't hurt Adonis, and he couldn't hurt me. And wasn't that what I saw in him? Gods, how pathetic. "You're the exact same. None of you think I'm *real*. That I can feel. That I'm some*one* not some*thing*. But you're wrong. I'm real, and I—"

"Whoa. I *never* said—"

"You were supposed to be different." Breaking off, I gasped for breath. "But you're not even *nice*." I swallowed hard. "I was *so* close to giving in to Zeus. To giving up. But then, you . . . I thought you believed in me, trusted me. And no one had ever—" I took a deep shuddering breath. "But it was all lies." I leaned against the half-wall, hoping the steadiness would offset the spinning room. "You don't believe in me, you don't even *know* me."

"Aphrodite..." Adonis moved toward me, but stopped when I flinched. He held his hands up, taking a step back. "You need to—"

I talked over him between gasps of breath. "Do you want to know what Poseidon has over me? What he thought I might be willing to—" If I could just breathe, I might finish this sentence.

"Will you just—"

"You!"

Adonis froze. "What?"

I slid down the wall until I reached the floor, and drew my knees to my chest. "He threatened to kill you, unless I—"

"No." Adonis stumbled backward, his hands going to his head, as if he was ready to plug his ears if he didn't like what he heard. "No. No! You didn't."

"Of *course* I didn't, you jackass." I was going to pass out, or suffocate, or something if I didn't catch my breath soon. "But I considered it. And for what? You don't see me. No one sees me; they just see the *thing* Zeus made. But I'm more than that. I've *got* to be more than that." I drew in one sharp breath after the other, in rapid succession, trying to get my lungs to fill with air. "I'm real. I know that I'm—"

Adonis knelt beside me, pushing something into my hand. "Breathe into this."

I shoved the plastic bag away. "Never try first aid again."

"Right. Bad idea. It's supposed to be paper, isn't it?" He pocketed the bag and tapped at the screen of his phone. "Okay, so this says you need to—"

"Adonis."

He looked up from his phone, gold hair falling into his eyes. "Yeah?"

"Stop . . . pretending to"—I broke off with a gasp—"care." I looked up at him, my voice pleading. "Just—I need you to go away."

"Aphrodite, I can't leave you alone right now." He waved his phone. "I think you're having a full-fledged panic attack, and if I leave you alone—"

"*Please.*" The rapid beating of my heart pounded against my chest so hard I felt like if I looked down, I'd be able to see the organ trying to break free from my flesh. "I—just—please!" I raked my hair back, hands trembling. "I'll heal. I need—I just need—"

"Aphrodite . . ." He knelt beside me.

"*Leave me alone!*"

My hoarse shriek had him jumping backward, startled. "Okay, okay." Adonis climbed to his feet. "I'll be right upstairs if you need me." He paused when he reached the staircase. "Oh, and Aphrodite?" The demigod turned, his gold eyes locking on mine. "I'm not pretending."

I waited until he walked all the way up the stairs before I tilted my head against the wall, and closed my eyes. *What's wrong with me?* Gods didn't get panic attacks, not like this. I'd woken up from nightmares, sick and gasping with fear, but within a few moments, my healing would kick in and the worst of it would stop, leaving me unsettled, but *functional.* This was different.

Realm sickness? I wondered again. Surely this went beyond minor discomfort. *Worry about it later; breathe now.*

Right. All the knowledge mankind had accumulated over the years for self-coping with panic attacks clicked into place.

Deep breaths, Aphrodite, I coached myself. *In one, two. Out one, two, three, four.* I focused on breathing from my abdomen and eventually calmed down. Was anything I'd learned tonight any worse than what I'd already gone through? Poseidon's revelation put a different spin on my entire life, sure, but Zeus's manipulations were all in the past.

Of course Zeus shaped who I was. Even if he hadn't hand-sculpted my personality, his actions, the threat of him lingering over me, had shaped my entire life. But Zeus couldn't hurt me now.

You stood up to Zeus. You can handle anything. Ares's voice echoed in my mind.

I opened my eyes. The similarities between Poseidon and Zeus put me on edge. He outranked me, he ruled the realm I was stuck in for the moment, and he was intimidating. But at the end of the day, he was nothing compared to his younger brother. Poseidon was powerful, sure, but Zeus had been powerful too, and in the end, I'd done the impossible.

I'd fought back.

Even in my darkest hour, I'd found the strength to resist Zeus. I'd given Adonis the credit for that, built him up as a symbol, but *my* strength bought the second the demigod needed to knock me out.

Standing, I walked to the kitchen, and grabbed a water from the fridge to alleviate my Sahara-dry throat. I drained the bottle, then grabbed another, and forced myself to take slow sips while I pondered my predicament.

After a moment's deliberation, I grabbed the key card off the countertop and strode out the door, shielding the room behind me as the door closed.

I refused to be afraid of Poseidon. And I was going to make sure he knew it before the night was up.

Chapter XIV

I DIDN'T EXPECT Poseidon to hang around on board, but I'd be stupid to try summoning him without checking to see if he was still at the bar first. Unfortunately, searching for his power signature required a level of calm I didn't possess in my current state. I forced myself to take a deep breath, trying to feel at ease within the safety of the writhing crowd. Music thudded through the room, reverberating through the floor. The cramped, close quarters of the club and the press of people against me made my chest tighten. Closing my eyes, I took another deep breath and inhaled the scent of alcohol, fruit juice, sweat, and the ever-present briny smell of the ocean that seeped into the fabrics on the ship and latched onto human skin. Bright, multicolored lights danced across my closed eyelids.

"Okay," I murmured as the tightness in my chest eased. My eyes fluttered open, and I looked around the club with a renewed sense of purpose. He wasn't in the cluster of tables by the door. Nor did I find him on the dance floor. My eyes traveled the polished wood of the bar curving around the club, searching for inexplicable gaps.

There.

I zeroed in on an unoccupied length of the bar, the sheer amount of people-free space tipping me off more to Poseidon's location than his power signature. When I approached him, the shield flickered, allowing me to step across the barrier.

"I'm sorry." He didn't look up as the shield re-formed behind me, bringing the music of the club to a quiet murmur.

If singing kittens had erupted from his cranium, I wouldn't feel more surprised. "You're . . . sorry?" The words were so simple, considering what he'd done, that I somehow felt more insulted than if he'd said nothing at all. "For what, Poseidon? Assaulting me last night? Threatening to kill my friend if I didn't sleep with you? The horrible things you said? *This?*" I held out my arm, showing off the purple welt his handprint had left. "I'm a goddess, Poseidon. I heal pretty quickly. Do you know how much pressure you have to apply to even leave a mark on me? Much less one that takes *this* much time to heal?" If I'd been human, my arm would have shattered.

He closed his eyes, deflating into a defeated figure nursing a glass of ambrosia. "Yeah, I do. I don't know what got into me. I'm—"

"You don't *know* what got into you?" My voice rose to a shout. "Let me give you a hint." Snatching his glass off the bar, I threw the ambrosia down. The blinking shot glass hit the ground with a satisfying smack. "You are too powerful for this crap."

"—the hell?" Poseidon sprang to his feet, his features twisting into a distorted mask of rage. I grabbed the bottle next, but he reached out and caught my arm, shifting his grip above the bruise when I winced. "Have you completely lost your mind?"

"You don't get to not know what you're doing. You run a realm, for crying out loud!" Wrenching my arm free, I stepped backward, shaking droplets of ambrosia off my shoes. "I meant what I said before. This is a new pantheon. Persephone—"

"Has no authority here." Poseidon's eyes glittered with challenge.

"We're *all* playing by new rules. That means you don't get to threaten or coerce or *assault* me when things don't go your way."

"Or you'll what?" The happy, multicolored, flickering lights dancing over Poseidon morphed into menacing flashes. "What exactly do you think you can do to stop me?"

"Not me." I shook my head for emphasis. "Her. You gave Persephone a natural right to your realm when you refused to take back Triton's powers." A thought gave me pause. "That was intentional, wasn't it? You're using her as a safety net. You know that if you screw up badly enough, she'll step in and make sure your realm is still safe. You can't *do* that, Poseidon. You don't get to be depressed."

"I can do whatever the hell I want," Poseidon growled, towering over me. "The only people whose opinions I valued are dead. They're all dead. Amphitrite, Demeter, Tri—" He cleared his throat. "Triton." His voice softened so much I almost didn't catch his last words. "How am I one of the last ones standing?"

"We are gods. We have responsibilities, obligations." I tried to inject some sympathy into my tone but failed. Forty-eight hours ago, I could have conjured some, but I'd learned a lot about Poseidon in the past two days. He didn't deserve my pity. "You have a realm to run and enough power to do some serious damage if you get more than a little tipsy." I slammed the bottle of ambrosia down to the ground. Instead of breaking, it hit the floor with a hollow thunk before rolling under the bar. I glared at the bottle, disappointed the ambrosia didn't live up to its dramatic potential, before I turned my attention back to Poseidon. "Crippling grief is a mortal luxury. You don't get to wallow."

Pot, meet kettle.

Shut up! I argued with the snarky side of my brain. *The last twenty-four hours were hardly typical and I don't rule a realm.*

Realm-rulers didn't get to place their friends and family above the fate of everyone else, no matter how much more they mattered. Hades had been

Aphrodite

willing to break the world to find Persephone. That's why gods didn't do the whole family thing. Because balance is hard and we didn't trust ourselves not to fail.

Maybe Poseidon's generation was defective. I considered all the drama, jealousy, and angst permeating mythology since they had come along. Maybe the Titans had a point when they tried to put a stop to his generation.

Poseidon glared at me with so much vehemence that, for a second, I wondered if he could hear my thoughts. "I've seen you with that demigod. Don't pretend not to care. I warned you he might be a threat—"

I rolled my eyes. "If you had proof he was actually a threat, I'd act on it."

"How vague."

"At least I'm not so wasted, I don't know what I'm saying. Gods! That is so dangerous."

"Yeah, well, I'm not going to listen to Zeus's latest blow-up doll lecture me on what it means to be a god. I have given up more than you'll ever—"

I tilted my chin up. "I never met Triton, but I know for a fact Demeter would hate you for using her as an excuse for your stupidity."

He shook his head and returned to his seat. "They already hated me. My son died. And it took me weeks to realize he was even missing." Poseidon cleared his throat and ran his fingers along the wooden bar. "And Demeter... I always thought we would—That I would find a way to fix things, to make things right."

"You can't. And you won't ever be able to." The words came out blunter than I'd intended, but no less true. Persephone's mother and Poseidon had been an item for centuries until she broke things off. He didn't take it well. I didn't know all the details—the interpersonal drama amongst the gods hadn't been included in my knowledge base—but I knew it was bad. Demeter had left the Olympian council and disappeared into her own realm, refusing to even speak to Poseidon again, until her daughter went missing and she needed his help. And now Persephone, the nicest god in the pantheon, would barely look at the sea god unless he demanded her attention. And even then, it was with a blatant distrust Poseidon seemed to take as a challenge. Watching him try to prove himself to her was disconcerting, at the least. "But you can do everything in your power not to sink lower. A small consolation, maybe, but better than you deserve."

Poseidon blinked. "You have a way with words."

They work better than a sledgehammer. Words were my weapon of choice when charm wouldn't work. "Then maybe you should listen." I sat next to him, holding his gaze. "And see that I am serious. Pull. It. Together. And if you ever so much as touch me, or gods help me, Poseidon, even look at me with ill intent again, I will *invent* new and exciting ways to hurt you."

The look on my face must have convinced him I was serious, because I saw something, not fear precisely, but something like caution, flicker in his gaze.

I flashed my teeth in a cold smile.

Poseidon's eyes widened in alarm.

I . . . wasn't that good. When I turned to see what could possibly alarm the sea god, my heart stuttered in my chest. *Impossible.* Four passengers separated from the writhing mass of the crowd, their eyes wide, pupils fully dilated. Charmed.

Like, *really* charmed. The sheer power pouring through them made my hair stand on end.

My eyes dropped to the long, glittering silver stakes in their hands. Olympian Steele: the only weapon in existence capable of killing gods.

Chapter XV

ALL IT TAKES IS a scratch. I couldn't breathe. Four humans against two gods should be a nothing-battle. Poseidon could probably handle them alone. With his eyes closed. In seconds. But if Olympian Steele, named for the shape of the blade, not the metal, broke our skin at all, we were dead. No. *I* was dead. As soon as they broke the shield, Poseidon would teleport.

But why come after us like this? They could have nicked me any time I'd been off my guard in a crowd. Poseidon too.

To send a message maybe? That they're armed, dangerous, and can come at us from anywhere.

Maybe. But to what end?

Does it matter? You. Are. Dead. Surely one of them would at *least* get a scratch in. *Move!* I told myself. Instead, I sat as though glued to my stool a smile frozen on my face. To an outside observer, I might even look calm, but only because of the paralyzing fear pumping through my veins. I was dead. Even if I somehow got away right now, I was dead. I was stuck on a ship full of passengers that could be charmed. Who knew how many of those weapons were out there?

They could all have one. My gaze swept the crowded bar. *Every single one of them could have one.*

"Okay." Poseidon stood in a slow, controlled movement and raised his hands in surrender. "Message received, loud and clear. You're off limits."

What? Poseidon thought they were under *my* control? My fear eased as I saw an opportunity. A very, very slim opportunity, but anything was better than certain death. Right now, I had information he didn't have. These humans weren't mine. Right now, the threat—*my* threat, in his mind—stood in front of him. Next time, he might not see them coming and that would worry him. But would it worry him enough? I had to try.

"Promise me neither you nor your agents will ever act with the intention of harming me, Adonis, or anyone else I declare off limits."

The passengers raised their arms in unison and slashed at the shield with an eerie accuracy, the strobe lights turning the fluid motion jerky. How were they seeing us if we were shielded? *The same way you figured out where he was, probably. Big empty stretch of space in an otherwise crowded room. Either that or they noticed you wandering over here and vanishing from sight.*

Yeah, that hadn't been terribly subtle.

The shield shuddered, but held. One of the humans, a boy with shaggy brown hair, didn't look old enough to get in the club. He wore jeans, a blue cotton T-shirt, and sneakers. Next to him stood a man with a comb-over, glasses, and a tacky brown suit. My gaze slid to the next passenger, a brunette in a striking hot pink dress, then to the man with black hair, thick, black-rimmed glasses, khakis, and blue-collared shirt.

Poseidon edged closer to me and away from the passengers. Sweat beaded along his forehead from the exertion of holding the shield. "I promise neither I nor my agents will ever act with the intention of harming you, Adonis, or any other individuals you declare off limits unless you or they try to harm me."

"Physically." I didn't want Poseidon to be able to come after us for hurting his feelings.

"Unless you or they physically try to harm me," he agreed with a nod.

The shield flickered, and I struggled to keep my face composed. "Swear protection too, and that you'll stop with the self-destructive behavior and start behaving responsibly."

The passengers bore down on the shield, unrelenting. I glanced around the bar. No one seemed alarmed by the four people slashing at thin air with silver stakes. Were the rest of the passengers behind another shield, or were they all charmed? What the hell were we dealing with? And how drunk did Poseidon have to be to attribute this to *me*?

He always thought it was me. The realization hit me like ice water. Of all the known gods, only I had enough charm to pull this off. *I bet that's why he didn't want me investigating in the first place.* Persephone would never believe his suspicions, so rather than voice them, he'd come up with a way for her to figure it out for herself. No wonder I couldn't access all my powers here. He'd probably capped them on purpose.

In a twisted way, his theory almost made sense. The first of the demigods went missing shortly after my creation. I'd been working with Zeus at the time, against my will, yeah, but Poseidon couldn't know what Zeus had ordered me to do before he died. Plus, Zeus had obviously found a way to get in and out of Poseidon's realm unnoticed. How else could he have gotten Triton?

Oh, gods. He thought I had something to do with killing his son.

"I swear. Now call them off!"

Every second the shield held bought me an opportunity to become a little less helpless. "And any unconditional favors I request in the future. Anything I want that you have the power to provide."

Poseidon gave a strained laugh. "You want fealty too? You can forget that."

"Not fealty." Shared power was way too personal. Even if I was the one in charge, the thought of being bound to Poseidon at all gave me the creeps. "Favors."

Music surged around us at full force and the pulsing crowd sharpened into focus. *Oh crap, oh crap, oh crap.* My resolve wavered, but I took a deep breath and forced myself to wait for Poseidon's response. *Say something,* I mentally begged him. Even if I never actually used the favors, having them to hold over him would give me a measure of security so strong, the benefit outweighed the risk of death. I'd be safe. Between being sworn to Persephone, and *owning* Poseidon, no one, god or otherwise, would ever be able to threaten me again.

Well, except the four little humans with their magic daggers. *They* would still be a problem.

Poseidon hesitated, probably wondering if he should give me what I wanted or just teleport away. Right now, the threat stood in front of him. Next time, he might not see them coming. "Three favors. Anything within my power, so long as your request doesn't harm me, my realm, or any other god, granted without condition."

Three favors were two more than I'd hoped for. "Deal. And it doesn't count as a favor unless I say the phrase 'Poseidon, I'm calling in a favor.'"

He repeated the whole vow, caveats and all, after me. Then the shield broke. "Call them off!"

"First tell me what you did to me."

"What?"

"You did something to me. What?" I demanded.

"I don't know what you're talking about."

"It hurts when I use my powers and something's off, I—"

"Chaos's Balls, you probably just have realm sickness or something. I've got nothing to do with it. Call them off, Aphrodite!"

Moment of truth. It was time to test if his vows held. "They aren't mine."

Poseidon turned to me, his jaw gaping in disbelief. For a precious second, he stood there, staring in shock. "Are you *kidding* me?"

"You promised to protect me," I reminded him. Inclining my head toward the charmed passengers, I added, "Now would be a good time to start."

Chapter XVI

"YOUR KIND ISN'T welcome here," the dark-haired man growled, pushing his thick glasses up his nose with his index finger. The kid with shaggy hair and the balding man stepped around him, Olympian Steele gripped tight in their hands. I couldn't take my eyes off the glittering stakes.

Poseidon let out a string of curses that would shock any sailor. "Get behind me." He held out a hand, ready to push me back if I didn't comply. His trident appeared in his other hand with a flash of gold so bright in the darkness, I found myself blinking away sparkling dots. "And get ready to run."

"Run?" I demanded. "Why can't we teleport?" Poseidon could grant me authorization in a second.

"And leave your demigod as collateral? My vows prohibit that, thanks to you."

I laced my voice with as much sarcasm as I could. "We could always *go get him*."

Pink Dress attacked first, with all the grace of a zombie. She leapt forward, hacking and slashing at the air with the Olympian Steele before she even got within a foot of Poseidon. She was *trying* to miss. The flashing lights illuminated a wild struggle in her dark eyes. She was resisting the charm the best she could, but what hope could a mere mortal have over a divine force of will?

"And risk 'porting straight into a trap?"

Poseidon had a point. You couldn't shield yourself while teleporting. We might be able to throw up a shield the second we arrived, but we'd be vulnerable for that second.

"We're dealing with this now," Poseidon declared.

I summoned my charm, gritting my teeth against the pain ripping through my stomach. *Gah!* What *was* this? The charm slid off the passengers like water. Swallowing hard, I stepped back, bumping into a barstool. Run? From humans?

Poseidon dodged an attack from Baldy, then seemed to remember me and threw himself between the two of us, trident whirling to block his Steele. "We're going to talk about the bargain we just made later."

"Talk all you want. Your promises are still binding." I threw up a shield, power flaring to life within me. Gods, that *hurt*. Gritting my teeth, I ignored the gut-wrenching pain and pushed the shield at the charmed passengers just as Shaggy joined the fray, Steele shattering my shield in a second.

I froze. Fighting wasn't in my skill set. Unlike Persephone, I'd never seen the point in spending my spare time learning self-defense or honing my powers so I'd be ready for a combat situation. My charm could quell gods. Why would I ever need anything more than that?

Poseidon shoved me to the side, intercepting the Steele with his trident. Baldy leapt to Shaggy's aid, slashing at Poseidon, but Poseidon sent him flying into the bar, crashing into a wall of bottles with enough force to shatter them. Baldy hit the ground with a thud, alcohol and glass raining around him. The bartender, unperturbed, kept pouring drinks. What the hell? Everyone else danced or stood around in unconcerned clusters. Was the whole club charmed? Holy Hades, what kind of power were we dealing with?

Don't just stand there. Do *something.* Taking a deep breath, I tuned out the pulsing music and concentrated. With effort, I picked out several more charmed passengers as well as a shield enveloping the entire bar. "Poseidon, break the shield!"

A wave of power swelled from Poseidon. The shield shattered. My stomach wrenched as I blanketed the room with charm in a desperate bid to gain control of the passengers before they panicked and fled. They could come in handy.

Gods! The effort of channeling my powers sent me doubling over in agony.

Gritting my teeth, I pushed past the pain, concentration breaking when another passenger lunged at me, knocking me to the floor. Rolling out of the way, I slid across shattered glass. The broken bottles sliced my skin. I leapt to my feet. The uncharmed passengers became aware of the fight in their midst, and rushed toward the door screaming. "Crap!" Pushing past the pain, I refocused my power on the crowd as the music shut off and fluorescent lights flickered on.

"Are you cut?" Poseidon spared me a glance, throwing up a shield to gain the half-second to determine whether or not I was all right.

"Not by Steele." Taking a deep breath, I forced my charm to take hold of the other passengers. "Help me!"

The bar came to life as passengers threw themselves in between me and the Steele-wielding zombies.

"Go," Poseidon shouted, trident swinging in a wild arc. Pink Dress ducked around the blow, slashing at Poseidon, but got intercepted by a crew member acting under the influence of my charm. I ran, Poseidon on my heels. The crowd split in front of me, forming a narrow hallway that closed in behind us. A living shield.

Scattered within the crowd, I could pick out the passengers who weren't under my control waiting for us to get close enough to strike. "Red dress!

Glasses! Waitress behind the table!" I shouted warnings to Poseidon as soon as I picked out the passengers who would attack, glancing back to gauge his success.

Poseidon's trident flashed. *Now* I understood why Demeter and Hades had been so determined to get him on their side against Zeus. Poseidon wasn't just powerful. He fought in a way most gods were too complacent to even consider. I couldn't tell where his powers stopped and his physical prowess began. Green lightning erupted from the trident, followed by a punch, a kick, a shield inverted around a passenger to restrain them. He seemed to be everywhere at once until they tried to strike back, and then he was nowhere.

"You're incredible!" I hadn't meant to speak out loud, and, by rights, I shouldn't be audible over the fight, but somehow, Poseidon still heard and shot me a grin.

"You sound surprised. I thought that was common knowledge." His grin faded. "Watch out!"

I ducked as another charmed passenger broke through the crowd, slashing at the place where I'd been with the shimmering stake. Poseidon was there in a flash. The passenger went flying into the wall as limp as a rag doll.

We broke free of the bar and dashed through a hallway decorated to resemble the night sky. If anyone thought it odd we ran like our lives depended on it, I didn't notice. "Where are we going?" I cried.

"Water."

Right. I veered toward the atrium as the hall opened up into a lobby full of gift shops, tables, and photographers posing random passengers in front of pretty backdrops. The charmed passengers followed right on our heels. "This way!" I rushed across the atrium and up the curved, golden staircase.

I screamed as a hand closed around my ankle and yanked me down the steps. For a second, all I could focus on was the stake centimeters from my face. The weapon didn't move. My gaze shifted up the arm of the passenger carrying the Steele. His face contorted in a grimace of agony. With a violent jerk, he was flung off of me, and slammed into the wall propelled by an invisible force.

"What?" Leaping to my feet, I found Poseidon. He had one arm up as he cast and recast a shield to keep the passengers at bay almost as fast as they slashed through it, and the other, stretched toward the man, trident extended. "How did you do that?" Telekinesis was not in our skill set.

"Salt water." Poseidon panted, the strain from casting a new shield every time Steele broke through evident on his face. "Run!"

I scrambled up the steps, my mind reeling. There were whispers, rumors, that the original six were capable of manipulating the human body via built-in fail-safes. A control for each god. Water for Poseidon, trace minerals from the earth for Demeter, and the four aspects of the soul for the rest. But

I'd only heard rumors. Precious little information about human creation passed down the bloodlines.

And no one could say for certain whether those same controls were built into us. *Forget that for now. How have you not been cut?* I'd been knocked over, pushed, and outright missed a statistically improbable number of times not to have sustained a single injury from the Olympian Daggers.

This fight didn't make *sense*. I'd been on this ship surrounded by these people for the last day and a half. Why hadn't someone taken me out then?

Maybe I'm not the target.

What if I was just in the way? Had they addressed both of us, or just Poseidon at the beginning of the fight? He'd stayed behind a shield almost the entire time he'd been on board. Maybe they'd attacked like this because taking down his shield would be noticeable no matter what they did. If you can't go for surprise, go for strength?

I burst through the exterior door and slammed into the railing, gasping for breath.

"Stay against the rail." Poseidon slid to halt in front of me.

"Here?" I took a nervous look around. The bit of deck we occupied reminded me of a sidewalk. The narrow strip of white wooden planks and painted metal rails ran parallel to the main lobby, separated by windows and glass doors. The charmed passengers stood in the open doorway, hacking at Poseidon's shield. Soft Caribbean music and laughter came from the pool farther down the deck. I glanced at the exterior steps, wondering if we should run up one more deck.

"Here." Poseidon's shield broke and I felt the power ricochet back to him. "Can you break the charm?"

I hesitated. I'd never succeeded in freeing Persephone from Zeus's charm, no matter how hard I'd tried. And I'd tried hard. "I have some theories."

Poseidon nodded. "Try then. I'd rather not have to kill anyone."

"Really?" It wasn't as if I thought Poseidon enjoyed death and violence. Much. But I didn't expect him to care one way or another whether the people attacking us lived or died.

Poseidon shrugged. "I don't want to give Hades any excuse to come to my realm."

Right. Gods had to respond to divine causes of death. It figured that's what Poseidon would worry about right now. The sea god turned to the door. "I'll buy you as much time as I can. You may want to duck."

I dropped to my knees, my hands going over my head as a wall of water rushed above me, whipping around the deck as the charmed passengers poured through the doorway.

Go inside, nothing to see here. My stomach twisted as I let the command blanket the ship, fueling the order with every bit of power I could manage.

Get to your room and stay there until morning.

The effort of maintaining hold of so many passengers twisted my stomach into painful knots. *Oh, gods, this hurts.* Water roared around me, disrupting my concentration. Squeezing my eyes shut, I waited until I sensed the passengers under my control begin to retreat across the ship. I imagined doors closing, and gave them a few seconds to get settled, making sure to imprint a strong desire in their minds to stay put until sunup before releasing them from my charm. Even out of my control, they would most likely obey the subconscious command.

I narrowed my focus to the passengers under foreign control heading toward this deck.

How many were there in total? I gave up counting at thirty and shifted my attention to the eight fighting Poseidon.

I could sense the charm holding them, but something about the power signature seemed off. Charm was like a thread of power extending from god to man. A *thread*. But the charm holding the humans hostage wasn't a solitary thread but many, woven together like a rope.

"There's more than one controller," I blurted, realization hitting me like a tidal wave.

"What?" Poseidon shouted.

My answer got swallowed in the roar of the water. Baldy lunged at Poseidon, but got whipped away by the current. The water animated and whirled around Poseidon, suspended in the air like the arms of an octopus, lashing out every time one of the passengers got too close. But he wouldn't be able to keep up the fight forever. I gritted my teeth and focused on gathering more power.

We weren't dealing with another deity like me or a super-charged Titan. This was something else entirely. What did Zeus say? *"You think you saved the world by killing me, but you've doomed it. What's coming is worse. And Hades, they're armed."*

They're armed. Plural. We were dealing with a group. An army, even.

I kept my eyes closed, tuning out the screams, grunts, and occasional flashes of green lightning to separate each power signature I found connected to one of the charmed passengers. The threads of power were braided together in an intricate chain of charm.

But the woman in the pink dress *did* fight the foreign control. Maybe she wasn't the only one. I opened my eyes for a second. The jerky movements of the passengers confirmed my theory. Gritting my teeth against the gut-wrenching pain that came with using my powers so close to Poseidon, I focused on a single thread of charm, ignoring the rest of the rope for now.

The individual threads were weak.

"Aphrodite," Poseidon snapped. "Any time now!"

More passengers joined the battle. I hadn't opened my eyes to check, but I could sense them. How many? Ten? Twelve? "I'm trying!" I focused on channeling my power through the gaps between threads of charm. Sweat bathed my face. Using my powers shouldn't *hurt* this much.

Almost. I pushed at the gaps, pouring more and more power into the effort. The charm snapped and my eyes flew open. "Got it!" I called triumphantly. "I've—" I broke off with a gasp. The passengers hung suspended in a wall of water before Poseidon. Their mouths open, faces frozen in contorted expressions of pain as they'd desperately tried to drag air into their lungs but failed, finding only water. Their dead eyes burned with accusation.

"No." Poseidon stepped backward and the water crashed to the deck, bringing the bodies to the ground with a sick sounding thunk, Olympian Steele still clutched tight in their dead fingers. "You didn't."

Chapter XVII

"YOU DROWNED THEM?" I stared at pile of bodies in horror. Between the shock of seeing the narrow deck littered with former passengers and the sudden power vacuum from dropping my charm, my senses went into overdrive. The glaring lights of the ship set the water on the corpses' skin glistening, creating a jarring illusion of movement against their unnatural stillness. Water dripped onto the gleaming white floor. Cheerful music played over Poseidon's ragged breathing.

There was too much noise, too much light, and not enough *space* on this narrow strip of deck. Good gods, they were all dead. Earlier tonight, they'd been dancing and enjoying their vacation, and now they were dead. I drew my knees to my chest and took in a deep breath.

"What the hell was I supposed to do? You sure weren't helping." Poseidon worked a muscle in his jaw. "We need to find out what just happened. Why were we attacked? Who was controlling them? And why did you just *sit* there like some useless human?" He strode across the deck, his eyes flashing with irritation. "You let me think they were under your—" He paused. "What's wrong with you?"

Confused, I followed his gaze over my shoulder. The lacerations from sliding across broken glass crisscrossed my back. They weren't healing.

"Did you get cut with—?"

"No." I stared at my scratches, willing them to heal, but nothing happened. "Uh... I had to use a lot of charm to try to break the control. Maybe..." I trailed off, trying to make my thoughts coherent.

"You getting enough worship?" Poseidon looked embarrassed to ask such a taboo question. That just wasn't the sort of thing gods discussed.

I was though, wasn't I? "Have you *seen* me? I get enough worship walking into a crowded room." I raked my hair back with my fingers and took a deep breath. "My powers *are* harder to access here, though." I didn't even try to keep the accusation out of my voice. "Care to fix that?"

"Harder to access?" Poseidon grabbed my hand to pull me to my feet. "You have permission to be here, they shouldn't be—" He swore when my knees buckled, catching me before I could crumple back on to the deck. "Look—" He propped me against the railing and watched me for a moment to make sure I wasn't going to fall. "I have to get rid of the weapons. I'm going to take them to Hephaestus and gather as many gods as I can. Do you think you can—?"

"What—?" Persephone's voice tore Poseidon's gaze back to the center of the deck where the bodies lay in a dripping heap, "have you done?"

"Watch out!" Poseidon reached for her, but Hades intercepted him. "*You* don't have permission to be in my realm," Poseidon reminded Hades.

Hades shrugged as he knelt to study the bodies. "Divine causes of death require a divine response. What happened here? Watch out for what?"

While Poseidon filled them in, I waited for the deck to stop spinning. Once I felt steadier on my feet, I picked my way through the bodies, gathering up the Steele. As long as the blades didn't break my skin, I'd be fine. "What should I do with these?"

"Give them to me," Poseidon and Hades demanded simultaneously.

I turned to Hades.

"Wait, hang on." Poseidon unbuttoned his garish, Hawaiian print shirt and passed the abomination to me.

I held my breath as I wrapped the Steele in his shirt. One slip-up, and I'd be dead. "Okay, here." I passed the dangerous bundle to Hades.

Persephone knelt next to each body, touching each passenger and, I assumed, releasing their souls. When she finished, she stood. "So, what's the plan?"

"There were charmed passengers who never attacked." I swept my hair off my shoulders. It was so hot out here. Was I the only one who felt this hot? "We can't know if they were armed or not, but we should probably assume that they were."

Hades shifted, angling himself to see the door. "We need to make sure there aren't any more weapons on the ship."

Poseidon nodded. "And we'll need to question everyone. If Aphrodite's right about this being a large group—"

"I am." I was either going to throw up, or pass out. Spots filled my vision. I stepped back, blindly groping for the white railing. When my hand closed around the cool metal, I leaned against the bars.

Persephone frowned down at the bodies. "This is a huge ship. Searching it and talking to everyone is going to take more time than we have."

"Not if we have enough help," Poseidon said. "I'm giving a temporary blanket teleportation authorization for my realm. Gather everyone you can. If there are more weapons, we need to keep them isolated here."

"I'll drop the souls by the Underworld and take these to Hephaestus." Hades shifted the bundle of deadly weapons in his hands. "Persephone—"

"I'll get everyone. Poseidon, let's make sure no one else can leave, though. Would you maintain a shield around the ship?"

"They can break shields." I shook my head, trying to disrupt the buzzing in my ears so I could focus.

"But Poseidon will know if they do. Aphrodite, keep everyone in their rooms as best you can." Persephone didn't take her eyes off the bodies. "It'll be easier to search, and maybe we can keep more people out of the line of fire if another fight breaks out." She let out a deep breath. "What do we do with"—she cleared her throat—"the uh, the bodies?"

"I'll handle it." Poseidon reached out, as if he wanted to touch her, but stopped when her green eyes narrowed at his outstretched hand. He dropped his arm to his side. "We'll meet in Aphrodite's room."

There were more details exchanged, room numbers and such, but I couldn't focus.

"Be back soon." Persephone smiled in my direction, and I did my best to grin back at her before she and Hades vanished.

"Keep a shield around us so no one sees this," Poseidon commanded.

No one should be out and about, thanks to my earlier charm. But I took a deep breath and cast a shield anyway. My stomach twisted, and my already swimming vision went Technicolor. I thought I heard something splash behind me, but couldn't be sure over the roaring in my ears.

"Okay, you can drop it." Poseidon's voice came from somewhere behind me, but I kept pouring power into the shield. There was a lag between the words I heard and my ability to react to them. "Aphrodite?"

His hand touched my shoulder, and I jerked in surprise, dropping the shield. My knees gave way. Poseidon swore, sweeping me off my feet before I could crash to the floor. I felt myself being lifted, felt my body burst apart then re-form in a sickening lurch. For a second, or possibly a century, everything went black.

"—not breathing!" Adonis's fingers probed my neck for a pulse. *Where did he come from?* He sounded worried, and oddly, that made me feel better.

Worship. I realized as my head cleared. *Kind of.*

"What did you do to her?" Adonis's voice brimmed with rage. His hands left my shoulders and I sensed him moving away from me. "What did you do?" The swish of fabric, and the thud that followed, sent me scrambling for consciousness.

Poseidon sounded ice-cold. "Get your hands off of me before I remove them."

No! I tried to open my eyes, to bolt upright, but a wave of pain, so intense I cried out, shoved me back under.

"Move!" Calloused hands as old as the sea gripped my shoulders, pouring power into me. The energy burned through me like molten glass. Crystallized. Shattered. Pain ripped through me. I dragged air into my lungs in a strangled gasp that became an anguished scream. My back arched and I fought to free myself from Poseidon's grasp, to make the pain stop. Anything!

"Stop!" Adonis's panicked shout echoed my thoughts.

"She's breathing again, isn't she?" The pain stopped, the pressure on my shoulders eased. Poseidon said more words, but I couldn't understand them.

". . . wrong with her?" Adonis asked. His hands cupped my face, tilting my head from side to side. "Come on, Aphrodite. Wake up." He brushed my hair from my forehead.

". . . much power during the fight."

"Fight?"

"But surely she wouldn't burn through her whole reserve in one battle?"

Adonis's voice rose with frustration. "What battle? What happens if she runs out of power?"

". . . dies," Poseidon replied, as if the answer should be obvious. I was almost surprised he didn't follow up with a "duh."

I wished I could giggle. Duh is a silly word.

"What?" Adonis's horrified voice pulled my attention back to the conversation at hand. "No. You guys live off *worship*."

"Worship fuels our power. The lack of worship wouldn't kill us if . . ." Poseidon's voice faded into indistinct murmurs as I lost the ability to track the conversation. I thought I heard Persephone's name, then the slamming of a door, but I couldn't be sure.

I heard a sigh then the couch dipped with Adonis's weight. "Aphrodite . . ." He sounded so worried that I *tried* to respond. "Come on, Aphrodite. *Please.*" He gripped my hands in his. "Come on. Wake up. *Please* wake up." He repeated the words like a mantra, gripping my hands so tightly, they hurt.

I'm not sure how long we sat like that. But gradually, my ragged breathing evened.

"Please, please, please," Adonis breathed.

Opening my eyes, I squinted against the light. Adonis sat hunched over me, balancing on the edge of the white couch cushion, squeezing my hands in his for all he was worth. A feeling I couldn't identify flooded my chest. Something safe and warm and soothing. Like I was home. As if someone like me could even have one, could belong somewhere. I hadn't felt that in a long time. "That hurts," I croaked.

Adonis's eyes flew open. "Gods!" He yanked me to him in a crushing embrace. "You're okay." His lips brushed my forehead when he spoke. "I thought—sorry." He let me go and scooted back a bit. "Are you okay?"

"Yeah," I gasped, dizzy. "Adonis. . . . *Thank* you."

"Don't." He jerked his head. "Don't thank me. I—Gods, Aphrodite—I—"

The door opened. "I said to bolt this," Poseidon grumbled as he entered the room.

"Where's Persephone?" Adonis stood. "I thought you were going to get her."

Poseidon shook his head. "No need. I figured if you took your focus off me, something like *this* would happen."

"And if you were wrong?" I sat up, reaching for a pillow to prop behind me.

Poseidon gave me a long look, and I read the answer on his face. He'd promised to protect me. Not run for help. If I died, the vows he'd sworn died with me. Poseidon moved one of the white-upholstered chairs closer to the couch and sat down. "You said something about your powers being harder to access here. You thought I'd done something to you? What did you mean?"

Adonis sat on the edge of the couch, shifting so I could stay stretched out. He gripped the cushions on either side of him in a way that could be for balance, but also acted as a kind of barrier between me and Poseidon.

Cleverly done. I watched Adonis from the corner of my eye. "It just . . . hurts when I try to use my powers here." I stared at him, heart pounding as I realized with absolute certainty he wasn't behind this. "I know sometimes gods can cap—"

"Not like that." Poseidon shook his head. "I granted you full access to my realm. You can do everything but teleport and attack me directly." He rubbed his chin. "Proximity?"

I brought my knees up to my chest, giving Adonis a bit more room. "That's what I figured at first, but then it stopped mattering if you were nearby or not."

Poseidon raked his hair back. "This doesn't make any sense."

"How long has this been going on?" Adonis's voice sounded strained.

Poseidon can't hurt you, I wanted to tell him. But I couldn't bring myself to say it out loud. Right now, Adonis thought he was protecting me. Pointing out that it was actually the other way around in front of Poseidon seemed rude. "Since yesterday."

"*When* yesterday?" Adonis looked like he wanted to ask something else, but he glanced at Poseidon, his eyes giving away how nervous he felt.

Poseidon wasn't paying attention to him. He frowned, deep in thought. "Did Zeus ever say anything to you about"—he hesitated—"an expiration date?"

My breath caught. "He never said anything, but . . ." That didn't mean I didn't have one. Zeus hadn't planned on keeping me around for long. He'd intended to force me to swear fealty and give him all my powers. Then again, he'd also been working with a pretty specific timetable. "Is that even possible?"

Poseidon shrugged. "Humans have them."

Scientists had never been able to figure out why stem cell function and frequency degraded with age. There was no *reason* for the human body to function perfectly one day and a little less perfectly the next. Humans only died because they were designed to.

A phone buzzed. Poseidon fished Persephone's pink phone out of his pocket.

"We're ready." Persephone's voice erupted from the speakers. "Drop the shield."

Were my powers getting harder to use each day until they failed completely? I looked over my shoulder, trying to see the scratches. They'd healed at some point. Would healing take a bit longer every day, until I stopped being able to heal all together?

Was I mortal? No. I'd know, wouldn't I? Surely I'd be able to sense my body dying with every breath.

"Done," Poseidon said into the phone, before hanging up without so much as a goodbye.

"You know if she thinks I'm in trouble, she'll do something stupid." I was linked to Persephone. She could give me powers, as well as take them away. Power was our life force. I wasn't going to be responsible for Persephone losing any of hers.

Poseidon hesitated. "Are you asking me for a favor?"

"No." I didn't understand Poseidon's obsession with Persephone, but I knew he wouldn't say anything to her, whether I asked him to or not. Especially if she could save me. The sooner I died, the sooner he'd be out from under my thumb.

Chapter XVIII

THE SOFT KNOCK on the door sent me cowering into the bathroom. I couldn't let *everyone* see me all weak and trembling, much less sweaty and gross.

You've been through a battle, the rational side of my brain pointed out as I studied myself in the mirror and groaned. The cuts and bruises might have healed, but that hadn't done anything to disguise the crusty blood crisscrossing my skin or the dried sweat plastering my hair to my face. Even my dress looked dirty.

Scrubbing my face in an attempt to salvage my appearance, I wondered, on a scale of one to ten, how stupid casting a glamour would be right now. Voices filled the stateroom and I swore.

Stop stalling, I commanded myself as I wove my hair into a complex braid. But I couldn't seem to keep myself from lingering. The familiar motions of putting myself back together again grounded me. I needed that after what I'd just been through.

I glanced beneath the counter where I'd stashed one of my bags and searched for something thick to wear that wouldn't expose much skin in case we encountered any more Olympian Steele. Yeah, *not* exposing skin was rarely my goal when getting dressed.

"You'll do," I muttered, slipping the thigh-length, form-fitting sweater I'd brought in case I got cold over my head and pairing the gray wool with some leggings and knee-high leather boots. I'd be hot, and not in the sense I preferred, but I'd been lucky enough tonight. Fabric wouldn't protect me from being stabbed, but at least I'd have less exposed skin to be scratched or nicked.

"Okay," I breathed, eying myself in the mirror. Satisfied with what I saw, I opened the bathroom door.

Muses, Graces, and every living, full-blooded deity except Hephaestus filled the suite. How had Persephone managed to gather everyone this quickly? They crowded around the coffee table, listening as Poseidon brought everyone up to speed. My eyes landed on Ares and I swallowed hard, remembering the way he'd held me the last time I'd seen him. *Fool me once,* I thought wryly.

Drawn by the power of my gaze, Ares looked up. "Hey!" He separated from the group of gods and rushed to the steps to meet me. "Heard you survived battle. Well done." The concern in his dark eyes belied the jest in his voice. "You make it out unscathed?"

I forced myself to grin. "Can I call myself a war goddess now? 'Cause I could rock the warrior princess look. Trade this in," I plucked at the side of my leggings, "for one of those spiky leather skirts. It could work."

Ares laughed. "I wouldn't trade your heels in for combat boots just yet, but I could get behind the leather skirt idea." He touched my elbow and drew me toward the rest of the gods. "Sadly though, if the old man of the sea's face is any indication, we'll have to talk shop later."

"Oh." Poseidon mocked. "Don't flatter yourself. We wouldn't wait for your input."

"Well, in that case . . ." Ares shrugged and turned his attention back to me.

"Quit flirting, Ares." Athena shook her head, flashing me a rueful smile.

"Jealous?" Ares teased.

Athena's grey eyes swept over Ares in a cool appraisal that ended with a snort of laughter.

"Ouch." I laughed, leaving Ares's side in favor of giving Athena a hug. "Good to see you in the flesh."

"You all right, half—Er, Adonis?" Ares asked, stopping himself before calling the demigod half-breed. "You're looking a little out of sorts."

Adonis jerked his gaze away from me as if surprised it had landed there. "No, ah, I'm fine. Just trying to remember something. Can I see that?" Adonis moved between Poseidon and the coffee table to study the map, oblivious to Poseidon's glare. "Here? You're sure this is where the disappearances happened?"

I moved behind Adonis and looked over his shoulder. "I mean, I can't determine the *exact* spot based on the information I found. But somewhere around here." I noticed Artemis and squealed, giving the shorter goddess a hug. "Where's your other half?"

"Oh, Ryan stayed home. I wasn't sure what I'd be 'porting into." She tossed her dark hair over her shoulder and shrugged. "Thanks for asking. He'll be happy to hear that you asked about him."

Persephone and I were likely the only gods who didn't refer to the human as her pet. I took a moment to greet the Muses, the Graces, and every other god I recognized from Demeter's place last year. I felt ridiculously happy to see them all alive and whole and smiling.

"That just figures," Adonis muttered.

"What figures?" Ares asked.

"May I?" Adonis grabbed a pencil off the table without waiting for permission and drew a line from Miami, Florida to San Juan, Puerto Rico.

Poseidon groaned and sat on the couch with a roll of his eyes.

Adonis added a line from San Juan to Bermuda, then from Bermuda back to Miami. "From right here?" He pointed to the lower center of the triangle.

I gave him a quizzical look. "Somewhere around there. Hang on." I swung by the kitchen counter and rifled through the giant stack of papers I'd accumulated. "Okay, so these"—I handed Adonis a handful of pages—"are the routes of all the ships the demigods went missing on."

"This is all of them?" He separated the pages, gold eyes narrowing as he counted the sheets.

"There are only so many routes, dimwit." Poseidon shook his head. "Or did you think every individual cruise sailed willy-nilly through the ocean?"

Adonis ignored Poseidon and put the printed, blue maps on the table, separating each sheet. "What's with the little arrows?"

"Those are days at sea. This"—I plucked another map from the stack—"is where I traced all the routes." I set the paper down on top of Poseidon's map. "And put an 'X' on the last point the demigods' cards were scanned, and another 'X' at the next port of call. They most likely went missing somewhere between the two, and absolutely went missing before the cruise ended, because they never scanned out."

"So you changed the color of the line with that last scan?" Adonis asked.

"Yeah." I flushed, conscious of all the gods pressing around me to get a better look at my map. The room felt cramped with this many people present. Too warm.

"Nicely done. So they all intersect . . . here." He circled the small area on the map.

"Which is a lot of ground—Er, water."

Adonis nodded. "But still," he said, pointing at the circle floating in the lower half of the triangle he'd drawn. "Come on, you have to see this."

"Shapes?" I glanced at Poseidon. "Humans have known about shapes for a while, right? Or did Zeus scramble that bit of history for me?"

"Yeah, we know *shapes.*" Adonis laughed. "But you really don't know what this is? Come one, I thought you knew everything except for like, good music and stuff."

"She knows nearly everything *real,*" Poseidon interjected. "The myths surrounding the Bermuda Triangle aren't—"

"Any more outrageous than the ones about you," Adonis added.

Poseidon rolled his eyes again. "There's no pyramid at the bottom of the triangle, no magic, no lost city. Statistically, there are no more vanished planes or ships or people there than any other spot in the seven seas, when you account for the fact that it's one of the most well-traveled routes in the Atlantic."

Adonis shrugged. "Except for the hundred or so demigods who vanished in the last year, you mean? The ones no one remembers going missing?"

Poseidon scowled. "Coincidence."

"Coincidence?" Adonis pushed his golden hair off his forehead, giving Poseidon a skeptical look. "If everyone's been charmed into forgetting the disappearances, how do you know there's not an even higher number of—"

"Either way," Athena interrupted, her voice stern enough to shut both the boys up. "We need to figure out who and what we're dealing with. What are we facing here? A god? A Titan? Something new? Can they teleport? If so, what's keeping them on the ship?"

Poseidon shook his head. "I put up a shield blocking teleportation as soon as you all arrived."

"My money's on a Titan." I shuddered, remembering how much charm I'd had to use to try and snap the passengers out of attack mode. "I've never seen anything like this, the entire bar—"

"Whole club," Poseidon corrected. "Not just the people sitting near us. Not a single head turned when those bottles broke. But you said we're dealing with more than one controller using a . . . charm chain?"

I nodded. "Created by a group of people who can use charm. More than are in this room right now, and we're the last of Zeus's known divine offspring. But Titans can create more gods, right? That charm has to be coming from somewhere."

"We can create more gods, too," Persephone added.

"None of us pass on charm, though. It's our lifeline." I had enough to spare some for myself if I ever wanted to reproduce, assuming I even could, but I had more charm than most. The others *needed* every ounce of their charm to generate enough worship to survive. "Ares, any of your kids get charm?"

"I've never passed on charm."

We went around the room, confirming what I already knew. "See," I said when the question came round to me. "It can't be from us."

"Wait, let's just get this out of the way," Persephone suggested. "*I* haven't charmed anyone aboard this ship. Ares?"

"I haven't charmed anyone aboard this ship."

I waited until the statement circulated the entire room. "Obviously, I have. But not to attack us. Any Titans missing from lockup?"

"Not to my knowledge," Hades said.

"You spent the last few centuries convinced Zeus was in the Underworld," Ares reminded him. "You may want to double-check."

Hades grimaced. "Aphrodite, weren't you worried Zeus created more gods like you? It doesn't sound likely, but—"

I frowned. "Hundreds of them?"

"They don't have to be as strong as you if they have numbers on their side," Artemis said.

"We should look into both possibilities," Persephone said. "Any Titan in particular we should be looking for? Who gave Zeus his charm?"

Crickets.

Okay, not actual crickets. We were in the middle of the ocean, after all.

"Rhea," Poseidon said finally.

"That's how she was able to convince Cronus to eat a rock instead of Zeus," Persephone exclaimed. "That whole myth makes so much more sense now. Okay, so I'll head to Tartarus and—"

"She's not in Tartarus." Hades ran his fingers through his hair. "We couldn't—wouldn't—She's not there."

"Then where is she?" I asked.

Poseidon and Hades exchanged a glance.

"I'll check in on her," Poseidon promised. "She can't teleport, so if she is behind this, which I doubt, she'll be shipbound. Plus, Olympian Steele is almost as deadly to her as it is to us."

Almost? Before I could ask about the qualifier, Athena spoke.

"While speculating has some uses . . ." Athena paused, waiting until all eyes were on her before she continued. "We should use our time wisely." She pulled a glossy map of the ship from the bottom of the stack of papers, and planted the thick sheet of paper on the table. "We need to search every inch of this ship and we need to talk to everyone so we can get some actual answers instead of wild guesses. Now, Aphrodite has done a wonderful job of keeping everyone in their rooms—"

"*Thank* you." I grinned at her, happy for the acknowledgement.

She nodded without missing a beat. "But we need to be absolutely sure we don't miss anyone, and we can't risk anything being hidden in areas we've already searched. So I suggest we take this deck by deck." She pointed to the middle of the deck where a small symbol indicated there were stairs and elevators. "We'll need someone to maintain a shield here and at the other exits."

"They can break shields," I reminded her. "With the Steele."

"Then we'll know exactly where they are." She flashed me a savage grin. "Hades, Poseidon, since you're our strongest two without charm, you are the logical choices for that task."

"And the rest of us?" Ares asked.

"Pair off." Athena divided up the decks by section, assigning some of us to shields and the rest to the search party. We'd search one deck at a time within shouting distance of one another. "We'll charm the passengers into forgetting we were ever there, once we finish their rooms."

"That won't work for Elise," I said. "She's immune to charm. I haven't been able to confirm whether Narcissus and Tantalus are immune or not, but they could be."

"We'll confirm that tonight," Athena said, unbothered. "And impress upon them the importance of their silence should charm fail."

Threaten them, she meant. I looked down, pointedly ignoring Adonis's heavy gaze.

"What if we don't find anything?" Artemis asked, her dark eyes glittering.

"Then we can hope we've already got all the weapons," Athena explained. "We'll figure out step two in a bit. Let's see if there's anything to be found first."

We settled on the questions to ask and the appropriate follow-ups, what to do if we found anything, and a dozen other practicalities before moving to the door.

"Coming?" I asked Adonis.

He shook his head. "I'm surprised you are. Shouldn't you *not* be using much power right now?"

"Persephone is going to do all the heavy lifting. The best thing I can do to recharge is to be seen by people."

Adonis didn't look convinced, but he shrugged. "See you later."

Chapter IXX

POSEIDON SHIELDED the room, locking Adonis safely inside. The first three decks were crew only, so we found a crewmember for Persephone to charm in order to get down to the sub-levels of the ship. Athena and Ares split off to search the people-free zones, while the rest of us started searching the crew's rooms.

By the time we reached the first passenger level, Persephone and I fell into enough of a routine to talk while we worked. Well, talk about other stuff instead of, "Do you think this opens?" Or worse, Persephone's bright voice wondering, "What's this for?" She was getting quite an education tonight going through people's private belongings.

The interior hallways on the lower decks tried to be well-lit, with recessed lighting in the low ceilings and track lights along the floors, but no amount of artificial light could make up for the lack of windows. Blue and tan lines on the carpet mimicked the effect of looking down at water near shore. So long as I kept my gaze latched on to the carpet, I wasn't so aware of the walls and ceiling less than an arm's length from either side of me.

"Are you okay?" Persephone asked as I marked the room we'd just finished searching off the map. She knocked on the door of the next stateroom. "It must have been awful when those poor people drowned. And gods know how many more were hurt in the fight." She gave a depressed shake of her head.

I made a noise she could take for assent. In truth, I wasn't all that upset about the passengers. Sure it had been shocking and terrible in the moment, but people died. It happened. And more often than not, death wasn't right or fair. I wasn't going to twist myself into knots over it. But if I told Persephone how I felt, she'd attribute my lack of grief to divine callousness.

But here was the thing. Humans were modeled after us. How else could they watch the news—a montage of war, death, and human suffering—over coffee, then go about their day as if nothing was wrong? People needed a certain level of callousness to get by without drowning in the horror story of life.

"I'll manage," I assured her after she charmed a couple into letting us search their room. This cabin looked much smaller than the room Adonis and I shared. The bathroom took up a little more space than a cubicle. The queen-sized bed left only a walkway of space around it, and the rest of the furniture clogged the entryway. Searching the actual room took less than ten minutes. Their luggage, not much longer. Nothing turned up. "So, I take it you haven't had a chance to chat with a Titan about your powers making 'stuff happen' like you wanted to?"

"No." Her bitter voice and the look on her face told me this topic was closed.

I frowned, torn between curiosity and her obvious desire to drop the topic. "How are you doing, anyway?" I watched Persephone out of the corner of my eye as we walked down the hall. "Since Zeus."

She knocked on a door. "Busy. All the realms, the god stuff, it can be pretty overwhelming. That's why—and I know you're mad at her for this—but that's why I'm so grateful for Melissa's 'no divinity allowed' policy." Persephone shot me an apologetic look. "She gave me a place to go where the entire planet isn't my responsibility. When I visit her, I can pretend all that stuff with Zeus never happened, and like, veg out, you know? Watch TV. Eat junk food. Gossip." *Be normal.*

That last bit wasn't spoken, but I knew Persephone well enough to know that desire was in there somewhere. Especially when it came to spending time with her favorite human. I waited until she charmed the next room's resident before saying, "I'm not mad at Melissa." Mad wasn't the right word for someone I'd considered a friend outlawing any references to *the* defining feature of my life. "I just . . ." I sighed, sweeping my hair behind my shoulders. "Persephone, we *are* gods. That doesn't disappear no matter who we hang out with. Life doesn't compartmentalize like that. I know we're both pretty new at this, but—"

Her green eyes glittered and she whirled on me, her chin held high. "I *know* what I am. And I've come to terms with everything that means, good and bad. I'm not ducking my responsibilities or wishing them away."

"Okay." I held up my hands in mock surrender as we moved into the next room. "But doesn't it bother you that she doesn't accept this *huge* aspect of who you are?"

Persephone shook her head. "She accepted that I was a goddess long before I did. She knows me, Aphrodite. Almost better than I do. *I* needed that space. I need a place where all of this"—she waved her arms—"isn't relevant." Persephone fell silent as we searched the next room. This one contained five beds. Searching through the luggage took nearly half an hour. When we emerged into the hallway, she gave me a thoughtful look. "Melissa's taking this psych class, and she says everyone assumes different identities based on who they're with. You talk about work stuff and act professional and different at work than you do at school, or with a group of friends versus strangers, or with your significant other. You speak a different language, even. She called it . . ." She trailed off, struggling to remember.

"Code switching?" I knocked on the next door.

"Yeah, that's it." There wasn't an answer, so Persephone pulled out the key we'd gotten from Miguel.

"Right." I went straight to the wardrobe, rifling through the life jackets. "But it's not about having different identities, it's using different aspects of the same identity. Nothing actually goes away when you're not—"

"I know." Persephone's voice echoed from the bathroom. "But I think the illusion keeps me sane. I talk to Melissa about nothing. Silly things, unimportant stuff. Human stuff. I talk to Cassandra and Helen about the same types of things, only that's Underworld stuff. And I talk to you about the Zeus stuff, or goddess stuff Hades wouldn't get."

"You don't talk to anyone else about Zeus? Even Hades?" I hated to ask about Hades. He and Persephone had hit equilibrium, so everything she knew, he knew, and vice versa. Hades could be listening to this entire conversation through Persephone now. Persephone swore neither one of them eavesdropped much. Not only would listening in be rude, but it was also difficult if they were trying to focus on something else. But still.

"Especially Hades." Persephone bit her lip as we moved on to the next room. "He's been different. I think . . ." She looked down, her hand frozen above the door. "I think after everything happened last year, it, I don't know, got to him."

I knocked for her. "We're going to look around your room," I told the startled man in a black bathrobe. "If there are any divine weapons, long silver stake-like things, you'll want to let us know now."

He blinked. "Um, okay."

We searched the room. "What happened got to *him?*" I dumped the man's suitcase on his bed. "*You* were abducted and tortured. What the hell does he have to whine about?"

Persephone closed the dresser drawers. "I kind of think that's the problem. Like, maybe he doesn't feel like he has a right to be upset or whatever because what I went through was worse. Only it doesn't work like that. We *all* went through hell last year. The things Zeus did were frickin' traumatizing. And not just for me. But I *can't* bring myself to talk about it with him. I need what Hades and I have to be separate, untouched. He's my sanctuary, you know? I'm safe there. Maybe not the healthiest approach, but . . ." She fell silent for a moment. "You're not the only one who has nightmares."

"Maybe you should try *not* sleeping." I winked at her and knocked on the next door. "Put Hades to use."

Persephone ignored the double entendre. "He definitely helps. I couldn't imagine waking up alone after—" She broke off. "I honestly don't know how you handle this all on your own."

"I just don't sleep."

Persephone shook her head. "We probably all need therapy."

I laughed. "Think Athena would charge us?"

Persephone giggled, and we both tried to ignore the fact that it *wasn't* silly. We were all so shattered and broken, no amount of therapy would ever be able to repair us to the point that the cracks didn't show.

"She probably would. So . . ." She let the word drag, her voice teasing as she shook a pillow free from its case. "How's *not* sleeping going, considering you're sharing a room with Adonis?"

I laughed, yanking open a suitcase. "Adonis and I are not together."

"Really?" Persephone pulled open the closet door. "Melissa thought you were head over heels for him."

I scowled, dumping out a beach bag and shifting through the contents. "And she still dated him? Nice."

"She felt bad about it." Persephone checked the pockets of a long jacket. "So . . . was she onto something?"

"It's complicated."

Persephone stopped in the middle of the hall and stared me down until my defenses crumbled.

"I think I fell in love with the idea of him. The reality's pretty disappointing."

"How do you mean?" she probed, as we moved on to the next room. A woman holding a sleepy-looking girl in footsie pajamas opened the door with a scowl.

"Do you have *any* idea what time it is?" the woman snarled. The child in her arms started wailing.

"We are so sorry," Persephone said, turning on the charm. "But we need to search your room."

"I can't charm him." I waited until Persephone finished questioning the mom before continuing. "Even accidentally. Everything he says and does is real, you know?"

"I do, actually." Persephone said. "Aphrodite," she scolded when I took a stuffed bear from the little girl.

"Baby jaguar," the little girl moaned. "*My* baby jaguar. Give him—" She fell silent under the influence of Persephone's charm.

"You can hide things in stuffed animals," I explained, giving the "jaguar" a cautious squeeze. "He's clean. Here you go, kiddo."

The little girl snatched her toy from me, giving me a look so cutting, I stepped back.

"Anyway," I said, once Persephone convinced the kid to go back to sleep. "He can't hurt me. He's not strong enough. So we balance. And when the whole thing went down with Zeus, he saved me. He trusted me, believed in me at a time when no one else could."

"But?" Persephone prompted after a moment's silence, closing the door as quietly as she could so we didn't reawaken the sleeping dragon.

"That's not actually him. I put him on this pedestal and made him into a symbol. But it wasn't fair to him. He can't live up to that, you know? And the real Adonis wouldn't want to anyway."

Persephone nodded, knocking on the next door. "I get that." Another vacant room. Which meant no luggage to search. Still, we went through the drawers and furniture.

"Uh-huh." I couldn't imagine another being, least of all Persephone, "getting" something I barely understood about myself.

Wait, another vacant room? I paused in writing a giant "V" on this square of the ship's map, trying to put my finger on why so many unbooked rooms bothered me. Persephone flipped on the lights, and the thought fled.

"No, really, I do get what you're saying." She raked her hair back, her hand stopping at the top of her skull. "I used to get a crush on literally every guy who was ever nice to me and it wasn't *them,* you know?" She flushed. "I always felt out of place, so I'd get really grateful when I got any attention at all. But I was too shy to act on my feelings, thank gods."

And I wasn't. Yup. Got *that* subtext loud and clear. "You think I'm insecure and desperate for affection?" I wasn't sure how to take that.

She pressed her lips together and glanced down at the carpet. "I think you're lonely. I'm not explaining this well." She sighed. "I'm saying I get it. I know what it's like to feel different and alone, and I know what it's like to seize onto that one kind gesture and read *so* much into it that everything the person says or does becomes . . . more. And you're right, putting him on a pedestal isn't fair to him. But it's also not fair to you, because you end up putting all this stock into someone who maybe doesn't deserve it."

My throat went tight. "Yeah."

"Besides, there's always Ares," she teased.

"He's not interested." I held my hands up in response to the "oh please," look she gave me. "No, trust me, Persephone. I've been there. He's *not* interested. But even if he was, it may not be either/or, you know? You and Hades are just weird. The divine default is not monogamy."

She shrugged. "Your love life, your choices. Date no one. Date one person. Date thousands. Date who or whatever you want, but—" She pushed her hair out of her face.

"But?" I repeated, unsure what she was getting at.

"Be careful." Her voice rose in question to make it clear she was making a request and not an order that I'd be forced to follow. "The pedestals I put boys on were low, because all they'd done is act nice. But it still *hurt* when they said or did something to bring them tumbling down. Your situation sounds a bit more loaded."

I chose my words carefully. "I appreciate your concern . . ."

"But mind my own business?" Persephone flashed me an apologetic smile and ducked her head. "I'm sorry. I'm probably just projecting my own stuff on to you anyway." She knocked on the next door. "Oh, did you hear about what happened with Cerberus?"

Tantalus opened the door and grinned when he saw Persephone and me standing before him. "I have dreams that start like this." He opened the door and motioned for us to enter. "Come on in."

Chapter XX

I WALKED INTO Tantalus's suite and found myself in a mirror image of the room I shared with Adonis. After a moment's hesitation, Persephone followed me inside.

"You're sweating," I observed, looking Tantalus over. He wore dark flannel pants and a white shirt. His golden hair looked messy, and sweat glistened on his neck. "Something wrong?"

"Am I?" Tantalus pulled at the neck of his shirt. "Well . . . this room did just get quite a bit hotter." Persephone made a disgusted sound, and he turned his attention to her. "And who are you?" he asked. "I know I haven't seen you on board." He closed the door, using the movement to plant a hand next to her. "How about we get to know each other better?"

I grabbed his arm and dragged him toward the living room, noting that Tantalus's balcony door stood wide open. "Can you search upstairs?" I asked Persephone. "I'll question him and get started down here."

"Deal." The relief was evident in her voice.

"Question me?" Tantalus asked. "Search? What are—?"

I turned on my charm; surely using my powers once wouldn't hurt too badly. My stomach clenched, but the pain felt more like a dull throb than the usual knife-to-the-gut variety. "Yeah, we're searching your room, and you're going to truthfully answer everything I ask, then forget we were ever here. Oh, and by the way," I added once Persephone disappeared up the stairs. "You're welcome."

"For what?"

I pushed him toward the couch and motioned for him to sit down. "I just saved you from a world of hurt. Don't flirt with her. She's not interested."

He sat down, looking toward the steps, as though hoping to catch another glimpse of Persephone. "Who is she?"

"Not interested. That's all you need to know."

Tantalus raised his eyebrows. "If you're going to 'question me,'" he emphasized the phrase and gave me a wry look, "I have a feeling I'm going to need caffeine. Want a soda?"

"Sure." I followed him to the kitchen and took a seat at the bar while Tantalus rummaged through the fridge.

Since Tantalus was in the know, I deviated from the usual questions, taking a more direct route. "Are you trying to kill me or any of the other gods?"

"No." Tantalus gave me an odd look and poured soda into two glasses. "Rum?"

I declined. He shrugged and turned his back to me, pouring a shot into one of the cups.

"Do you know of anyone who might want to?"

"Nope." He put the drinks on the bar and sat across from me.

I took a sip. "Are you in possession of any weapons that could kill a god?"

"No!" Tantalus drew back in surprise. "Is there such a thing?"

"Not that you're going to remember." I ran him through the rest of the questions and finished my drink.

When I started searching the kitchen, Tantalus stood. "Can I help?"

"Nope." Standing on my tiptoes, I scanned the top of the cabinets. The boat lurched and I lost my balance, making me stumble back into Tantalus. "Sorry." I turned to face him as he steadied me.

"Sure thing." His eyes met mine, then widened in surprise. A broad grin broke out across his face, weakening my knees.

Yeah, okay. He acted arrogant and self-absorbed, but he also looked really hot. What girl wouldn't react to finding herself in his arms?

Tantalus tilted my chin up. "If I kiss you, you're not going to turn me into a plant or anything, are you?"

I laughed. "Well I won't promise anything, but . . ." I touched my lips to his, keeping the motion light and teasing. "Don't you think I'm worth the risk?"

"Hell, yeah." Tantalus yanked me to him, his mouth meeting mine with practiced skill. He was one *good* kisser, and I'd know. I closed my eyes and let all my frustration, anger, and fear from the last two days fuel my kiss. My teeth grazed his bottom lip and he let out a low groan, pressing me against the cabinets as his hands roamed beneath my sweater.

"Hey, Aphrodite?" Persephone called from upstairs.

What the hell was I doing? Breaking away from Tantalus, I struggled to catch my breath. I should be searching the suite, not making out with the incredibly hot . . .

My thoughts trailed off into oblivion as I stared into Tantalus's gold eyes. I yanked him back to me using the drawstring on his pajama pants. His mouth crushed against mine as he swept the countertop behind me clear. Something clattered to the ground and shattered.

Stop! I jerked my head, breaking off eye contact with him. "You're using charm," I accused, as I scrambled down from the countertop.

"Always." Tantalus shrugged. "I can't exactly turn it off. I gotta say"—he slid a hand down my arm, trying to pull me back to him—"it's nice knowing that was all you." At my puzzled look, he tilted his head, gold hair falling into his eyes. "Well, you're immune, right? I couldn't possibly charm a god."

Footsteps thudded over my head. "Aphrodite?"

"Rain check?" Tantalus suggested, releasing his hold on my arm.

I stared at him, reeling in shock. He had charm? So, he was a son of Zeus. Three of Zeus's demigods on one ship? What were the odds? How many kids did Zeus have? And if Tantalus always used charm, how come I hadn't sensed him using any before?

How come I couldn't sense him using charm now?

And how could he have charmed *me*? No one could charm me, except maybe Persephone. But if my powers were fading, maybe all the rules were changing. I needed to test my immunity, but in order to do so, I needed someone who knew what they were doing.

"Hey." Persephone rounded the corner into the kitchen. "You okay?"

"I'm done in here." I moved away from Tantalus. "Did you need help with something?"

Aphrodite

Chapter XXI

THE REST OF THE search went by in a blur. I couldn't keep my mind on the task at hand. Not even when we searched the shops. It was pretty bad when even designer clothes couldn't hold my attention.

"So now what?" Ares asked, when Persephone and I joined the rest of the group huddled on the top deck at the very front of the ship. From here, we'd be able to see anyone coming, and the constant wind made a shield unnecessary for blocking sound. The ocean still looked black as pitch, but the horizon showed signs of dawn approaching. We'd already dismissed the Muses, Graces, and minor deities, instructing them to don glamours and blend in with the passengers, keeping their eyes open for trouble, so our group consisted of just us seven. Artemis, Persephone, and I claimed the window ledges while Ares, Hades, Poseidon, and Athena stood.

"I can't believe we didn't find anything," Artemis grumbled from the ledge next to mine. The three windows were set so deep into the wall overlooking the miniature golf course that they made pretty good benches, despite the inward slant.

"That's good, right?" Persephone sat tucked into the ledge on my other side. Not that I could see her very well around Hades, who leaned on the wall between us. "It means there were no more weapons."

"Maybe." Athena raised her voice to be heard over the air rushing around us. She leaned against the white rails of the ship, an entire person-length away from Poseidon and Ares. "But on this whole ship, someone should have known something. We didn't even pick up any stray power signatures. Whoever is behind this might have found a way to circumvent our shields."

"Either way, they know we're on to them." Poseidon's gaze focused on the sea.

"Pretty sure that cat was out of the bag *before* they attacked us with Olympian Steele." I wondered if I should broach the topic of my missing powers and the possible loss of my immunity. They couldn't count on me right now, and allowing them to think otherwise would be a bad idea. But before I could speak up, Persephone leaned around Hades, extending a hand. "Where to?"

I blinked at her hand, unsure what she wanted from me. "What?"

"You're done here," Poseidon said before Persephone could clarify.

"You can go home. I don't need you anymore. They know I'm on to them. I no longer have reason to be subtle."

"You were going for subtle and you sent *her?*" Ares shook his head and flashed me a grin. "No offense, Aphrodite, but you stand out."

I accepted the compliment with a shrug, turning my attention back to Persephone. "I'd like to stick around." I leaned against the cool glass of the window. "I've already established a rapport with the demigods. I think they'll tell me if something—"

"You charmed an entire room full of people into protecting us, nearly broke the charm affecting the attacking passengers, then charmed a ship's worth of passengers into staying in their rooms while we searched," Poseidon said, sounding impressed despite himself. "I think it's safe to assume you're no longer under cover. No one is going to assume you can be charmed into forgetting anything."

"Which means they'll be focused on her. That doesn't have to be a bad thing," Artemis said. "I could keep an eye out, see if anyone is watching her too closely."

"You guys do *see* her, right?" Ares waved an arm at me. "*Everyone* is going to watch too closely. Every head in every room turns when she walks by. That's what Zeus was going for when he made her."

"This is bigger than some missing demigods. Zeus said something was coming, something bigger and *armed*. I, for one, don't want to be caught off guard." Artemis looked at me. "Do you mind? Being our diversion?"

"Uh . . ." I needed to tell them. If I could be charmed, I was completely vulnerable. But could I risk them sending me away? Adonis and the other demigods were in danger. He wasn't wrong in his estimation of their importance—or lack of—to most gods. I glanced at Poseidon for guidance, but he pointedly ignored me, scowling down at the waves.

"How much time do we have?" Ares asked, crossing his arms.

"I'm not sure exactly." I wiped at the salty beads of water coating my face from the damp sea breeze. "If the patterns hold, the demigods will go missing somewhere between midnight and six a.m."

Ares glanced down at his watch. "It's already seven."

Artemis sputtered with laughter but I just stared at him, waiting for him to catch on.

He closed his eyes. "You meant next midnight . . . Yeah, I gotcha."

"And this is why we don't bother waiting on your input," Poseidon muttered, his navy eyes churning in time to the waves. "So, we need to—"

"Let it happen," Athena suggested.

"What?" Hades jerked forward in surprise.

Athena's grey eyes went flat, and her face took on that passive patient look I'd only ever seen in her expression when she grew super annoyed at having her advice questioned. "We need to know more about what is being done to the demigods, who is using them, and where these weapons are coming from. The surest way to do that is—"

"Use them as bait?" I didn't like the sound of that any more than I liked the idea of me being a diversion. But I wasn't surprised.

"No. *Be* the bait," Athena explained. "There are four demigods. Let's replace them. When they take them, they get us."

Huh, who would have thought Adonis and the goddess of wisdom would be on the same page, idea-wise?

"What do we do with the real demigods?" Persephone asked.

"Hide them in the Underworld until this is over," Athena suggested. Demigods were the only living beings who could go to and from the Underworld uninvited.

"Adonis and Elise can't be charmed," I added. "They might not go for it."

"I think we can leave Adonis." Athena mused. "If we do all get taken, it might be good to have a real demigod on hand who can do the talking."

"You mean the lying." If Persephone tried to mask the disapproval in her voice, she failed.

"Precisely." Athena touched her hair as though checking to make sure the wind hadn't damaged her severe style. As if a bun that tight could be dislodged by anything less than a tornado. I made a mental note to give her some tips later. Practical beauty was a thing. "Adonis has proven he can hold his own and is trustworthy. Those of us with charm will need to replace the demigods, and one of us will have to replace this assistant woman. From what I've observed, she's close enough to notice minor changes in Narcissus's behavior. As for the rest of us, we can use glamours to blend in with the passengers."

I looked up. There was no way I could keep up a glamour. "I—"

"Oh, not you," Athena clarified, smoothing her taupe power suit. "You've already been seen on this ship. It would be suspicious if you vanished. I think Artemis has the right idea. Let's let whoever's behind this waste their time watching you. With any luck, they'll never see us coming."

"I could replace Elise." Artemis's dark eyes were narrowed in thought. "The height difference is going to be a pain. What is she, five-seven, five-eight?"

"Wait, we can glamour height?" Persephone sounded so excited that we all paused to look at her.

"The further we are from our original form, the more power a glamour takes to maintain," I explained. "Height is a big one, because it impacts your entire skeletal structure. It wouldn't be practical day to day."

"Oh."

"I'll replace Tantalus," Ares said, getting us back on track with a wicked grin.

"This isn't a good idea," Poseidon objected.

"Do you have a better plan?" Persephone asked him.

"Yeah. Sink the boat. Get the weapons safely out of human hands. If whatever is behind all of this survives drowning, then we'll have learned more about the nature of it. If not, you and Hades can sort it all out in Tartarus."

Persephone stared at him for so long that Poseidon shifted, and rubbed the back of his neck. She turned, not saying a word to him. "Athena, your idea sounds wonderful. Ares, Artemis, thank you for volunteering." She looked to me. "I'll check in as much as I can, but for now—" She cast Poseidon a stony look. "If you *dare*—"

"You're not queen of this realm," Poseidon reminded her. "This ship is scheduled to reach your realm in two days—"

"Tomorrow," I corrected. "Well, like in an hour."

Poseidon shook his head. "At a private island, small enough to shield. But this ship will make port at Nassau in two days and that is an island too large to monitor every inch of. Right now, we have whatever is responsible for the missing demigods and these weapons trapped on a boat. I'm not letting it escape from my realm. Two days, and this ship stops moving. In the meantime, I can play Narcissus. I don't think he's one of Zeus's. Have you ever seen him use charm?"

I shook my head. "But every other demigod on the ship can. And I've heard some things that indicate there's a good chance he can too."

"Just in case, I'll be Narcissus's assistant," Athena said, bringing us back to the focus of the conversation. "I can charm if necessary. We'll make the exchange after the shoot today. That gives us time to observe their mannerisms."

"Does everyone have a phone?" Persephone asked. "We might need to reach each other without waiting around for a dreamscape."

"I've got one," Ares said.

"Me too," Artemis chimed in.

Athena, Poseidon, and I said nothing.

"Be back soon." Persephone vanished.

After we'd worked out a few more of the logistics, she reappeared with a handful of smart phones, secure in their boxes. "The guy at the store swore they were fully charged and ready to go."

The store? What time zone did she teleport to?

"I programmed all of our numbers into the phones, so all you'll have to do is charge it every now and then and keep it on. Don't hesitate to text me with any questions. Uh . . . do you all know how to text?" She handed a silver phone to Athena, who scoffed.

"We might not be as young as you, dear, but I can assure you, cell phones are not beyond our comprehension."

Persephone looked doubtful, but handed Poseidon a black phone without argument, then handed me a gold one. "I should have picked up some cases," she worried.

"We can shield them," I reminded her. "Thanks, though." I pocketed the phone.

After nailing down a few last-minute details, everyone was ready to move on to their assigned tasks.

"Ares," I called, running after him before he could get too far away. "Can I talk to you for a second?"

"Of course." He followed me across the deck, out of sight of the golf course. We stopped walking when we reached a glass wall looking down to the next deck. "Is everything with Poseidon—?"

"Handled. But now I need a favor." When his expression went guarded, I laughed. "I just need to test something. Can you turn on your charm?"

I hated to ask *him*, but Persephone was too strong—her charm might have worked on me even if my powers weren't fading. I didn't trust Athena with my weakness, and I didn't know Artemis that well.

"Maybe. What do I get for this favor?" he teased.

I gave him a playful shove.

"Ouch." Ares laughed. "Not the payment I was hoping for. But yeah, sure." He waited a beat. "Happy?"

I frowned. "I can't feel anything. Charm me."

"Really?" Ares gave me a mischievous grin and met my eyes. "Yeah, okay. Take off your top."

Gods, this sweater felt itchy. I reached for the bottom of my sweater and his eyes widened, mischief shifting to alarm. "Stop." He grabbed my hands. "That wasn't supposed to work."

What wasn't supposed to work? I looked down at his hands wrapped around mine at the bottom of my sweater. "Ares, seriously?" I jerked my hands free and shoved him. "*That's* where your mind goes?"

"Of *course* that's where my mind went."

I narrowed my eyes at him.

"I stopped you," he reminded me. "I wouldn't—I didn't—"

"Are you blushing?" The tips of his ears, just visible through his mop of curly hair, were bright red.

"That's not a line I would—" he continued babbling. "Not with you. Not with anyone, but definitely not with—Are you—" He paused. "Are you laughing at me?"

I stopped trying to hold back and burst out laughing so hard I couldn't breathe. I clutched my stomach, trying to suck in air between giggles. He laughed for a moment, despite himself.

His laughter trailed off when he realized I wasn't stopping.

"I'm sorry," I gasped, still giggling, gripped by the sheer absurdity of my situation. "It's not this funny, I just—I just—" I couldn't stop. I'd made the frickin' god of war, battle, and bloodshed blush. *I* could be charmed. There was a distinct possibility I was dying. I'd been attacked and harassed and insulted and become a model, and—

I could be charmed.

And I was probably dying.

My laughter was no longer audible, though my shoulders shook with my hysterical gasps.

Ares hesitated. "Aphrodite . . ." He draped an arm around my shoulder and pulled me close to him in an awkward embrace.

Despite myself, I leaned into him, clinging to his cold jacket. Once my laughter stopped and shifted into deep, shuddering breaths, he pulled away. "How come I can charm you?"

I hesitated for all of a second. But I was in way over my head, and I needed an opinion on this from someone who wouldn't benefit from my death as much as Poseidon. Shivering at the cold, morning wind biting through my sweater, I filled him in on *everything* that had happened since I boarded the ship, and Poseidon's theory. When I got to my encounter with Tantalus, Ares clenched his jaw, but didn't comment. "Do you think Poseidon's right about me having an expiration date?" I asked, after I finished the whole story.

"I think it's possible," Ares admitted. "The way Zeus made you . . . it's like nothing any of us have ever seen before. Maybe you just weren't built to operate outside of your realm. I mean, there's got to be some reason Zeus tossed you into Poseidon's realm right after he made you. Maybe he was keeping you weak until he moved everyone else into place."

I narrowed my eyes, thinking that through. Zeus would have known placing me in Poseidon's realm would bring my existence to the attention of one of two gods. Poseidon, of course, who at the time would have used a land-based deity popping up in his realm as an excuse to talk to Demeter, and everyone knew it. But Poseidon wasn't the only one who would have noticed. Hades would have, too. After all, he had access to a prophet. Either way, all roads led to Persephone, who at the time had no built-in resistance to my charm.

"He didn't teach you to control your powers," Ares reminded me. "So you were weak in the ocean realm, but the second your feet touched land—"

"Wham." My powers came back without any thought or direction. Persephone had tried to drown herself to get away from me. Hades had to transfer more power her way, just to return her to sanity. "That might explain why my powers are harder to access on the ship, but . . ." I frowned. "This doesn't *feel*/like I'm just disconnected from my powers. I had a full-scale panic attack last night. I've been getting claustrophobic, and crazy emotional. Something's *wrong* with me. I can feel it."

Ares drew in a deep breath and leaned against the glass wall. "I mean . . .

you've been traumatized. What Zeus did to you, the way he used you—" He worked his jaw, his eyes distant as if he was searching for words. "That doesn't go away just because you heal. It's always there, hence the nightmares. With your powers in place, you could wake up from that and be fine in a matter of seconds. But without them..."

"I'm getting the physical side-effects." I considered, rubbing my arms for warmth against the cold wind. I wanted to argue, but if any god knew trauma, it was War. "That tracks. Well, with any luck, your theory is right and I'll be good as new once I get to the island today, and—" I stopped when I saw Ares shaking his head. "What?"

"This island's too small to be considered fully outside of Poseidon's realm. You may improve a bit, but the real test will be Nassau. In the meantime—" He shrugged out of his jacket and draped the garment around me. "See if this helps."

The gesture felt oddly intimate. Ares and I had progressed *way* past hugging on our road trip last year, but having his jacket around my shoulders felt *really* good on a different level. Reassuring, somehow. The inside of the jacket retained Ares's body heat and smelled a bit like burnt cinnamon. I felt grounded for the first time since I'd stepped onto the ship. Almost like I was back in my realm. "This is your token," I realized.

Tokens were objects from a god's home realm that could act as a kind of conduit. Instead of struggling to draw power while in a foreign realm, a god could channel their power through their token, neatly avoiding all the yucky side-effects I'd felt since I set foot on Poseidon's turf. Unfortunately, Zeus had held back my ability to create one. I'd tried.

"Ares, I can't—"

When I started to slip my arms out of the sleeves, Ares tugged me toward him using the edges of the jacket, and zipped it, his fingers never deviating from the tiny piece of metal. When he reached the hollow of my neck, he paused. I tore my gaze from his hand and looked into his eyes.

"I can make another one. You, I can't replace. Be careful?"

My heart stuttered at the words unspoken, the silent promises in his eyes. I'd been *so* mad at him, and it was easy to stay angry while he was gone because he wasn't around to object. But I couldn't hang on to my rage anymore. "Gods," I managed to whisper. "You make it hard to hate you."

"I try." His lips twitched up in a smirk.

I leaned into him, tension easing out of my shoulders when his arms wrapped around me. "I miss this," I admitted, keeping my gaze fastened to his shoes. "Us. Can we just go back?"

He squeezed my shoulders. "Aphrodite..."

"I don't have expectations," I said, hurriedly, unable to stop talking now that I'd already stooped to desperation. I couldn't sink any lower, so why not keep drowning? "I know I'm a mess. So if it was just a fling..." I waved my hands. "So what? It was a *great* fling. You didn't need to—"

"It wasn't a fling. Not to me."

"—leave." The word was out of my mouth before I processed what he'd said, and somehow, knowing I hadn't misinterpreted or overstepped, made me feel worse. I looked up at him so fast I almost clipped his chin. "What?"

"It was more." He glanced down at the deck, then looked back up to me, a fire burning in his eyes. "*You* were more."

"Stop it." I moved away from him, shivering when I stepped out of his arms. "You don't need pretty words or grand gestures. I'm a sure thing, remember? I never asked for more, never expected it from you. So don't insult me by trying to pretend that I actually mattered. I was *fine* with—"

"You do matter." He stepped toward me, then seemed to think better of it.

"I told you *everything*." I couldn't keep the raw pain out of my voice. "And you *left*. For over a *year*. Just slipped away in the middle of the night like a coward. You don't do that to people who *matter*."

"You're right." He dropped his hand. "You're absolutely right. You didn't deserve that."

"I know," I said unzipping the coat and holding it out to him. "So don't do it again."

Chapter XXII

I RETURNED TO the suite, feeling numb with exhaustion and pain. I'd never felt this tired before, mentally, physically, or emotionally. Gods, if being human felt like this, maybe those short life spans were a mercy. With effort, I pushed Ares out of my mind. I couldn't muster up the energy to be angry with him anymore, and the alternative hurt every bit as badly. Best not to think about him at all.

To my surprise, Elise lounged at the bench near my door. "Oh, gods." Her eyes widened when she saw me. "You look like crap."

"Well, it was a long night." I slid my keycard into the slot and turned the knob, pleased Poseidon had already removed the shield around the room. "Come in?"

She followed me over the threshold, careful not to let the door slam, and raised her eyebrows as she took in the suite. The wall of windows allowed bright, morning sunbeams to stretch across the carpet. "Wow. This is huge."

I shrugged, flopping down on the white couch and putting my feet up on the wicker table, too exhausted to care about maintaining appearances. Where was Adonis? The squeal of the pipes turning on and the rush of running water from the upstairs shower answered me before I could even voice the question. Adonis's showers could take years, so if I could send Elise on her way, maybe I could get a bit of rest in before we headed to shore. "Elise?"

"Uh . . ." Elise jerked her head away from the paintings of sea foam and turned her attention to me. "I realized I never told you where to meet us for breakfast. We were all gonna meet up in about . . ." She pulled out her phone and glanced at the screen. "Thirty minutes? I can tell the girls to push it back if you need more time. With all the equipment and stuff that needs to be set up, it'll be a bit before we're needed on shore."

Crap, I'd forgotten about breakfast. "Yeah, sure." As much as I wanted to rest, I couldn't pass up an opportunity to find out more about Elise, even if she would be going to the Underworld in a few hours. Plus . . . I kind of liked her. She was randomly friendly, and I knew that had nothing to do with my charm. "Just give me a few minutes once he gets out of the shower. I have to change and at least wash my face." And either text Poseidon to reapply the shield, or drag Adonis to the Lido deck with me.

"Of course." She moved in front of me, pushing back the coffee table so she could perch on the fragile-looking wicker. "So . . . Tantalus interrupted us before you could answer me back at the club. And then a bunch of gods searched everyone's room last night and no one remembers. I know you guys don't just go around doing that unless something *really* bad is going on, so—"

"How could you know if we do or not?" I leaned forward. "Most people forget when we charm them to. This could be a nightly occurrence and unless someone like you happens to be there, people would never hear about it."

She frowned, glancing up the stairs when the water shut off. "Yeah, okay, maybe. But I've gone my whole life without seeing a god, and now I'm on a ship full of them. That makes me nervous. Should I be?"

"No, because we're getting you out of here." Maybe I was making a mistake in trusting her, but she deserved to know she was in danger, and I felt too tired to come up with a plausible half-truth to get her off my back. So, instead, I brought her up to speed.

"You're . . . helping us." She leaned back, looking dumbfounded. "I don't know what to say."

"Thank you?" I suggested with a yawn big enough to crack my jaw.

"Yeah." She had an odd expression on her face. "Thanks."

"Elise?" Adonis stood at the top of the staircase, dressed in a pair of shorts and a T-shirt. His hair looked strange when damp. Like liquid metal. "What are you doing here?"

She looked up at him, and in that moment, I recognized her from the magazines, billboards, and glossy posters in the mall. She modeled makeup or facial wash or something. Strange how I hadn't remembered before.

"Adonis." Her voice went perfectly neutral. Pleasant, yet distant. "We need to talk." She turned to me, the fake warmth in her eyes creeping me out. "Can we have just a minute? We won't leave the room, I promise. You can even shield it."

"Of course," I agreed, only slightly surprised she knew about shields. "I'll go take a quick shower and then we can grab breakfast."

"Uh—" Adonis protested, but I darted up the stairs and into the bathroom before he could articulate his objection. She couldn't charm him, and she wouldn't be able to leave if she tried anything. Plus, these rooms weren't soundproof. If Adonis needed me, I wasn't far.

Can you shield the room again for a few minutes? I texted to Poseidon. *Something came up.*

Done, he replied.

The passengers who were killed last night haven't been noticed yet, I texted back. No way the boat would dock, business as usual, and no chance every single one of those passengers was traveling alone. Someone should have noticed by now, and my charm to keep everyone calm and in their rooms would have worn off at dawn. *Is that our doing, or does that mean something else with charm is already on board making people forget?*

He didn't respond for a long moment. *Be careful.*

I swallowed hard, set down the phone, and turned on the water. Not us, then.

"... thinks we're in *danger!*" Elise's voice rose over the spray of the water I'd just turned on, whipping toward me like daggers.

"I *know*, okay ... should have told ..."

"People died! This isn't the time for secrets."

I stepped into the shower and their voices faded to indistinct murmurs. The scalding hot water was just what I needed to wake up and unknot the tense muscles in my back. Gods, these last few days had been brutal. Humming to myself, I scrubbed my skin with enough fervor to leave it raw. As if ridding myself of the sweat and grossness from searching all those staterooms last night would make the tension and fear wash away with it. Satisfied I was squeaky clean, I turned the water to cold. Any sleepiness I felt before fled under the freezing water. I gasped, my heart pounding, and turned off the shower, reaching for one of the white fluffy towels.

"How can you do it?" Elise demanded. "Pretend to care and then not warn—"

I scowled, finding the towel damp, and stepped out of the shower, dripping and cold to search for one Adonis hadn't already used.

"Here we go," I murmured, grabbing a shorter towel off the rack by the toilet. When I wrapped the terry cloth around me, it *almost* closed. "What is this, a washcloth?" What was the point of a towel this size? Seriously? "Oh well." I flipped my hair and started scrunching it dry.

"I *do* care." Adonis's voice exploded through the suite. "Do you think it was an easy decision? That I want anyone to get hurt? It's all screwed up, and I'm *sorry*, okay? I should have told you. I shouldn't have—" He took a deep breath before continuing at a lower volume. "Given the stakes, I don't know what else I could have done."

He had a point. The more people who knew the situation, the more likely my presence here would be noted as a threat. Of course, last night blew those concerns out of the water, but I hadn't thought to give Adonis the go-ahead to warn his friends.

Dry enough, I opened my suitcase, searching for beachwear. I slipped into my aquamarine bikini and pulled a sheer, white swimsuit cover on over it. There was no point in doing anything to my hair beyond a quick comb-through because the stylists would be working on it in what ... ? One hour? Two? I glanced at my phone. I'd been close. An hour and a half. Sliding into sandals, I inspected myself in the mirror.

"Not bad." My skin still looked flushed from the shower, and my damp curls hung around my face. I teased my hair a bit, trying to achieve what Melissa groused was my "annoyingly perfect, carelessly sexy" 'do. Not as easy without a glamour but—

"Don't!" Elise sounded near tears.

I sighed, studying the mirror in an attempt to find something, anything else that would make noise and use up some time. I was trying to give them privacy. The least they could do was keep their voices down.

"I don't want to be a part of this," she continued. "You shouldn't be either. When we leave, when we're safe, we can—"

"Oh, screw it," I muttered, opening the bathroom door. They'd had way more than a minute anyway. "We need someone who can lie," I explained, ignoring their surprised looks as I descended the staircase. Whatever. If they didn't want me involved in the conversation, they should have whispered. "So if he wants to stay—" My eyes met Adonis's. "He's welcome."

"Well." Elise crossed her arms with a huff. "He certainly can lie."

"Elise." If Adonis was trying to keep the frustration from his tone, he failed.

"*Adonis.*"

By the Styx! Was this what their relationship had been like? *Elise, Adonis, Elise, Adonis.* This conversation sounded like something out of one of the overly emotional animes Persephone watched. I considered throwing my name in there for variety, when Adonis seemed to recover his vocabulary.

"We're going to fix this."

Elise's glare could have frozen flames. "You'd better." She looked at me, tucking her hair behind her ears again. A nervous gesture, I realized, as she spoke. "I have one shoot today, but after that, I'll tell everyone I'm not feeling well and head straight back on board. If you meant what you said about getting me off this ship and out of the middle of all this—" She waved her hands around, eyes glittering with unshed tears. "Then that'll be a good opportunity."

"I do," I assured her.

She nodded. "Then let's not waste any more time. I'll cancel breakfast. Adonis, order room service, you know what I like. Make sure to get an energy drink for her." She motioned to me. "No offense, but you still look like you're about to fall out. And you should probably get whoever is going to be playing me here as well. There's some stuff my doppelgänger is going to need to know if she's going to have a prayer of pulling this off."

Chapter XXIII

AFTER WHAT TURNED out to be a tense, yet informative breakfast with Elise, Artemis, and Adonis, I couldn't wait to get off the boat and explore the cruise line's private island. Instead, I got swept along to another photo shoot. Adonis promised it would only last a few hours before another batch of models took our place. That was a few hours ago, so with any luck, we were almost done.

I was lying on the beach, posed on top of Adonis, and feeling absolutely jittery while a makeup artist arranged my hair so my red curls didn't block his face. The sun reflecting off the brilliant white sand hurt my eyes. At least, that's how I justified keeping my gaze focused on Adonis's bare skin. Despite the sun beating down on us, the cool breeze coming off the ocean kept us from breaking out into a sweat. Mostly.

What a beautiful beach. If I craned my neck, I could see the ocean, about half a football field's length away, water sparkling like liquid tourmaline. Voices caught my attention from my other side, and I glanced over to see one of the assistants fiddling with a light board. Another noise caught my ear and I turned, earning a sharp tug from a stylist named Trish as she messed with my hair.

"Could you *please* stay still?" Trish asked.

"Yeah, for real," Adonis added.

"Sorry." I flushed, realizing I was all but bouncing with uncontained energy. The fact that energy drinks could impact me at all didn't speak well for any chance of improvement once we hit real land, but rather than focusing on the negative, I decided to enjoy the novelty of the experience. If energy drinks could impact me now, could I get drunk? What else had changed? Could I—

"Seriously," Adonis complained.

"*Sorry.*" I said again. Geez, what was with him? He'd gotten all cranky and introspective after his argument with Elise. Instead of indulging his angst, I turned my attention to Trish. "So how does this sell jeans?"

"They sell your swimsuit, too." Trish sprayed my hair with something that smelled like a chemical version of a tropical paradise. "Not that it's likely to be in the shot."

Adonis and I both wore the company's signature jeans, but where he was shirtless, as per the norm, I wore a striped bikini top that actually looked pretty cute. If they didn't let me keep the swimsuit, I'd have to pick one up the next time I visited the mall.

Did their ad convince me to buy their product while I was in their ad? How meta.

"Okay, we're all ready." Trish stood, inspecting us from every angle, then made a beeline to the cabana the modeling agency had rented so we'd have a stretch of private beach.

As soon as she walked out of earshot, Adonis returned to his favorite topic of the day. "You think you're dying." His deep undertone brought me back to reality with a crash. "So why are you still here? If I were you, I'd want to have fun, you know? Hang out with people who . . . I don't know—"

I flashed him a sarcastic grin. "Do more than barely tolerate me?"

Adonis winced. "Yeah."

He had a point, but I felt too tired to dwell on it. While the energy drink certainly energized me, my head was still buzzing, and though the cuts and scratches had healed last night, my body still felt sliced and diced. A smarter goddess would probably take the hint and leave. Getting attacked went way above my pay grade, especially if my time actually was limited. But no, I'd stick around. All for one stupid demigod. Sometimes I wondered if Zeus's programming went deeper than I thought. Deeper than even Poseidon implied. Zeus had bred loyalty into me. Subservience too, though that one had a harder time sticking.

"Near death has pretty much been my state of being since my creation." I shifted my weight to my hands so there wasn't quite so much skin-to-skin contact going on. Damned distracting stuff, but somehow I couldn't bring myself to mind. "I can't just drop everything because of some theory. Poseidon could be wrong."

Adonis propped himself up on his arms. "Your shield broke when we were on the balcony."

"Someone distracted me," I teased, planting a hand on his bare chest and pushing him down on the sand.

We both fell silent for a series of shots where our faces were visible, but the second we were angled away from the camera, Adonis picked up right where he'd left off. "You wince every time you charm someone or put up a shield. You didn't used to do that."

"Watching me pretty close there, eh, Adonis?" I wiggled my toes in the warm sand. Were they almost finished setting up? I glanced toward the photographer, but he looked engrossed in a conversation with one of his assistants.

"You had a panic attack last night." Adonis's serious voice drew my attention back to him. "I've never heard of a god getting those."

"Maybe I was panicked," I snapped, losing my patience. What did he want me to say? Everything sucked, and at the rate my powers seemed to be abandoning me, I'd be dead by dawn? What good would dwelling on the obvious do? This would either pass or it wouldn't.

"Aphrodite, I'm worried. You stopped healing." His hand rested lightly on my back, and I winced, remembering the patchwork of scratches I'd gotten from sliding across the broken glass last night.

I leaned into his touch, accepting the apology in his voice. "I healed eventually."

"You stopped breathing. Do you have any idea how—" He looked away. "I didn't know what to do. I thought—I thought you were—" He took a deep breath, jolting when I touched his arm.

"I'm breathing now. You actually kind of saved me, again." I tilted my head and flashed him my most dazzling smile. "Thanks, by the way."

"No!" Adonis took a deep breath and exhaled with a forced calm before adding in a much quieter voice. "No, I didn't. So don't thank me. And next time you might not—"

"Who said there's going to be a next time?"

The photographer ambled over and rearranged us, moving Adonis, and talking me through the poses. By the time he finished, Adonis and I both faced away from the camera, my head on his chest, his arms wrapped around me. I let myself relax against him. When Ares touched me, I could feel power pulsing through him, leaving him hot to the touch. In his arms, I'd felt like a moth drawn to the fatal flame. I'd never wanted so badly to burn. Adonis lacked that heat, but his arms felt steady and firm. There was a comfort here I desperately needed right now.

When Adonis spoke, I could feel the words reverberate through his chest. "You should get off the ship. Ask Persephone to teleport you somewhere safe while we're in this realm. Anywhere but here."

I didn't tell him I'd turned down that exact offer last night. This was the third time in as many days that Adonis had asked me to leave. If he asked again, I might have to take the request personally. "I'm not leaving."

"You were attacked and charmed—"

I gave an exaggerated groan, and sat up, straddling him per the photographer's instructions. "I told you, I might not have been charmed when I made out with Tantalus."

"Yes, you were." Adonis propped himself up on his arms and leaned toward me in a half-sitting position. "You wouldn't have kissed him otherwise."

That was a pretty big leap. "What makes you so sure?"

"Because . . ." He trailed off, rubbing the back of his neck. "You're not subtle when you want to kiss someone. The way you look at me, the way you looked at Ares last night . . ." He glanced down at the sand. "A blind man could see it. You're a lot more transparent than you think."

I gave him a level look. "Then you know I'm not going anywhere."

"Don't stay here for me. Please, Aphrodite. Not for me."

"You're *really* worried," I realized, shocked at the level of concern in his voice. I tried to inject some levity into the conversation. "And here I thought we weren't friends."

"I told you, I'm not pretending." Adonis flashed me a playful grin for the camera and gripped me tighter before he rolled over. I half-laughed, half-shrieked with surprise at finding myself lying on the sand beneath him.

"I care." Adonis worked his arms free, planting one on either side of me to support his weight. "I don't know exactly when that happened or to what degree. I've mostly tried to ignore it. But then . . ." He broke off with a sharp shake of his head.

"But then?" I encouraged, brushing his hair back from his face.

"You stopped breathing." Adonis's voice wavered. "The way I felt, in that moment . . . I can't ignore that anymore. If you stay for me, and you get hurt or worse, I couldn't live with myself." His gold eyes bored into mine, full of fear. "Please, Aphrodite. *Please* go."

"And if I left and something happened to you?" I wouldn't insult him by asking him to leave, even though I knew Persephone would hide him in the Underworld with the others if I asked. Adonis wouldn't hide while demigods on the surface went missing. Everyone in his family was a demigod. "What do you think that would do to me?"

"Aphrodite . . ." He hung his head and his forehead brushed against mine. "I'm not. . . . I'm not w—"

"They said that's a wrap. *Hello?*"

Elise's voice sent Adonis scrambling to his feet in shock. I glanced around, surprised to find all the equipment being broken down and no one except Elise actually focusing on us.

Adonis tilted his head. "You're not—"

"No need to announce it to the world." Her face might belong to Elise, but the smile sure didn't. "Just wanted to check in with you guys before I head back to the boat." She turned around, slow, with her arms out. "How do I look?"

"Just right." I grinned at Artemis. "Be careful, will you?"

"You, too."

"I will." But somehow, I doubted all the caution in the world would be enough.

Chapter XXIV

ONCE ELISE AND Artemis made the switch, all Adonis and I could do to help was stay out of the way and look "normal."

"I think they stock this water with sand dollars." Adonis's hands were full of the sandy disks, an expression of delight lighting up his face.

"Probably." The water looked so clear, I could see reflected ripples making a patchwork pattern along the sandy bottom below. If I squinted, I could make out nearly a dozen sand dollars within splashing distance. Sunlight fractured upon hitting the crystal-clear water, sending rainbows sparkling in the rise and fall of the gentle waves.

Grinning, I plucked the largest sand dollar from Adonis's fingers and sprang away from him.

"Hey!" He splashed after me. "There are like, a hundred other ones you could get." Adonis threw a shard of a sand dollar at my head. "Get your own."

The sand dollar hit my head with a thunk before crumbling and splashing into the sea. I kicked my feet, splashing Adonis. "But I want this one."

"Never!" He laughed, sending a spray of water in my direction.

I held the sand dollar at arm's length above my head. "I'll throw it!"

"Don't you dare." Adonis lunged toward me and looped an arm around my torso to pull me to him and try to grab the disk from my fingers. I pushed backward off the sand bar. We went under, pushing and pulling at one another until we tumbled into the shallow water, sand scraping at my back.

He grabbed my hand, looking at me in askance when he found my clutched fingers empty.

"I dropped it," I admitted.

He burst out laughing. "Bet I find it first."

"You wish." I dove into the water.

The hours stretched into eternity. We went scuba diving, played volleyball, and lounged on the beach. Clouds wisped into thin lines in the bright blue sky. Fragrant pink blossoms bloomed beside tiny, spiky palm trees and thick cedar pines. And for a little while, I felt as if we'd frozen one perfect day in paradise.

Then the sun started to sink into the aquamarine waves, and the warm, euphoric feeling I'd enjoyed all day froze in my chest. Whatever was happening to the demigods would happen tonight, and I might not be able to stop it. I eyed Adonis, swallowing hard at the sudden pressure on my chest. It wasn't just him who'd be in danger tonight. Ares, Artemis, Athena, even Poseidon were making themselves targets and I was powerless against whatever was coming.

Suddenly, I wanted nothing more than to head back to the room. I felt sick with fear and cold, too. I shoved my worries out of my head and focused on the physical instead. The sun did a pretty good job of drying my bikini, but my hair still felt damp. Between the dying daylight and the constant sea breeze, my sheer swimsuit cover didn't stand a chance against the chill.

I brushed sand off my legs and arms, to no avail. The beach looked beautiful, but the white granules got everywhere, and the powdery substance clung to my skin like foundation. A flicker of flame caught my attention down the beach.

A group of models sat around a campfire. Snatches of laughter and conversation made their way to us on the wind, but we weren't close enough to make out words.

"What are they doing?" I narrowed my eyes, trying to see clearer. Judging by the laughing and jeering when someone poured a shot, they seemed to be playing some kind of a drinking game.

"They're playing Truth." Adonis yawned, stretching in a way I found incredibly distracting.

"What, like Truth or Dare?" I forced my gaze to his face.

"Just Truth. We ah . . . cut the dares after some . . . incidents. It's a stupid game," he explained. "Everyone thinks the whole thing is dumb, but, you know . . ." Adonis shrugged. "It's something to do to wind down after a shoot whenever we're stuck on location. They ask questions, and if you don't answer or if you lie, you have to drink."

"How would they know you're lying?"

"Tantalus charms them into being honest, not that they realize it. Not the best game to play if you're an impostor who can't lie, though." Adonis eyed Tantalus, squinting to see him in the distance. "So I'm guessing Ares hasn't taken his place yet?"

I texted Ares.

He's always in a group, he replied. *If he doesn't go somewhere alone soon, I'll have to wait until he gets back to his suite.*

I frowned at my phone. "It's still him."

"Tantalus probably hasn't been alone." Adonis scowled at the fire and let out a deep breath. "He tends to stay in a crowd. What if he stays in a group the whole night? He might not even go back to his room alone."

"He didn't have anyone with him last night."

"Probably still hoping for a shot with you."

I could use that. I texted Ares my plan, then pulled off the swimsuit cover, folding it into my bag. "Stay here."

"Aphrodite, don't." Adonis followed right on my heels as I approached the fire, blazing green and blue thanks to the sea salt.

"Mind if I join you?" I flashed Tantalus a smile.

"Please." Tantalus stood and reached for my hand, pulling me to the spot beside him. "We're playing a game. I'm winning, but it's not too late to join in."

"If by winning, you mean well on your way to passing out drunk." The brunette next to Tantalus gave him a playful shove.

"Was that not the point of this game?" He grinned, then turned his attention to Adonis. "You can join too, have a seat. Play a round. You pass, you drink. You lie, you drink."

"Isn't the ship leaving soon?" Adonis asked. "Maybe we should head back."

"It's not going to leave without us," Tantalus said with such certainty that I wondered who he'd charmed to make that arrangement.

He motioned for one of the crew to grab us some shots. "Pass on whatever questions you like except mine. I *really* want to hear your answers."

When I hesitated, his eyes bored into mine. "Come on. It'll be fun."

The sooner the game ended, the sooner I could get Tantalus alone and Ares could make the switch. I relaxed, sitting on the log Tantalus indicated, joining the circle of seven other models. The air shimmered with heat from the blue and green flames rising from the salt-coated driftwood and the smoke bit at my taste buds. The musky campfire scent always reminded me of the fires Ares, Hephaestus, and I grilled hot dogs on during our road trip last year. Unlike the bulk of that trip though, not a single cloud marred the sky, allowing the crisp moonlight to beam down and reflect off the pure white sand.

"Violet, I believe it's still your turn." Tantalus motioned for her to ask a question.

Violet, a dark-haired model, turned to me. "We'll start small. Ever kill anyone?"

The girl next to her burst out laughing. I gave her an icy smile then turned to Violet, waiting for the laughter around the fire to die down to a nervous silence. "Pass." I took a shot.

Tantalus's laugher sounded a bit forced. "Good one. Adonis, what was the last lie you told?"

A long look—one I couldn't decipher—passed between the two of them. "I apologized to Elise."

That drew a few hisses and snickers from the group of models. I looked around at their smiling faces and realized Elise was not well-liked. Huh. I hadn't cared for her either at first, but she actually seemed pretty nice. Friendly, even.

Tantalus stared at Adonis. "You gonna make me say it?"

Adonis clenched his jaw and took a shot.

"I thought so." Tantalus turned to me. "Who was the blonde you were with last night?"

"Pass." I reached for another shot, but Tantalus grabbed my hand, hard enough to hurt.

"Who." He met my eyes. "Was. She?"

"Persephone." I filled him in on as many details about her I could think of, forgetting the words even as I spoke them.

Adonis glanced from me to Tantalus, his face darkening. "Stop charming her; let her go."

"When I'm done with her. Oh, and don't worry. No one is going to remember anything you or I say to or regarding her, isn't that right, everyone?" He met each model's eyes before settling on me.

"Yeah," I said, chiming in with everyone else. Wait . . . Why did I say that?

"We're just having fun." Blue-green firelight flickered across Tantalus's golden features. "Nothing unusual going on, right?"

Every head around the circle nodded.

Adonis worked his jaw. "Tantalus . . ."

"Careful, Adonis," Tantalus cautioned. "You're getting awfully close to crossing the line here. Look, *you* don't have to play. Go back to the boat. I'll get her back to you, eventually."

Adonis sat next to me, his expression stony.

Tantalus leaned forward, gaze intense. "Why were you searching the ship?" His voice sounded so low, I almost couldn't hear him over the crackle of flame.

He shouldn't have remembered the search. Either he was immune, or I'd been so charmed out of my mind, I only thought I'd made him forget. Good. I couldn't imagine why I'd ever want to charm him into forgetting anything. "We were attacked by charmed passengers with Olympian Steele. We needed to make sure there was no more left on the boat."

"Why are you on the boat to begin with?"

My phone buzzed, vibrating in my bag, and setting my beach tote glowing with a cool blue light. I blinked, staring at the bag. What did I say? Why—

"Hey!" Tantalus's sharp voice brought my attention back to him. "I asked you a question."

Right. I scrambled to remember. "Demigods are going missing. We're trying to figure out where they're going and why."

Tantalus made a surprised sound. "Any leads?"

"We know the demigods will go missing tonight, but that's about all we know." My fingers dug into the sand, feeling the powdery granules slide against my palm.

"Tell me everything you've found, and everything you've planned so far.

Aphrodite

Who is working with you, and what can they do?"

"Tantalus," Adonis objected. "Enough."

Words spilled out of my mouth, impatient and eager. When I finished, Tantalus turned to the next girl. "What's your favorite color, Andrea?"

"Blue."

He made his way around the circle, each question more innocuous than the last. I dug my toes in the sand, frowning. Did he ask me a question? Or did he skip me? Not that I minded being skipped in this game, but. . . . He'd asked me something, hadn't he?

I looked to Adonis for clues, but he wouldn't meet my eyes.

"My turn," the brunette next to Tantalus announced. "What the hell kind of a name is Tantalus? Like, seriously, why do you all have such weird names?"

Tantalus's face darkened. "It's Greek. And Nikki was a weird name once upon a time. Naming trends have to start somewhere."

"No offense, but I somehow doubt your parents are going to be trendsetters in the baby name sphere." She laughed, giving Tantalus a good-natured push, and continued around the circle. When she got to Adonis, she asked, "Are you and Tantalus related?"

The two demigods exchanged looks, but Tantalus answered. "Not to our knowledge, why?"

Well, actually they were. But I guessed Zeus would be rather hard to explain.

She flushed at the challenge in his voice. "Well . . . I mean, you're both Aurums. I've heard it can be genetic."

I resisted the urge to roll my eyes at the human explanation for demigods.

"I'm sorry," Violet interrupted. "Aurums?"

"You know," the brunette said. "People who look like them. All gold and stuff."

"Most of the time, it doesn't run in families." Tantalus's smirk looked less than friendly. "Aurumnism is a genetic abnormality that absolutely anyone can be born with, no matter what their ethnicity or family history."

"We prefer people with Aurumnism," Adonis added.

What, were they reading from the same pamphlet? Both their answers sounded super rehearsed.

"What's the difference?" Violet asked.

Adonis glanced down at the sand, his face flushed with embarrassment. "Person-first language is a bit less dehumanizing."

"Dehumanizing?" One of the other models laughed. "You guys, like, rule the world. How many famous people have it? Like one in ten?"

"At least," Andrea chimed in. "Seems like every other movie star, model, or singer has it."

"My history prof told me that you guys were held up as gods in most ancient societies."

"We also made handy sacrifices. And today, we go missing and die a lot thanks to human trafficking and crazy people who think we're some kind of unnatural abomination." Tantalus's voice sounded dry. "Let's move on." He gave the brunette a pointed look.

"Yeah, okay." Nikki turned to me. "What's your number?"

"Uh." I frowned, trying to remember the number to the phone Persephone gave me. "Seven o-six—"

She laughed. "No, no. I mean your *number*. How many people have you slept with?"

"People?" I mused, leaning back, enjoying the way the words made my lips tingle. *After one shot?* Even if my divine tolerance decreased to human levels, I shouldn't be feeling tipsy yet. Right? What was in these things? No more passing for me. "Hmm . . . I don't know that I've—"

"Beings," Tantalus corrected so I couldn't equivocate. When Nikki shot him a puzzled look, he turned on the charm. "Don't ask."

I felt ultra-aware of Adonis sitting next to me. And I wasn't sure I wanted him to know my number. Against my better judgment, I downed a shot.

"Aw, come on." She pouted for a moment, then stopped when Tantalus whispered something in her ear. "Okay. Adonis . . . "She laced her fingers together over her knee, and fluttered her lashes with a come-hither look so impressive, I found myself taking notes. "What is your room number?"

Adonis gave her a sideways grin at the obvious invitation in her voice, took an inward hiss of breath, and took a shot.

"Ouch," cried another model. There were snickers and jeers around the campfire and Nikki turned bright red.

"It's occupied," Adonis offered by way of apology. She followed his gaze to me and shrugged.

"Your loss," she replied with as much dignity as she could muster, and moved on to the next question.

"Pass," the next model replied.

"Third pass," Tantalus cried. "Lightning round, who are the unlucky victims?" He spun an empty beer bottle in the sand and grinned when the mouth came to a stop pointing at Adonis. "Heads or tails?" He flipped a coin in the air.

"Heads," Adonis said.

The quarter landed in the sand with a thunk. Tails.

"Two minutes, double shots so pass or lie at your peril." Tantalus filled a few extra-tall shot glasses and placed them in front of Adonis. "What's the most horrible thing you've ever done to another being?"

Adonis took a shot.

Aphrodite

Tantalus grinned. "Biggest regret?"

"Meeting you."

I frowned and looked between the two of them. What was *this* about? Each question was more hostile than the last. The air felt thicker with tension than smoke, and no one looked as if they were having fun anymore.

Tantalus leaned forward. "How's your little sister?"

Adonis ground his teeth and took another shot.

"She still auditioning for a role on *Teen Mom*?"

I raised my eyebrows. A couple of the models cleared their throats and looked away. I had a feeling there was a well-known story here, and no one looked too thrilled with Tantalus bringing up the subject.

"Shut up."

"Oh . . . that's a yes, I take it. I'm not surprised. She was a great lay."

"I said, shut up!" Adonis sprang to his feet, sand flying everywhere. I stood, ready to intervene, then reconsidered. Tantalus earned whatever Adonis chose to throw at him.

"Whoa, okay. Minute's up," Violet declared. "Your turn." She motioned to the blonde whose pass had triggered the lightning round.

"Yeah, okay." She turned to Tantalus. "What the hell was that? Buzz kill much?"

Tantalus grinned, and even though I couldn't sense power coming from him, I could tell he used charm, because everyone relaxed visibly.

Adonis shook his head. "I'm out of here. Aphrodite, come on." He turned to me, then paused, sucking in a deep breath and sank back to the sand. "Or . . ." He held up a finger. "I'll wait. What's in those shots?"

Tantalus's smile looked predatory in the flickering firelight. "Something special."

"Let me get you some water," Andrea murmured, reaching into the cooler. She passed the water bottle to Adonis, but he didn't seem to notice because he was staring at Tantalus with a startling intensity.

"Most skin shown for a photo shoot?" the blonde asked me.

I blinked, bringing my attention back to the game. "Less than Adonis." That got a few laughs. Leaning back, I described the outfit I'd worn today.

"A bikini top and jeans?" The blonde laughed. "Aw, you are new. Where did you come from anyway? I've never seen you before."

"That's more than one question," Tantalus interjected. "Moving on."

When my turn came around again, one of the male models asked, "How old are you?"

I smiled at him and raised my glass, but Adonis grabbed my arm. "Don't."

My smile faltered and I looked at him, but he was still staring at Tantalus. "Yeah," he said after a moment in a slurred voice. "Nobody's going to remember this conversation."

My mind went blank. Blinking rapidly, I tried to clear my fogged thoughts. Something was happening here. Something important. I needed my wits about me. But I couldn't. . . . Wait. What did I just think? Something was wrong?

Adonis struggled to his feet. "How much . . . ?" He took a deep breath and clenched his fists, as if he was trying to keep from swaying. "How much did you give her?"

"What do you care?" Tantalus rose to his feet in a smooth, uninhibited motion, and moved toward Adonis. "You know what she is. You hate her kind more than most."

"She's not like them." Even I winced at the wistfulness in his tone. Adonis didn't believe I wasn't "like the other gods," any more than I did. I was a goddess, no matter how much he wished otherwise. I wasn't going to change.

And I shouldn't. I didn't see my divinity as something I should be ashamed of. If he couldn't—*Aphrodite!* Some clear and functioning part of my mind tried in vain to keep me in check. *On a scale of one to important,* that *doesn't even rank. Break the charm. Now!*

"Don't kid yourself, Donnie." Tantalus pushed Adonis. There couldn't be much force behind the shove, but Adonis went sprawling. "She's exactly like them." He turned and met the eyes of each person around the circle. "Keep him out of my way." His eyes found mine and my mind cleared. What was there to be confused about? I'd just do whatever he said. "How about you and I go someplace more private?"

Adonis grabbed my hand. "Aphrodite, stop!"

Had he forgotten the plan? I needed to get Tantalus alone. I slipped free of Adonis's grip, stood, and followed Tantalus into the night.

Chapter XXV

COME ON, APHRODITE! You're the frickin' goddess of charm. Break this. Despite my mental struggle, I still hadn't broken free when Tantalus led me into one of the small, three-sided beach huts.

"Stand here." He pushed me against the wall in the back corner, my feet scuffing over the wooden slats of the floor.

Though I stood still, my mind felt like a battleground. I struggled against the charm, pain flaring through me every time I tapped into my powers. Panic flooded my system. My breathing quickened, and I felt like the dingy, wooden walls of the hut were closing in on me. Through the open wall, I could see the moon glittering over the ocean. Despite the small hut being maybe the size of a parking space, freedom felt so far away.

Come on! This was just charm. I'd overcome worse. My head spun, stomach twisting as my vision blurred. Still, I called upon more and more power. *Finally,* the charm snapped and my abilities flared to life within me. I gritted my teeth against the pain and channeled as much charm into my gaze as I could. "Stop—"

"Ah, ah, ah." He clamped a hand over my mouth. "No fighting back."

The sheer power behind his command slammed into my mind like a sledgehammer. Was he *that* strong, or had I just become that weak?

Did it matter? I was screwed either way.

He stared at me for another moment, pushing more energy into his command, and gradually, my mind eased. Fight back? To what end? I stared at Tantalus in mute adoration, unsure why I'd ever wanted to fight against what *he* wanted.

Tantalus moved his hand away from my mouth and I mourned the loss. Did I do something to upset him? How could I fix this? Tears brimmed in my eyes, and I couldn't seem to catch my breath. Why did I always screw everything up?

"I need a favor." He studied me for a long moment, his expression uncertain.

Oh, thank gods! I leapt at the chance to redeem myself, despair dropping off me like a lead weight. Beaming, and thrilled beyond words that he'd deigned to speak to me, I took a deep breath. "I'll do any—"

A shield shot up around me, slamming me into place and cutting off my words. Tantalus made a strangled gasping sound. Black veins crisscrossed over his face, blood vessels bursting. He flew away from me and hit the opposite wall with a thud. I struggled against the shield, or tried to, but a wave of dizziness pushed me back into place. Tantalus sprang to his feet and smacked into a five-foot tall bit of blond fluff with glittering green eyes. Vines sprang from the ground, breaking through the wooden slats in the floor and wove around Tantalus. He blinked out of view as another layer of the shield surrounding me clicked into place.

"No!" I struggled against Persephone's shield. "Persephone, stop!"

"Aphrodite?" Ares moved in front of me, and the shield Persephone cast to hold me into place shattered.

"Did he hurt her?" Persephone didn't take her eyes off Tantalus. "*Ares.* Is she okay?"

Of *course* I wasn't okay. Tantalus was about to get torn apart by the world's shortest goddess, and nothing I could do would stop her. "Please, Persephone. Don't hurt him!" I lurched forward, trying to stop her.

Ares held me back. "Aphrodite, I'm sorry about this."

Why did he keep saying my name like that? He sounded so frickin' contrite, that I actually wanted to kill him. "Let. Me. Go," I growled, looking him full in the eye. But of course, my charm didn't work.

Black energy sparked between Persephone's fingertips as she stared down Tantalus. So much power charged the air that her hair seemed to float, as if gravity worked differently around her. "You can speak now. Drop the charm, and maybe you'll be able to move too."

"First, tell me why he's been watching me all day." The demigod jerked a finger toward Ares. Tantalus didn't look nearly frightened enough. Maybe he didn't think the tiny blond standing before him was really a threat. Demigods didn't sense powers the same way full-blooded deities did. Or normally did. While I could almost see an aura of power crackling around Persephone, I couldn't feel the energy.

"Aphrodite, look at me." Ares winced as my fist found his face with a satisfying smack. "This isn't you. You can break this; you just have to remember to try. Talk to *me.*"

"*Shut up!*" I kicked Ares as hard as I could.

"I shielded her for a reason," Persephone called over her shoulder. "Why'd you break it?"

Ares tightened his fingers and raised his voice so Persephone could hear him over my enraged cursing. "Because you should never shield anyone who's been charmed like this. I've seen people break bones or worse trying to get free."

"Good to know." Persephone flashed Tantalus a grin so cold, she must have picked it up from Hades. "Yeah, you're not in a position to negotiate here. Drop your charm, or I will end your ability to use it."

She was going to kill him. "Persephone," I screamed, trying to twist free of Ares. "*Please.* Stop! Don't!"

"Why did you search my room last night?" Tantalus didn't seem the least bit disturbed by my outburst. "What do you want from us? I know demigods are going missing, and now there's something wrong with Elise and Adonis. Neither one of them would spend a minute with a god if they had a choice in the matter."

"Let him go!" I kicked, hit, and clawed at Ares, to no avail. "Don't hurt him!" Gods, I felt useless. What good was being a goddess if I couldn't keep even one person safe?

"Answer me," Tantalus demanded. "Or I swear by the Styx, I'll tell her to drop dead."

Tantalus and Persephone blinked out of sight as a new shield slammed into place between us. I couldn't even hear them anymore. "No! Persephone," I screamed, trying to push past Ares, but he didn't budge. "Please, Ares! Please! Let me go to him. *Please,* Ares. Let me go. If you let me go, I'll do anything you want, Ares, please. I'll do anything!"

Ares clamped a hand over my mouth.

I kneed him in the groin and slammed my elbow into his stomach. "Let me *go,*" I shrieked when Ares's grip loosened. Twisting free, I lurched forward, and then froze as the charm broke and sanity thrust back into my brain. "Oh, gods." My knees buckled and I crumpled to the floor. "Oh, *gods,*" I said again as Ares knelt beside me.

"You're back now." Ares wrapped his arms around me. "It's over."

My vision blurred, and I couldn't stop shaking. Never again. I'd never wanted to feel that way again, and now—"There was nothing left of me; there was nothing left."

I was going to be sick. "Persephone, where's Per—?" I tried to stand, but as soon as Ares's arms slid off me, the weight of my promise to Ares hit me like a bag of bricks. Anything. I'd promised him anything.

"She took Tantalus to the Underworld to snap his charm over you." Ares glanced at where they'd been. "She'll be back."

Anything. Anything. Anything. The word echoed through my mind. An unconditional promise. No limits, no expiration date. I sank back to the ground as the full horror of what I'd done pierced through me. The rough floor bit at my knees, then arms, as I slid forward, head in my hands. "Oh, my gods."

"Hey, hey." Ares scrambled forward, ducking his head almost to the floor to be level with me. "I would *never* call you on that. When I ask something of you, react exactly as you would without your promise in place. Got it? It weighs *nothing.* I would never do that to you."

I wouldn't hesitate to use an unconditional promise, no matter what the circumstances were when it'd been given. I'd bound Poseidon in what, two seconds into his misunderstanding? No wonder Ares had left that night. I was every bit the monster Zeus was.

"Think you can stand up?" Ares looked me over. "You've got to feel freezing in that." He snapped his fingers, and his jacket appeared. He draped it around me.

I sighed as the warmth enveloped me. "Thank you." I took his hand and struggled to stand, swallowing hard. "I feel weird, Ares."

"Adrenaline, probably. I've got you." He supported my weight as I sagged against him, then frowned, pressing a hand to my forehead. "You're warm."

I didn't feel warm. Ares's jacket kept most of the shaking at bay, but I still felt as if I'd been carved of ice.

"I think—" I swallowed hard, dizziness overwhelming me. "I think something's wrong with me."

Worry flickered across his face. "Well, let's fix that." Power surged from his fingertips to my skin.

Pain. Blistering, white-hot agony. My screams echoed off the rafters.

"Aphrodite!" Adonis's voice sounded faint over my screams. I had some awareness of him rushing into the hut, but most of my focus went to the torrent of agony crashing though me.

"I was trying to heal her," Ares protested. "What happened?"

"I don't know," Adonis said, squeezing my hand. "For some reason, that makes it worse."

I squeezed his hand back, and Ares's arms tightened around me, but I couldn't manage words. A shudder wracked through me, chased by another wave of pain so intense, I cried out.

Ares gathered me into his arms and lifted me, damsel in distress style, as he headed back toward the boat.

"Tantalus dosed her with something," Adonis explained, following right on Ares's heels.

"What, in case charm wasn't enough?" Ares sounded disgusted. "Find out what was in her drink. I'm getting her back to—Get out of my way."

"Where were you?" Adonis demanded. "You were supposed to be watching us. You were supposed to grab him the *minute* he got away from the crowd—"

"Something came up on board. The others needed my help. I texted half a dozen times for you guys to hold off." Ares tried to move around Adonis, but Adonis blocked him.

"Give her to me. You can go get the drink."

"Seriously?" Ares demanded. "Look, we don't have time for—"

"Then don't waste any. Give her to me."

"Can we not do this?" Ares groaned. "This isn't a love triangle. I have too much self-respect for that crap, and I *know* she does. You should, too. But either way, right now is *really* not the time to assert whatever—"

"You actually think—?"

"I don't know what to think," Ares snapped. "I don't know what's wrong with her. She shouldn't get charmed, or drugged. And she shouldn't stop breathing. I have watched gods *die*, and I've *never* seen anything like this. We have to help her, but you keep standing in my way."

I wanted to say something to stop the arguing, but words were beyond my capabilities at the moment. The pain was subsiding, slowly, but in its wake, I could feel my body shutting down in a desperate effort to recover.

"Just because I'm not jumping to follow your orders doesn't mean that I'm not worried or that I'm jealous, or any other explanation you want to come up with to assuage your divine ego." Adonis's voice dripped with anger. "Think whatever you want, I'm not leaving her with one of you."

"She *is* one of us." Ares drew back. "And it was one of *your* kind who mixed drugs and alcohol and charm—"

"Oh yeah, because gods never do anything like that. It's not like my entire *species* exists because of gods tricking, charming, or straight-up forcing—"

"Are you defending Tantalus?"

"No, I'm pointing out that Tantalus is half *god*. He gets it from somewhere."

"Oh, so logically you assume his divine side—"

"Zeus used mind control to make her do whatever he wanted. Hades was willing to sacrifice a *planet* to get his girlfriend back, and Poseidon threatened to kill me if she didn't sleep with him. So yeah, I'm pretty sure Tantalus gets 'evil douche bag syndrome' from your side of the family."

"Poseidon did what?" All the good nature and cheer I'd grown used to hearing in Ares's voice evaporated.

I couldn't stop Adonis from telling him. By the time he finished, we were back onboard, surrounded by Persephone, Poseidon, and everyone else. Except Hades. Where was Hades? Had I blacked out? How did we get here? Ares couldn't teleport onto the ship. When did everyone else get here?

Conversation flowed around me, brimming with urgency, but I couldn't keep up. The words whirled about in a vortex of confusion.

"What do you mean, gone?" Ares demanded.

"—looked everywhere."

"—combing the island and the ship, but we need—"

Looked everywhere? Looked everywhere for who? "Adonis." I tried to sit up, but dizziness pushed me back down. "Where's—?"

"I'm right here." He gripped my shoulder and I leaned into his touch, relieved he wasn't missing.

"I'll shield the room." Poseidon's voice broke through the haze of my panicked thoughts. "You'll be stuck inside until we find—"

". . . understand," Adonis said.

My panic eased. Poseidon would keep us safe. We'd be okay. Now if only I could just . . .

Before I could complete the thought, darkness swallowed me whole.

Chapter XXVI

I COULDN'T BREATHE. Tears swelled my throat, and the pressure of having him on top of me, crushed against my lung, made it impossible to take a single breath.

"Oh, sweetheart,'" Zeus murmured. "Don't cry. Never cry. In fact . . ." He sat up, and the pressure on my chest eased. Something dark glinted in his unearthly blue eyes. A cruel grin spread across his face. "Don't just lie there. Enjoy yourself."

I had no choice but to comply.

I bolted up in the bed, Ares's jacket sliding off me and onto the floor. I couldn't breathe. I couldn't breathe!

"Aphrodite?" Adonis reached for me, and I batted his hands away, still desperate to draw in air.

"Don't *touch* me," I gasped, ripping the covers off and stumbling out of bed. When he reached out to steady me, I shouted, "*Stop!*" I tried to throw up a shield between the two of us, but failed to summon enough power. Right. My powers weren't working, and I could be charmed, and I couldn't heal. *Helpless.* I felt completely helpless and I couldn't *be* helpless, not again, not ever again. My heart slammed against my chest, beating so hard and so fast, my stomach twisted with the wrongness of the sensation. Dizziness overwhelmed me, and my head felt as if I'd bounced too high on a trampoline. Wind rushed past my face as I fell backward through the sky, only I wasn't landing. Jitters buzzed through me, making my extremities feel the way static looked. Why couldn't I pull enough oxygen into my lungs?

You're fine. You're going to be fine. You just had a bad dream. Zeus is dead. I was. . . . I was. . . . I was going to be sick!

I dashed to the bathroom, slamming the door behind me and throwing the lock. My stomach heaved, and what felt like everything I'd eaten in the last year splashed into the toilet. Trembling, I sat back.

Adonis pounded on the door. "Are you okay? Hey, answer me."

I flushed the toilet and climbed to my feet. Mouthwash would help. After a long minute of gargling, I spat into the sink, then swished some water to get rid of the burning, mint sensation. As I raised my head, I caught sight of myself in the mirror. Oh, this wouldn't do at all. Ignoring Adonis's persistent pounding, I grabbed the washcloth and ran the white square under the water. I wiped my face, then my hands, then my arms, but the skin where Zeus had touched me still burned, as if he'd left some kind of a brand on me, and no amount of scrubbing helped.

I could still feel him, his breath hot against me, his sweat stinging my skin, his weight pressing against my chest. Gods, I couldn't breathe. *Yes, you can,* the rational side of my brain pointed out. *If you couldn't breathe, you'd be unconscious by now. Stop overcompensating; you're going to make yourself sick. Control this. Breathe in, one, two. Out, one—*

No! That's not enough. My body was long past rational reasoning. I tried in vain to drag more air into my lungs as darkness threatened to overtake my vision.

"Aphrodite!" The door shuddered under Adonis's blows.

I had to get the memory of Zeus off me. My hands shook as I edged past the Jacuzzi tub and to the shower stall. I turned on the shower as hot as I could stand, then climbed into the stall, bikini and all. Grabbing the loofah on a stick, I stepped under the scalding spray, scrubbing my skin raw.

All the scrubbing in the world wasn't enough. Nothing would ever be enough. Sinking to the floor of the shower, I drew my knees to my chest, ducking my head so the scalding water didn't hit me in the face. Tears pricked my eyes but never spilled over. I felt broken, hollow, as if all my tears had been stolen from me, leaving me empty and soulless.

Steam filled the bathroom, thickening the air and obscuring the gleaming white tiles. The water dulled the sound of Adonis pounding on the door again. Buzzing with over-oxygenation, I felt detached, numb. My shoulders slumped, muscles relaxing against the shower wall. I didn't feel real.

I heard a crack, and then a splintering boom as the door burst open. Adonis reached into the shower and shut the water off, sucking in a pained breath when the hot water dripped on his arm. He yanked a towel off the rack and pulled me up and out of the shower.

"By the Styx." Adonis wrapped the towel around me. "You really got burned. Hang on." He moved toward the counter, steam swirling around him. "I think there's some aloe in here somewhere. What happened?"

"Bad dream," I managed to gasp.

"Must have been one hell of a dream." The steam cleared a bit, escaping through the open door, and I could just make out Adonis rummaging through the cabinet, a warped reflection of the demigod looming over himself in the foggy mirror. Adonis held out a green bottle of goop. "This will help."

I took the bottle of aloe vera gel from him, twisting the top. "Persephone, Ares, the others," I remembered, heart slamming in my chest. "Something's wrong." The bottle bit into my hand as the lid clicked uselessly without opening. "What happened?" I yanked on the lid. "Where is everyone?" I gave up on the stupid lid. "And why can't I open this?"

"Aphrodite, breathe."

"I'm trying." I gasped. My heart beat against my chest in jerky flutters, and I felt all keyed up. I wanted to run for my life, only there was nowhere to go, and, even if I got there, I'd be screwed anyway. "Why?" My voice cracked. "Why is this happening to me? What's wrong with me? I can't . . . I can't do this, be like this. I'm a goddess, I'm supposed to be a *goddess.*"

"Look at me." He took the aloe and set the bottle on the countertop behind him. "Take a minute; calm down." Adonis gripped my shoulders, careful to avoid the worst of the burns.

I shook my head. Couldn't he see that I was *trying?* Calm was eons away. I'd be calm when my world made sense again, when the rules of my reality stopped getting rewritten.

"Stop." Adonis's golden eyes bored into mine. He moved my hand to his chest. "Breathe when I do." Charm. I didn't have to be able to sense power to recognize the effect. I took a deep breath and exhaled when he did. "Okay." Adonis tucked my hair behind my ears. "It's okay. You're okay. Calm—"

I clapped my free hand over his mouth. "D . . . don't do that. Don't tell me how to feel. Please. You don't know what that's like, losing that line between what you think and feel and, and what someone else tells you to."

"I won't, I won't," he assured me, guilt, pity, and horror flashing through his eyes in quick succession. "I'm sorry. I didn't mean—Just breathe with me, okay?"

That, I could do. The gleaming white tiles of the bathroom seemed to fade away as I looked into his eyes. *But he's charming you*, the panicked part of my mind objected, but Adonis's power was too strong for panic to hold much sway. Besides, I could trust Adonis. Between the mind-numbing charm and his arms around me, I felt safe. *This isn't real. Eventually, he's going to remember he can't stand you, and he's going to look away. And then where will you be?*

"It's going to be okay," he whispered, and I ached to believe him.

Extreme steam and hyperventilation don't play well together. My knees couldn't support my weight. We sank to the floor, leaning against the damp wall, huddled and wet and clinging to one another. I don't know how long it went on, but for a few minutes, all that seemed to exist were his eyes locked onto mine, his heart beating beneath my hand, his arms wrapped around me.

"Better?" he asked, once my breathing evened out. When I nodded, he said, "Everything's fine." His voice sounded soothing, and his eyes never left mine. He took another deep breath, waiting until I followed suit. "Persephone and the others are fine. Last I heard, they were looking for Hades."

My back stiffened. *Looking* for Hades? Persephone and Hades were connected. They could sense one another. She should never have to *look* for Hades.

"Take a breath, relax." Adonis reminded me. When I complied, he continued. "Narcissus and his assistant went missing before Hades and Athena could make the switch. Poseidon shielded our room and everyone is searching the ship. But without Artemis and Ares to help—"

"Wh—what happened to them?" I asked, panic breaking back through. "Why can't they help?"

"It . . . would blow their cover." Worry flickered in Adonis's eyes. "Remember?"

Oh yeah. They were disguised as Tantalus and Elise. Right.

"It's going to take a while to search the ship," Adonis continued. "Persephone said she'd swing back by in the morning, whenever they finish. Still okay?"

I nodded.

"Good. It was about ten, last I looked, so we have a long wait until morning. How about we find you some dry clothes?" He tried to move away from me, but I held on to him.

"Please," I whispered, not even sure what I was asking for. Adonis mattered to me. I could trust him. I needed something real. *Someone* real.

"Aphrodite . . ." Pity flickered in his eyes.

"*Please*, Adonis."

"Okay. Just . . ." He leaned back, shifting positions. "My foot's asleep."

Once he got comfortable, he pulled me back to him. I leaned my head against his chest, soothed by the sound of his steady heartbeat.

His hand stroked my hair. "You're okay," he said again. "Everything is going to be okay."

I closed my eyes and let myself believe the lie.

Chapter XXVII

HOURS LATER, A blast of thunder so strong the entire boat shook sent the lights in the bathroom flickering in one bright flash before they died. I lifted my head and looked around, blinking in confusion as my eyes tried to adjust to the darkness. "Adonis?"

"Hmm?" he asked, hand still rhythmically stroking my hair.

He fell asleep, I realized, ducking under his arm and standing. "Are the lights on a timer?" Stupid question. I'd heard the pop of the bulbs before the power failed. My fingers crawled over the bumpy wallpaper until they reached the light switch.

"Dunno," he said with a jaw-popping yawn. "Why?"

I swallowed hard as the boat lurched back and forth with a nauseating frequency and flipped the switch a couple of times, but nothing happened. "The lights went out."

"It's night time."

Sound logic, that. "Maybe it's just these bulbs." I groped for the doorknob, and ended up banging my knuckles. I couldn't adjust to this level of darkness. Even my eyes couldn't work in the total absence of light. I tried to open the door, but Adonis's weight held it closed. "Can you move?"

"Wait, what's going on?" Adonis stretched and climbed to his feet. "Gods," he muttered as the boat was hit by a strong wave. I heard a hollow *thunk*, indicating he'd bumped into the hot tub, followed by some cursing. He jerked in surprise when his hand brushed mine and something clattered off the countertop to the floor. *Aloe,* I realized as the bottle bumped against my foot. I kicked the plastic container out of the way so neither one of us would trip over the bottle of green goop.

Adonis found the light switch and flipped it up and down. "What happened to the lights?"

"I don't know." I got the door open and breathed a bit easier. There wasn't much light from the windows, but the starlight did provide enough to make the complete blackness fade into more of a fuzzy, navy blue. The furniture even gained outlines. Major improvement.

Lightning flashed, illuminating the suite in white-hot light for a span of three eye-blinks. "Rain dance?" Adonis joked.

"Maybe later." I laughed. The rain hit the window with so much force, each individual drop sounded like it weighed a ton.

Making my way along the wall until I reached the nightstand, I groped blindly for the lamp. The clicking sound of me twisting the knob filled the air, but no light. "Power's out."

"Can't be," Adonis objected. "We're on a ship."

"Listen." I took my own advice. Not a single sound rose over the rain and wind. "No A/C, no fans, no background noise. Everything is down."

"No, it's a cruise ship." Adonis still sounded befuddled. "They have generators and stuff to keep this from happening. We can't lose power."

"Afraid of the dark?" I teased.

"No. You don't get it." Adonis's voice took on a panicked edge. "*Everything* runs off power on ships like this. We're lucky enough to have windows so the darkness isn't total. What about the interior rooms? Or the elevators, or—" He broke off, probably remembering we'd spent the last couple of hours curled up on the bathroom floor, thanks to my *un*divine panic attack. "It's probably nothing," he corrected, clearing his throat. "Everything will be fine. I bet they'll have it fixed in no time."

If even a fraction of the people on board thought along the same lines as Adonis, there would be mass panic. And Persephone and the others were out there, wandering around a dark ship packed full of scared people who could be armed with Olympian Steele. I dropped to the ground, groping blindly until I found Ares's jacket, slipped it on, then stood and picked my way across the room toward the stairs.

"Aphrodite." Adonis caught my hand as I walked by, but I tugged free. "Where—?"

"Find your phone." I clung to the banister, my toes pointed in search of the next step. "We can use it for light."

"Yeah, okay. Maybe there are some candles or something in the kitchen."

"Oh, there's an idea, add *fire* to the equation." Gods, I hoped no one had brought candles on board. The last thing we needed was to be on a boat, without power, in the middle of the ocean—on fire. I stumbled over the last step but caught my balance and headed for the door.

"Right. Hang on, don't the life vests have some kind of flashlight on them?" Adonis's phone lit up in his hand and he moved to the cabinet that held all the life preservers and pointed the phone down at the floor. "Do you see this?"

I didn't have to glance at the floor angling beneath us to feel the boat was tilting.

Adonis swore, dropping to a crouch as the floor rose to meet him.

"Move," I shouted, jerking him away from the closet as the life vests and shoes tumbled out. We scrambled up the incline. I threw open the door and smacked into Poseidon's shield with enough force to push me back into Adonis's arms. The shield! I'd forgotten about the shield.

"No!" Slamming my hands against the barrier did nothing to combat the overwhelming weight of the darkness and ocean surrounding me. The boat continued to tilt. If we capsized, we were screwed. "Poseidon," I gasped. Poseidon had to drop the shield. I scrambled for Adonis's phone, snatching the slim device out of his hand.

"What do we do?" Adonis demanded. "We can't get out! What do we do?"

I dialed Poseidon's number. No signal. "Crap." I passed Adonis the phone, thinking fast. The crashing sound of dishes thudding against the inside of the kitchen cabinets gave me an idea. "Keep trying to call him."

I dashed to the small bathroom under the stairs, struggling to keep my feet under me as the boat continued to rise. Blasts of lightning illuminated my path. Reaching the bathroom, I pawed through the darkness until I found where the small water glass had landed, unfortunately still whole, beneath the sink. Slamming the tumbler into the tile until the glass broke, I grabbed a shard and dashed off toward the balcony.

"What are you doing?" Adonis yelled as I struggled to pull the balcony door open.

"Getting help!" I ran onto the balcony, pausing as the full force of the wind hit me. Cold raindrops hit my skin like dozens of tiny, stinging needles. I took a deep breath and made my way to the edge of the balcony, slicing my palm against the glass as I walked.

My hand shook as I held my palm over the rail, letting my blood, glittering maroon in the darkness, drip down to the sea, and hoping against hope some actually landed in the water. *It's not enough.* A drop or two hitting the ocean *would* be enough, but the wind whipped toward me, nullifying the odds of the tiny droplets of blood reaching the sea. Gritting my teeth, I edged down to the corner of the balcony where the boat dipped closest to waves and dug my nails into the cut.

"Poseidon," I yelled, pouring as much power into the invocation as I could.

The wake my powers left hurt so badly, my insides seemed to shatter into shrapnel, tearing through my body in search of escape.

"I've got you." Adonis's arms wrapped around me, pulling me to him as my knees gave out. "Watch out!" The boat continued to tilt and the deck furniture pitched toward us. Adonis yanked me down, covering my body with his as the wicker furniture tumbled off the deck. He grunted as a table leg slammed into his side before clattering over the bars and crashing into the shield.

The boat stopped. Hovered. My breath came in pants as I stared at the sloped deck floor. After what felt like an eternity, the deck leveled out.

"Oh thank gods," I gasped, still clinging to Adonis. He held me just as tight, his fingers biting into my sides.

"You're bleeding," he said.

"It'll heal . . . eventually." The waves batted the ship back and forth like a volleyball. "Are you okay?"

"Yeah." Adonis helped me up, and we made our way back into the suite to see if we could get out the door.

It was still shielded. "I hate this," I whispered, pressing my forehead and hands against the shield, my shoulders slumped. "I feel so useless. What if the others need help? How can you stand feeling like this all the time? Being so helpless." My voice caught on the last word.

"We're not helpless, and I'm sure the others are fine. Just . . . busy. This might even be good." He didn't sound convinced. "Yeah, we can't get out, but no one can get in, either. So long as the boat doesn't sink, we'll be fine."

The fact that Poseidon hadn't shown up or broken his shield didn't bode well for his control on the situation. Something big was happening. "Olympian Steele can break shields."

"I doubt anyone will break into this room when 'Elise' and 'Tantalus' are making themselves easy to get to, and a bunch of gods are wandering around on board," Adonis said. "But even if they did, Poseidon would know, and he'd teleport here, and—" He broke off. "I don't want to rely on Poseidon."

I laughed. "You and me both."

"So let's not." Adonis took a deep breath. "Look, we know what we can't do. You can't charm, but even with charm, you couldn't break the hold on the passengers last time, right?"

He had a point. Even if my powers were working, I'd never figured out how to charm someone already under another god's influence. "I can't heal you or me if anything—"

"You wouldn't be able to heal from Olympian Steele, anyway." Adonis shrugged. "No big loss. What is Olympian Steele, anyway? I mean, I get it's a type of metal, but beyond that? I don't know much." He kept moving as he spoke, shifting around, balancing on his heels, and running his hand across the shield, as if the barrier might vanish at any time and he wanted to be ready to rush to the lifeboats. His gestures were nervous, keyed-up. But he was trying to hide his fear.

For me, I realized. He felt terrified. Who wouldn't? But he was trying to stay calm for my sake.

"They're um, they're made of adamantine, which almost everything divine and metallic is. Gates, thrones, Poseidon's trident, you name it." I dove head-first into the distraction of explaining obscure facts as much for myself as for him. Once I began to talk, the words kept coming, flung free from my tongue by nervous energy. "Steele refers to the type of a weapon. It's, you know—" I outlined the stake-like shape in my hands then remembered he couldn't see me. "Like a type of dagger. Or pick. Hephaestus came up with a pretty no-frills design because they were just prototypes. But he had a whole line planned. Chthonic Steele, Primordial Steele, Elemental Steele. 'Course, he never got that far, once he realized what he'd created."

Adonis leaned against the shield, his shirt brushing against my side. "So, if the materials don't make it deadly, what does?"

"They don't channel power like most divine weapons. They have their own, and it kills us." Feeling my way to the couch, I took advantage of the darkness to adjust my bikini. I moved forward, feeling along the floor for my luggage and found my bag caught against the couch. "Gods have one weakness. Our own powers. We can't turn them against ourselves, instinct shuts that down, but we can't heal from them either. When we pass on our powers, we pass on our weaknesses. That's why our kids can kill us."

Adonis nodded. "Hence every myth ever."

I snorted. "Pretty much. Something in that metal resonated with the power it was infused with and that confuses our ability to heal. It's as if we've been struck by ourselves, no matter who made the weapon. Only it spreads like—like venom. Specific details about how Hephaestus created the Steele didn't pass down the bloodlines, for obvious reasons. All I know is, the way he forged the power into the metal circumvented the whole immortality thing. He took the power back into himself and destroyed them all to protect us." I shuddered, remembering the writhing mass of Hephaestus's face. "Really messed him up, too."

"But if he destroyed them all, where . . . ?" Adonis trailed off, waiting for explanation.

"And that is the million-dollar question." I smiled at him. "To say we were surprised when Steele popped back up is an understatement. Our best guess is that Zeus figured out how to make it."

Adonis tapped on the shield, filling the air with hollow-sounding thunks. "Okay, back to the problem at hand. Being powerless doesn't make us helpless. People get by without powers every day."

"Against other *people*. The scales are kind of tipped here." I felt his gaze on me, heavy and expectant, and I turned away, digging through my bag. "I'm not even strong enough to leave the room."

"You're smart. You'd have to be to have survived Zeus. And what did you do to Poseidon? He's afraid to look at you now. Your powers didn't help with that, so what did?"

"I don't know. A willingness to do things that would never occur to anyone with any comprehension of right and wrong." I sat on the couch, drawing my knees to my chest and told him all about the forced promises. "I've hurt people, Adonis. I've done terrible, terrible things. But before, I could always say I was under Zeus's control. What I did to Poseidon was like Zeus-caliber bad . . . only, that was all me."

"To hell with Poseidon. If there's any justice in the universe, bad things will never stop happening to that dickwad."

He didn't get it. "But *I* still did it. And I'd do it again. Because that's how I survive. I hurt people, and I get hurt, and I run away from fights I can't win."

"Sometimes, being nice and doing the right thing is a luxury." The couch dipped as Adonis sat beside me. "Sometimes, you have to use whatever advantage you've got."

"Funny, that sounds kind of like the exact opposite of everything you've ever said about me using my powers before now."

"Against *people,*" Adonis clarified. "People you already have the advantage over. I'm not saying you should starve or end up on the streets instead of using your charm. I get that you just kind of popped up in the world with nothing. You have to get by until you have something behind you. It's the frivolous stuff you do that I can't stand. What you did to Poseidon isn't like that. You didn't have a choice."

I shook my head. "Persephone wouldn't have done it, even before she came into her powers. Ares didn't do it when he had the chance. As far as I can tell, it didn't even cross his mind."

"Persephone had two of the most powerful gods in creation protecting her until she came into her powers, and has the entire pantheon backing her now. Ares has had centuries to build up power, wealth, and anything else he'll ever need. Don't let them set your moral compass. They have the advantage. Of course, they don't want you to feel good about taking that from them."

I frowned. "They're not—"

"They're using you, Aphrodite. Poseidon treated you like a thing, something disposable, something he could use until you forced him to see you otherwise. Just like Zeus, just like the others. They're all still using you. Why else would they send the newest god with the most limited powers to investigate, when they didn't even know what they were up against?"

"I volunteered," I reminded him. "Charm is kind of my thing, so it made sense. The second this got bigger than I could handle, the rest of them stepped in. They're all out there, Adonis." I motioned toward the door. "Trying to get to the bottom of this while we're shielded and safe."

Adonis drew in a deep breath. "I'm just saying, you shouldn't feel bad about what you did to Poseidon. Look, if you were even half as selfish as you think you are, would you still be here? You could have left the second Persephone got here. Why didn't you?"

Because I can't leave you. I chose another truth instead. "Because of all the terrible things I've done. I can't—If I don't do something to balance it—I—" I struggled for words. "I want to be able to look at myself in the mirror and not feel guilty for every horrible thing I've ever done. I want to be able to sleep without . . ." I waved my hand in the general direction of the bedroom, though he probably couldn't see the gesture. "I want to do more than survive, even if it kills me. I wasn't supposed to have much of a life, Adonis, so I want to be able to feel good about what I do with mine."

Adonis touched my hand, then felt his way up to my shoulder to give me a comforting squeeze.

I leaned into his touch. "I need you to promise me something."

"My promises don't hold as much weight as yours."

"Then it means more when you keep them."

He hesitated for a second. "What do you need?"

"If something gets in here, something that can charm, I need you to knock me out again."

Adonis shook his head. "I can't do that."

"Adonis, I'm not strong enough to resist charm right now. I don't want to be used to hurt anyone."

"You also can't heal," he argued. "I know your perspective on this may be skewed, but being hit hard enough to lose consciousness is actually kind of a big deal."

"I don't care! I'd rather die than feel like that again. You don't understand. You've never been charmed, but it's—"

"I am not going to hurt you." He grabbed my hands and met my eyes, starlight glittering in his. "I can't. Don't ask me to, please. But maybe there's another way. Charm takes eye contact, right?" Adonis spread his hands to indicate the darkness. "You don't have to make that easy."

Something in his voice made me tilt my head to study his silhouette. "What are you thinking?"

He grinned, his teeth glittering in pinpricks of light. "Practice not getting charmed? We could play a game to pass the time until the others get back. If I can charm you, my point. If you block it, yours." He shrugged. "First to seven points wins the game?"

If only it were that easy. Unlike demigods, full-blooded deities could blanket an area with power. Eye contact just made charm easier and strengthened control. Still . . . I needed to do *something*, however useless. My heart still pounded in my chest from my adventure on the balcony, and every time a strong wave hit the boat, I froze in fear until I felt sure the boat wouldn't tilt again. If I continued to just sit here, I'd go crazy. And given how tense Adonis sounded, he needed to think about something else, too. The guy didn't even like being confined in an elevator. "What would I win?"

Adonis grinned. "Getting a bit ahead of yourself, aren't you. Victor's choice?"

I could find ways to make that fun. I pushed off the couch and moved away from him. "Ready . . . set . . ."

"Go!" Adonis looked toward me. "Clap three times."

When I didn't clap, he swore. "Too dark." He stumbled over the edge of the couch, closing the gap between us. "Clap three times."

I squeezed my eyes shut. "Two-nothing." I squinted, trying to make out Adonis, but I couldn't see his silhouette. Where did he—

"Boo," Adonis whispered in my ear, and I yelped in surprise, spinning to face him. "Clap three times."

I clapped.

"One-two." His teeth flashed in a triumphant grin. "Clap three—"

I took off, tripping and scrambling over the furniture to get deeper into the suite. He'd have to find me to charm me. He managed to grab the collar of Ares's jacket, but I slipped my arms free and kept on.

"Three-one." Picking my way through the room in complete darkness was a challenge, but judging by the crashing and thuds behind me, I was navigating the obstacles better than Adonis.

There. I ducked into a nook under the staircase and tried to stay still and quiet.

He stumbled around for a few seconds, then a piercing light swept the room. His phone blazed in his hand. Cheater. I closed my eyes when the light came close.

White, molten light shone through my eyelids. "Clap three times."

I smiled. "Four to one."

He wasn't touching me, but he stood so close, I could almost feel him. My back brushed against the wall. "Cornered. I think you just lost."

I opened my eyes. Faking right, I sprang left and stepped right into the suitcase I'd stashed under the stairs. "Crap!" The bag slid out from under me and I slammed sideways into Adonis, knocking him off balance and sending us both crashing on to the carpet with a *thunk*.

"Ouch," he groaned, rubbing his head. "Are you okay?"

"Five-one."

His eyes glittered in challenge. "Clap—"

I straddled him, covering his eyes with my hands. "Six."

He wrapped his hands around my upper arms and yanked me off balance. I yelped, finding myself nose to nose with him, my hands sliding on the carpet behind his head to stabilize myself. "Clap—"

I touched my mouth to his, the motion featherlight. With a flick of my tongue, I opened his lips under mine. Adonis froze, hesitating for half a second, then kissed me back with ardor. His hands flattened on my back, pressing me against him. "Not fair," he groaned.

"Seven." I laughed, reveling in the knowledge I'd put heat in his voice. My reality might be breaking down, my powers fading, my charm gone, but this? This, I could still control. And I needed control right now. I propped myself up on his chest, grinning at him. "Face it, you've lost."

"Funny, it doesn't feel like it." He leaned up, his mouth capturing mine. His fingers knotted in my hair, and he eased back down to the ground, taking me with him.

We breathed each other in as the kiss deepened. His mouth moved against mine. When his hands slid down my waist, my heart pounded in my chest. His lips on mine felt like a promise I wanted to keep with a terrifying intensity. Without breaking the kiss, I unbuttoned his shirt and allowed him to sit up enough for me to work it down his arms before planting a hand to his bare chest and pushing him back down.

In the darkness, we were little more than shadows, but our hands explored what we couldn't see. I gasped when his hands slipped beneath my bikini top. "Gods," I groaned, burying my head in his shoulder.

"Wait, wait, wait." Adonis pulled away, and propped himself up on one arm. "Just . . ." He grabbed his phone, and light flashed in my eyes, searing my vision. I jerked away, holding up my hands to ward off the glow. "Sorry." He grabbed my hand, pulling me back down to him. "I'm sorry, I just, I had to make sure you weren't charmed. I had to—"

He stopped when my mouth covered his, his hands rising to cup my face with a tenderness that made my head spin in a whirlwind of emotions. This was more, so much more than fear, or regret, or pain. More than a pleasant physical distraction, more than a way to forget.

"Aphrodite . . . wait," Adonis's voice sounded hoarse, but he ignored his own advice, tangling our legs as his lips found mine again and again and again. Each kiss felt deeper, harder, and more desperate. His finger deftly untied the knots holding my bikini together. "I should—"

He sucked in a breath when I slid my hand down the waistband of his jeans. If he told me he didn't want me because I was a god or any other reason, I'd break. I'd do anything, be anything or anyone he wanted if it meant I wouldn't lose the way I felt right now. "Please," I whispered.

He put his hands on my hips and yanked me to him with a groan. I poured all my feelings into the kiss. We were pressed together so tight, I almost couldn't tell where I stopped and he began, but that wasn't close enough. Fabric gave way to firm flesh and heavy breathing. And this time, there were no interruptions.

Chapter XXVIII

AT SOME POINT in the night, we made it upstairs to the actual bed. And sometime even later, I let Adonis fall asleep. Sleep had to be the worst weakness we'd given mortals. Their lives were so short already—it seemed a tragedy to waste a third of it slumbering.

I snuck downstairs, drained a bottle of water, and slid back into the bed without disturbing him. He shifted, wrapping his arm around me. We lay with our legs tangled together, bodies pressed close in a way that shouldn't have felt comfortable, but somehow did. Staring up at the ceiling, I smiled, surprised by how happy I felt. Lying in his arms, with nothing to distract me from the rise and fall of his chest, the rhythmic sound of his heartbeat, and the way his body felt warm against mine, was nice.

As the minutes turned to hours, euphoria faded in favor of more pressing needs. The symptoms started small; minor aches and pains, a small bout of dizziness, some cold sweats, and a thirst that seemed unquenchable. But by the time I made my third trip downstairs by the shaky light of Adonis's cell phone for yet another bottle of water, my entire body shook with fatigue.

I couldn't do it. I couldn't make myself climb those stairs. Trembling, I opened the water bottle and took a sip, determined to relieve my Sahara-dry throat. *That's a bit better.*

My stomach twisted, and a wave of dizziness slammed into me. I stumbled, leaning against the wall and gasping as I waited for the awful feeling to pass. *Ares's jacket,* I remembered. I wasn't sure if a token from my home realm would help, but at this point, I'd try anything.

What was wrong with me? Last night, my symptoms had felt dull. Noticeable, but not debilitating. *Definitely not debilitating,* I thought, remembering all my fun with Adonis. No, this level of pain felt new. Whatever was wrong with me was getting worse.

I shuffled through the dark room at a slow, yet painful pace. My lips pressed together as a moan escaped my throat. Every muscle, every joint, every fiber of my being cried out in agony. Somewhere above me, Adonis slept on, unaware, and that pissed me off to no end. I wasn't sure why I felt angry, much less why I didn't call out for him. I guess logic and unendurable agony weren't great bedfellows.

"Gods," I gasped, leaning against the wall, fumbling with the kind of limp heaviness associated with the very ill, the drunk, or the undead. I sank to the floor and crawled instead. My too-hot skin cracked with each stretch and bend, as if each layer was being tanned, shrunk, then stretched over my bones. Cool leather brushed against my fingertips and I felt an iota of relief. I pulled the jacket to me, not even bothering to crawl the two extra feet to the couch.

I spent the night alternating between freezing and burning as I shook beneath Ares's jacket, taking small sips from my bottle of water. When I ran out, I didn't have the energy to get a new one. My head felt full of molten lava, and my veins seemed as if they were filled with granules of sharpened glass. Each heartbeat seemed to slice through my body with a wave of pain.

Delirium. Fragmented thoughts and memories played through my mind as the sun lightened the horizon.

"It's so cold," I moaned to Adonis, though the rational bit of my brain *knew* he was upstairs and I was not. What the hell, at least now I had someone to talk to. "How are you not cold?"

Adonis's gold eyes popped open. "You don't feel cold at all, you're—Gods!" He sat up in the bed, his hand brushing my hair from my forehead. "Aphrodite, you're burning up."

I couldn't stop shaking. "Feels like freezing."

"Well, here." He pulled the feather duvet back onto the bed and draped the cool fabric around me. "Better?"

Now I felt too hot, but I didn't have the heart to tell him, so I pulled him to me and kissed him instead. "That's better."

"Mmm," he agreed. His hands cupped my face, his thumb stroking my cheek as the kiss deepened. For a few minutes, I did feel better.

Then I shifted positions and the friction of the carpet beneath me brought me jerking upright in confusion. I wasn't on the bed. I was downstairs. "I should fix that," I murmured. My lips cracked when I spoke. I climbed to my feet, Ares's jacket sliding to the floor.

Clothing would be good. Persephone and the others would be checking in on us soon. I grabbed the jacket and managed to make my way to the suitcase beneath the stairs.

I blinked at the clothing scattered across the floor in confusion for a few moments before I urged my heavy limbs to cooperate with my efforts to get dressed. Once I pulled on a green dress, I raised the water bottle to my lips. Empty. With a sigh, I lurched to my feet, donned Ares's jacket, and shuffled toward the kitchen. Now that the sun was up, I could see the suite was a mess. When the boat tilted last night, everything fell. Including my massive stack of papers on the kitchen counter. A manila envelope with Adonis's name and old room number caught my eye from beneath the fridge.

Rooms, room numbers, empty rooms. Feverishly, I combed through the drawers, searching for Olympian Steele. Wait, no. I closed the drawer, trying to get my bearings. I wasn't searching the ship. I was in my room. There was nothing to find here.

Dozens of empty rooms. No luggage, no people. Something about the empty rooms stuck with me, so I paused to scrawl myself a note on the manila envelope below Adonis's name.

There are no other rooms, Adonis's voice snapped. Miguel had tried to escort him off the ship because they were at capacity.

"Augh!" I clamped a hand to my forehead, taking measured breaths. I couldn't . . . think. Gods, my head felt ready to explode. I could hear my pulse pounding in my ears, and the thought of blood pumping through my veins was almost too much for my nauseated stomach to bear. A whimper caught in my throat. I felt worse, so much worse. Why did everything hurt so badly?

What was I doing? Why were all these papers on the floor? I spotted our room key and knelt to grab the plastic card. I couldn't lose mine because Adonis had borrowed my spare. Upstairs, Persephone moved around. I could hear her feet treading on the carpet above.

Wait. No. Persephone wasn't here. That was Adonis moving around upstairs. My mouth felt as dry as dust. Right, water. The fridge didn't feel cold anymore and the light didn't flip on. *Power's out,* I remembered, moving to twist the cap the rest the way off the last water bottle.

I paused, hand poised and ready to open the bottle. Did I break the seal or was it already broken? I glanced at the empty water bottles littering the room, struggling to remember.

No, that was just something Adonis always did for me. Something nice and gentlemanly. Good thing, since these stupid plastic ridges hurt my palm.

"Water?" Adonis had asked, holding out a bottle. Over and over and over again. Always offering me drinks.

"Okay," I whispered, bringing the bottle to my lips.

Clarity burst through my feverish delirium before the cool liquid could relieve my parched throat. I backed up into the countertop staring at the water bottle in disbelief. Oh, gods! Something was in the water. My powers hadn't failed until my first night on the boat. *After* I drank the water. Then, every time I drank another bottle, they got worse. How many bottles had I drunk? My mind flipped through every single time Adonis passed me a water bottle, every single time I'd raided the fridge. The bottle shook in my trembling hand as I studied the water, searching for some trace of. . . . What? What could hurt a god, but leave a demigod unharmed?

A violent shudder wrenched through me, setting my entire body ablaze with pain. I gasped, mopping the sweat off my forehead with my free hand. My body sagged against the counter because I couldn't support my own weight anymore. I grimaced, clutching my stomach. I was missing something, a piece of this puzzle that would make everything else fall into place. But I couldn't *think* clearly enough to—

There! Tiny, almost microscopic, flakes of silvery specks inside the bottle caught the sunlight. What the hell was that? Steele? Impossible. A single scratch could kill me in a matter of heartbeats. Water made it to the human blood stream within five minutes of consumption. I'd have been dead days ago.

"Aphrodite..." Adonis stood at the entry of the kitchen. I looked up at him, dread filling the pit of my stomach when I saw the guilt written across his face. "Don't drink that."

Chapter XXIX

I DROPPED THE water bottle. The weak plastic dented upon hitting the floor and water sluiced free from the unsealed top. "What have you done?" My voice sounded weak and brittle, and my mind screamed for me not to ask. Because whatever he said next would be bad. So bad there would be no going back. That much seemed obvious by the look on his face and the twist in my gut. "*Adonis*, what have you done?"

He closed his eyes. "They told me it wouldn't hurt you."

Oh, gods. My breathing quickened as my feverish mind put the pieces together for the thousandth time in as many minutes. Only, this time, I couldn't breeze past the obvious. Couldn't blame someone else. Couldn't deny the one thing that would make this entire situation worse. He *knew*. "You . . . poisoned me? Why?"

"Aphrodite." Adonis moved toward me, papers crinkling beneath his feet as he crossed the threshold into the kitchen. "Take a deep breath."

"Don't!" I jerked away from him, but didn't have far to go with my back against the white cabinets. "Don't touch me. Don't come anywhere near me. Don't you dare." The room spun around me. Gripping the edge of the countertop, I fought to keep myself on my feet.

Adonis backed off. "Aphrodite, I'll explain everything, I swear. But you've got way too much of that stuff in your system. I have to get you to Jason so he can—"

Jason. I filed the name away to explore later. "I don't know how you missed this," I snapped through gritted teeth, "but we can't *go* anywhere. And even if we could, I wouldn't go with you. You drugged me! I'm—I could be *dying.*"

"They might have an antidote, or something." Sunlight filtered in from the floor-to-ceiling windows. The pale beams leaked across the white carpet, invading the wide, open room to outline Adonis's frame, lighting up his golden features in a way that, to my feverish state, seemed menacing, unnatural. He glowed with malice. "I can get us to Jason, you just have to trust me."

"Trust you?" Was he serious?

"Aphrodite, it wasn't supposed to hurt you, you have to believe me." Adonis's gold eyes met mine, pleading.

"Oh, gods, this wasn't even your room, was it?" More pieces I'd refused to put together fell into place, my mind suddenly clearer than it'd been all night. *I haven't had any water for hours. Maybe I'm healing a little?* More likely, shock had snapped me back to my senses. I'd be a wreck when the adrenaline wore off. But for now.... The room number, the empty rooms, Adonis's "lost" key. "You lied to keep us in the same room, and then you were a complete jerk about me being here. And then you *poisoned* me. Why?"

"It wasn't supposed to—"

"Then what was it supposed to do?" My heart slammed in my chest as adrenaline pulsed through my veins, making me dizzy and numb, yet hyper-aware all at once.

Adonis rubbed the back of his neck, looking so contrite, so frickin' remorseful, I felt like throwing something at him. "Take away your powers."

His words hit me like a punch in the stomach. I felt as if I'd been thrown off a cliff and could feel the ground rushing toward me at a million miles an hour. "That will kill me."

"I didn't *know* that." Adonis held his hands out. "I figured without your powers, you would just . . . be human. Alive, but on a leveled playing field. It wasn't supposed to be dangerous."

"*You* have powers. It's not a level playing field if you're uphill! And you can't just"—I waved my hands for a second, searching for words—"turn me human. It doesn't work that way. And gods without powers aren't human. They're dead! Power isn't all that separates us from humanity. We're . . . we're a different species. We're wired differently. You can't just . . . you can't—"

"Play god?" Adonis tilted his head and gave me a pointed look.

My mouth dropped open. "Are you seriously making puns right now? Is this . . . is this *funny* to you?"

"No!" Adonis's eyes widened. "Of course not. I'm telling you exactly what they're doing. They're playing at being gods. And unfortunately"—Adonis looked up at the ceiling and let out a deep breath—"they aren't much better at it than you guys. Innocent people got hurt, and they promised that wouldn't happen."

"You guys? Innocent people? Not much better? I was *attacked*, assaulted with deadly weapons, brainwashed, *poisoned*, lied to, tricked, and betrayed. They're *not much better* than we are? *We* are *not* a collective. Neither are you, Adonis. You don't get to hide behind this group, whoever the hell 'they' are. *You* drugged me."

"I didn't have a choice!"

I gritted my teeth against the pain and brought myself to my full height, channeling every bit of righteous indignation I could muster. "You're going to tell me who 'they' are, or so help me, Adonis—"

"There's no need to threaten me." Adonis's foot crossed from carpet to tile as he stepped into the kitchen, his hands in the air in a gesture of surrender. "I *want* to tell you everything. I've started to a thousand times. Last night before we.... On the beach, before you went off with Tantalus, after Poseidon went off on you in the club. I've *tried,* Aphrodite."

Not hard enough. We were rooming together, and had been with each other nearly twenty-four hours a day. He'd had dozens of opportunities. He'd just chosen not to use them.

Oblivious to my thoughts, Adonis continued. "And even before that, I tried as hard as I could to get you to leave the ship. I stopped giving you the water the night you stopped breathing, the minute I realized stripping you of your powers would actually hurt you. I poured all the water bottles out and everything. I didn't even know they replaced them. And Aphrodite..." He took a deep breath. "They knew, they knew I wasn't giving it to you. That's why Tantalus gave you so much last night. I know you're mad right now, and you have every right to be, but I wasn't trying to hurt you. I swear, if I hadn't done what I did, they would have killed you."

My head spun, and I touched my hand to my forehead, trying to sort through everything he'd said. Screaming at him felt so much easier than trying to puzzle this out, but I wasn't the only one at stake here. This information mattered. "Tantalus?" What did he have to do with this? "Adonis, who are 'they'?" I edged away from him when he pulled the fridge open.

"The demigods. We're not missing." He looked at the empty fridge, his face paling. "How many did you drink? How many were there?" Adonis looked me up and down, his eyes wide with alarm as he seemed to take in my sweaty skin and trembling limbs for the first time. "Aphrodite—"

"Yeah, I'm probably as good as dead," I snapped. "Do you think you could get as skilled at answering questions as you are at murder? 'Cause I asked you a few. What do you mean, the demigods aren't missing?"

He swallowed hard and bent to pick up the water bottle on the ground. I resisted the urge to kick him in the gut, but only because I wasn't sure I could remain standing. "We're being recruited. The demigods you're looking for left of their own volition."

"What?"

"When Tantalus and the others saw you charming your way on board, they got spooked, and...." He walked around the suite, picking up empty water bottles as he went. I could see the alarm growing in his features as he tallied the bottles. "I knew they had the weapons, okay. I didn't want them using them on you, so I promised you weren't a threat, and swore to keep an eye on you. They agreed to leave you alone, so long as I gave you this stuff that would strip you of your powers for a while. They didn't want you charming them because they aren't all immune." Adonis pushed the empty water bottles into the trash.

The room spun around me, and I couldn't pull enough air into my lungs. The demigods? Really? We weren't looking for a god or a Titan or a primordial or anything we'd ever considered to be consequential in terms of power? I thought of the charm, woven together from hundreds, *hundreds* of different power sources, forging an unbreakable link to the passengers.

Alone, the demigods were nothing, but together . . .

Especially when there were demigods like Adonis.

He certainly can lie. Elise's voice echoed in my thoughts. How did we miss this? How did *I* miss this? Gods, the Olympian Steele. I knew exactly where the rest of the weapons were. The only room I'd never finished searching. Tantalus's.

Assuming they aren't in Adonis's luggage. I'd never thought to search there, either.

I remembered the look of horror on Elise's face after Adonis explained we were trying to help find the missing demigods. *I'm not a part of this, and you shouldn't be either.*

"They call themselves the DAMNED. Demigods Against Major Nymphs, Elementals, and Deities."

"Nymphs?" Nymphs were all but extinct, and they'd never been powerful.

Adonis shrugged. "They were mostly fishing for something to complete the acronym. 'Cause they might change things on the surface, but they know once they die. . . . Well, you know. Hades."

Yeah, they'd be damned all right. The Lord of the Underworld wouldn't look too kindly upon members of a group that sought. . . . What exactly? Our extinction?

"Where is Hades?" I asked, remembering Adonis's offhand comment last night. Persephone could *always* find Hades unless they got separated by extreme circumstances, like Zeus's lightning and an entire realm of distance. *Or a bunch of bloodthirsty demigods armed with Steele?* No, if Hades died, Persephone would know instantly. There wouldn't be a reason to search.

Adonis shrugged. "Probably with the others by now. I told you; last I heard, they were looking for Echo and Narcissus. I'm sure they'll all be back soon." He paled. "I'll tell them everything."

Echo? Did he mean E? "Poseidon was right." I quelled the hysterical laughter bubbling up within me. The demigods were a threat. They were working together, and they were armed; they'd tricked us. All because we were too proud to consider that we might be dealing with lesser beings. "I should have let him sink the boat."

Didn't that just figure?

Adonis didn't seem to have heard me, because he continued trying to explain, his voice growing desperate. "They swore it wouldn't hurt you. I'm sorry, I'm so sorry, but I didn't have a choice."

Gods, Poseidon was right about Adonis too—he was a professional victim. "You could have *told me.*" My enraged shriek echoed across the room.

"And then what?" Adonis demanded, frustration giving way to anger.

"You would have told Poseidon, and he would have killed us all the minute he realized we were armed."

We? Only a moment ago, he'd said *they*. How deep into this was he?

Adonis backed away, moving across the tile line dividing the kitchen from the living space. "I couldn't be responsible for anyone dying. They're good people, just scared and angry, and they have a *right* to be. I . . . I didn't want anyone to die, you included."

"They attacked *me*." Or did he forget about the passengers wielding Olympian Steele?

"That was an accident. You'd already left the club and they didn't know you were coming back. Once I realized you'd left the room, I tried to warn you. I tried, but you didn't hear me. They weren't trying to get you, you were just in the way. They were trying to get to Poseidon."

"People *died*."

Adonis winced. "Do you think I'm not aware of that? I'm not on their side anymore, Aphrodite. No one was supposed to die."

"Except Poseidon, obviously." I stared at Adonis in disbelief. "Like that's somehow better?"

"Poseidon deserves it."

I shook my head. "We're an endangered species, Adonis. If *any* of us die, it hurts us all."

"I thought you weren't a collective."

"That's not what I—" Why explain anything to him? "Gods, you really hate us." I'd known that from the get-go, but I'd had no idea how deep his hatred went.

"I don't hate *you*."

"Only because you thought you could make me something different." I leaned against the countertop for support. "Something you can stand."

"No! That's not—"

"Three days ago, you could barely tolerate me. Now all of a sudden—"

"Three days ago, I didn't know you. Not really." The words seemed to explode from within Adonis, like if he put enough power behind them, the volume would force me to see reason. As if he could drown out the horrified voice in my head crying that he'd poisoned me, betrayed me, hurt me. But the truth couldn't be silenced. "All I knew was that you weren't psychotic like most of the gods, and you didn't deserve to be killed off as a precaution."

"*Most* of the gods? You've met almost all of them, Adonis. Does Persephone seem psychotic to you? Or Artemis? Or Ares? Or Hephaestus? Are you saying any of them deserve to be killed off as a *precaution?*" I spat out the word. "This is a new pantheon. Everything is different—"

"It's too little, too late. The gods have screwed around with us, our families, some of us for generations. Tantalus's entire family is literally cursed. It passes down his bloodline because of something that happened *centuries* ago.

There's no point in telling them the gods have changed because that's cold comfort to anyone who's already been hurt. They were going to kill you."

His words echoed around the room as we stared each other down, breathing hard. "What do you want me to say, Adonis? That what you did was understandable? That it's okay? Because it's not."

"I know. I just want you to understand I didn't have a choice."

"But you *did*. And you chose to drug me. You chose to *lie* to me. You could have trusted me instead of stabbing me in the back and—"

"I'm sorry!"

"—trying to remake me into something more to your liking. Something you can control. Gods, all that stuff you said last night about taking an advantage if you weren't given one. You were trying to justify what you did."

"No!"

"You slept with me," I cried. "Was any of that me? Or did you charm me into—"

"*No!*" Adonis looked horrified at the thought. "I even checked. You weren't charmed. I would never—"

"But if I'm drugged, it's okay?"

"*No!*"

"How am I supposed to believe you? You can lie!"

"Because I could charm you right now into believing whatever I say, and I'm not. I wasn't lying last night. You mean something to me. I think . . . I think I might even lo—"

"Don't." My voice broke as the feeling I'd found last night shattered within me, the shards ripping my heart, soul, and very being to shreds. For all the hell I'd lived through before, I'd never felt as empty and broken as I did right now. And I *hated* myself for giving him so much power over me. But I wouldn't make that mistake again. "Don't you dare play that card. Not after what you did."

"I love you."

He probably even believed it. But this wasn't love. I knew love. I'd seen it in Persephone's strength when she should have been broken beyond repair, in Demeter's sacrifice, in the way Hades's voice gentled every time he said Persephone's name and Poseidon's broke every time he said Triton's. Love could be pain and fear and strength and wonder and everything in-between. But it was *never* poison.

No. Adonis felt what happened when you tossed two people in a room, piled on emotional and physical disasters, danger, and mayhem, and threw in some guilt for good measure. He felt *something* toward me, maybe even something strong, but it wasn't love. Not if he could do what he'd done.

But it still hurt.

"I never meant for any of this to happen." Adonis moved toward me and something inside me snapped. He didn't get to look upset, and he didn't

163

get to act heartbroken. No. I was most likely dying, and not only had he caused it, but he'd watched while my powers deteriorated, sending me through a world of pain. And he'd said *nothing*. He'd lied to me and tricked me and betrayed me and tried to change me, all while pretending to care about me, and now he dared to say he loved me? Snarling, I grabbed the first thing I could reach on the counter and threw a heavy, ceramic cup at him.

"Get *away* from me." The mug hit the cabinet behind him and broke into pieces. "You are *everything* that you hate. In fact, you're worse!" After all his talk about how the gods were *so* bad, trying to make me feel ashamed of what I was.... And all that time, he'd been manipulating me?

"Aphrodite—"

"You're a *monster,*" I yelled so loud my voice went hoarse.

A knock at the door drew me up short. Miguel's voice filtered through the thick metal. "Is everything all right in there?"

Miguel could knock on the door. Which meant the shield was down. And that meant that something had happened to the barrier—or to the god who set it.

Persephone! She'd left with Tantalus. And Ares and the others. I needed to warn them. They thought they were helping the demigods, but the demigods were behind this whole thing and they were armed. All because I was too blind and stupid to see the danger right in front of me. I needed to fix this. To help them.

Gods, I was probably too late.

I couldn't fall apart right now. There was too much at stake. With effort, I shoved aside my hurt and anger so I could move on to more important matters. "They would have killed me?" My voice sounded numb, detached.

"*Yes.*" Adonis looked at me, eyes full of hope.

I'd have rather died outright. At least then, the others wouldn't be in danger. "How many demigods are on this ship, really?"

"Dozens. They . . . some of them can use glamours."

That shouldn't have been possible. Demigods couldn't glamour, but even if they could, it should have left a power signature. My ability to pick up on signatures had vanished almost instantly, but Poseidon had tracked me using my glamour. He would have noticed dozens of glamoured demigods. Poseidon's voice echoed in my mind. *If they're immune to charm, no telling what other oddities they have about them or what they may pass on. They're too dangerous.*

I closed my eyes. He was right. Gods help me, Poseidon was right. "Will they kill the other gods? Will they drug them?"

"I don't . . ." Adonis rubbed the back of his neck, looking sick with guilt. "I don't know. They don't trust me anymore, so they haven't been talking to me. It's not like their aim was ever to attack you guys. They just wanted to be left alone."

With an acronym like DAMNED, I somehow doubted that. But Adonis had believed what he wanted to believe, and now I was dying for it. But I wasn't going to let that happen to the others.

"Aphrodite, don't go out there!"

Oh, as if I would ever listen to another word he said again. I bolted out the door.

Chapter XXX

THE DOOR SLAMMED behind me, pushing me into a startled Miguel. "I'm sorry," I gasped, leaning against the door.

Miguel steadied me, studying my face. "Are you all right, miss?"

The doorknob rattled, and I clutched the cool silver knob. Miguel took one look at me and grabbed the knob, holding it closed.

"Aphrodite!" Adonis's muffled shout echoed through the hall and he pounded on the door. "I can help, just open the door."

"Um . . . miss?" Miguel eyed the shuddering door as Adonis's pounding persisted.

"I might pass out," I warned Miguel, adjusting Ares's jacket. "If that happens, promise not to leave me with him."

"I'm sorry, what?"

My head spun and I decided to work on making sense later. Right now, I needed to keep Adonis contained. I closed my eyes and poured everything I had, which wasn't much, into shielding the room. My stomach wrenched. Blood dripped from my nose and spots filled my vision, but the shield held up.

"*Miss*," Miguel cried out in alarm as my knees buckled, but he held on to the door. Smart man.

"S's 'kay," I murmured, leaning against the wall. Tilting my head, I pinched the bridge of my nose to stanch the flow of blood. Sunlight streamed through the glass skylight and the endless halls of windows. The tightness in my chest eased. I'd been afraid the entire boat would be pitch black.

I drew in a breath. "I need to—I just—" Poseidon. I'd tell Poseidon. He could locate any deity in his realm and teleport us all to one place. I only wanted to tell this story once. Taking a deep breath, I waited for the worst of the dizziness to pass. Once I felt certain I wouldn't collapse, I announced, "I have to get outside."

"Get to medical, it's . . ." Miguel eyed me, as if evaluating my ability to make it down to the bottom of the boat. "There is a door, straight down this hall that leads outside. Wait there, I will send someone to escort you the rest of the way." He reached for a radio strapped to his belt as the door shuddered. "Go."

Thankfully, my room wasn't far from an exterior hall. The adrenaline keeping me on my feet wouldn't last long, but I had to know. "What happened? Why is the power off?"

I could see in the struggle on his face that he wanted to ask what had been going on between me and Adonis, but wasn't a hundred percent sure he wanted to know. "Uh . . . there was a malfunction. The power should return shortly, and once it does, we'll be moving again."

"Thank you." I pushed off the wall and headed for the exterior door at the end of the hall. As I staggered down the corridor, I heard Miguel speaking rapid Spanish into his radio, and another crew member's voice speaking to a group of passengers.

"Try not to close your cabin door completely, because you may not be able to unlock your door again. Looters will be prosecuted to the full extent of the law. Ah, and if your facilities are not functioning, please urinate down the shower drain. Bags will be provided for fecal matter."

I pushed open the door to outside and sucked in a deep breath of the salt-tinged air. The white walls of the ship seemed to fade away as I gazed out at the never-ending stretch of navy blue. There were no waves. No wind. The ocean looked flat as glass, the lack of movement so profoundly *wrong* that I stepped away from the bars. "What?" I glanced up and spotted a few clouds lingering in the sky, but even those remained perfectly still. As if the world held its breath, frozen in time. I knew exactly which coordinates the boat had reached. I needed to find the others. Now. But the second Miguel's backup arrived and he opened the door to our suite, Adonis would charm Miguel into telling him exactly where I went. I couldn't be here.

Trembling with fatigue, I made my way to the stairwell and headed down, clinging to the white railing. I'd gone two flights when my shaking legs called it quits.

"Okay, then." I leaned against the rail and looked around. I could hear people murmuring on deck, but no one occupied this strip of walkway. "Let's try this again." Swallowing hard, I dug my nails into the scabbed-over slice on my palm and dug deep until bright red blood welled up from the indentation. I held my sliced palm over the rail and watched as my blood dripped into the ocean. The water looked so still, I saw each red drop hit the water a ship's length below. *Poseidon*, I focused my thoughts. *It's an emergency.*

Nothing happened. Minutes ticked by, and my concern grew into alarm. *I'm ready to call in a favor,* I added in desperation.

Still nothing. I repeated the ritual out loud with no better luck.

Persephone? I sent a prayer her way. *It's important.*

Nothing. "Okay, think, Aphrodite." *Something* had obviously happened last night. "They can't be dead." I'd feel my bond of fealty snap if something had happened to Persephone. As for Poseidon, a realm ruler's death was not a subtle event—there would be echoes of their death and realm-wide chaos.

My mind flashed to the tilting of the boat and the wild storm last night, but I dismissed the thought. Storms were common. Terrifying, if you happened to be out on a boat and locked in a room, but the chaos that reigned when a realm ruler died was the stuff of legend, not simple nightmares.

I'd *know* if Poseidon had died. Unless, of course, Poseidon had pulled a Demeter and willed all of his power to someone else. But the only person he would trust enough to give all his power to would be Persephone, and she wasn't answering either.

Ares! Hades! Artemis! Athena! I went through the list of every living deity I could think of. Nothing.

"Okay. . . . Now what?" I chewed my lip, drumming my fingers against the metal bars. Maybe Artemis and Ares had kept their heads down last night to keep their cover intact. If I—

"Aphrodite?" Adonis's voice filtered down from somewhere above me. I froze, holding my breath. He knew me, knew that, given a choice, I'd venture outside rather than stay in the stifling boat. Moving as quietly as I could, I opened the door and slipped inside, stumbling toward the dark staircase leading to the lower decks.

Sobbing filled the stairwell. Snatches of angry, frustrated, and frightened conversations flowed past me as I descended the steps. The lower I went, the darker the boat became. I couldn't see anything. The disembodied voices sent shivers up my spine. Or maybe that was the fever.

I groped my way along the stairwell, my hands on the wall as I shuffled forward until my toes touched the edge of the next step. There was something creepy about wandering around the cruise ship in the dark. Just knowing how many people were on board with me, many of them demigods intent on my destruction, how small this boat was compared to the ocean, and how *dark* this stairwell looked—it all pressed against me. Tangible fear. I'd never felt claustrophobic or suffered panic attacks before Adonis drugged me. But now, I felt like I was suffocating. Choking on air smelling of chemicals and mildew, sweat, and salt.

Somehow, I made it to Elise's room, hoping against hope Artemis would be there. If anyone needed to know the demigods were behind all the trouble, it was the deities impersonating demigods.

I pushed up the sleeves on Ares's jacket and pounded on the door for a solid minute, each knock louder and more desperate than the last. "Come on, come on. Open the door!" All the physical and emotional exertion was catching up to me, and my adrenaline high was wearing off. My head spun as I slammed my fist against the door one last time. "Come on!"

The door next to hers opened. Sunlight spilled into the dark hall, revealing an annoyed old man in a bathrobe with three long white hairs atop his head. "Would you cut that out," he snapped, glowering at me through wrinkled flesh. "Obviously, there's no one. . . . Honey, are you all right?" He seemed to actually see me for the first time.

Gods, how bad did I look if *that* was the reaction I kept getting?

"S-sorry," I stammered, backing away.

"Wait," he called after me as I made my way down the hall, but I ignored him. I was far beyond the help of mortals.

I found Tantalus's room and knocked. Warm and welcoming sunshine spilled into the hallway, bathing me in light when the door swung open. "Hey there." Ares had really done his homework in mimicking Tantalus's facial expressions. That familiar sideways grin lit up his golden face.

"Ares!" I threw my arms around him, so relieved to find him safe that for a second, my fever didn't matter. "Oh, gods. I was getting so scared. I can't find Poseidon, or Persephone, or Artemis, or *anyone* else. What happened?" I drew back an arm's length. "Actually, never mind, we have to get everyone together *now*."

"Whoa, whoa." He leaned back, ready to pull free of my embrace until he noticed to what extent I clung to him to stay on my feet. "Are you okay?"

I shook my head. "The demigods aren't missing, Ares, they're conspiring against us. They've got weapons and poison, and Adonis—" My throat constricted when I thought of Adonis. "He *knew*. He knew the whole time. I left him shielded in the room. Once we get the others, he can tell you the whole story."

"He knew what?" Ares shifted his grip on me as he locked the door. "Hang on, what about the demigods? Does this have anything to do with the power going out?"

"I don't know." I shrugged, wondering why he'd bothered to lock the door instead of putting up a shield. *'Cause Tantalus wouldn't be able to?* "You can drop the cover, Ares, there's no point. What *happened* last night? Where are the others?"

"They're just through here." He motioned past the entryway.

Through here? Why would they be hanging out *here?* I pulled free of Ares and rounded the corner. "Ares, you have no idea wha—" The room was empty.

He'd lied.

Not possible. Gods can't lie.

Demigods can.

Tantalus? But I saw Persephone 'port Tantalus away. I saw it. He was in the Underworld. Even if he'd somehow managed to get through Tartarus and escape, how could he possibly have found his way back onto a moving ship?

I felt him approach behind me. "You're going to—"

I closed my eyes, my stomach twisting as I thought of Adonis's charm avoidance game from last night. *Clap three times.* I pushed past the pain and fatigue to explode into action.

Gods, how many warnings had I missed? I snatched one of the blue sea foam paintings off the wall, ready to slam the heavy frame into his skull.

He dodged, not surprising given I was fighting blind. The painting crashed to the floor, glass frame shattering upon impact. "Fine," Tantalus groused. "We'll do this the hard way." Pain exploded across my face. He struck me hard enough to make me see stars, and I cried out in shock as I stumbled backward. But I didn't open my eyes.

His hands closed on my shoulders and he slammed me against the wall. I kneed him in the stomach and slipped free of his grasp, scrambling to get to the door. He knocked me to the floor. "Look at me," he shouted, his weight crushing me against the carpet.

"No!" My fingers closed over a piece of the shattered glass. I jabbed Tantalus somewhere in the torso, slicing open my own hand as I did so, and he grunted and loosened his grip. I pushed myself to the side, taking him with me as I rolled off the carpet and into the entryway. Gripping his hair, I slammed his head against the marble floor, over and over again, until his body went limp beneath mine.

Oh, gods. I took a deep breath and opened my eyes to the room swirling around me. *Stay conscious*, I ordered myself. It was easier said than done. I'd been in bad shape before I cast a shield, ran all around the ship, and fought off a demigod.

I needed to warn the others while I still could. *One divine cause of death coming up.* I grabbed a shard of glass and pressed it against Tantalus's throat. His eyes flew open.

"Stop," he ordered.

I dropped the glass and scrambled off him. "I'm sorry, I'm sorry, I'm so sorry." What had I been thinking? Why would I hurt him?

He winced as he pushed to his feet. I moved forward to help him and he grabbed me by the collar of Ares's jacket and slammed me into the wall. "Look at me, you stupid slut!"

Look at him, such a simple request. I'd never look away unless he asked me to. Why would I want to?

"Tantalus!" Adonis pounded on the door.

"When I'm done," Tantalus growled.

His fist slammed into my face, then into my gut. He punched me over and over again, his eyes wild with anger. Dimly, I was aware of Adonis screaming at a crew member to hurry up and open the door. The keycard beeped, the door flew open, and still I looked at Tantalus, desperate to do whatever he asked.

"Stop!" Adonis's voice sounded hoarse from screaming. He pulled Tantalus away from me, and I dropped to the ground, my eyes still desperately searching for him.

"Oh, gods, oh, gods." Adonis brushed hair from my face, his voice hitching in panic. "What did you do?"

"She legit just tried to slit my throat," Tantalus yelled. "You had one job,

Donnie. Just one job. Keep her"—he jabbed a finger toward me—"out of the way, and we'd leave her out of it."

"Look at this," Tantalus continued, lifting his shirt to inspect the damage. "She stabbed me. And probably gave me a concussion. Come on. Give me a hand. We can lock her up with the other ones."

Adonis tilted my chin up, his fingers probing my throbbing face. I tried desperately to see around him to Tantalus. "He—Gods, what did you do to her? The gods are going to kill us all for this. They're never going to stop."

"Stay still," Tantalus commanded me when I flinched away from Adonis. "There's no need to worry about the other gods. By the time we're finished with them, they'll be as helpless as she is." He motioned to me, and I concentrated on staying very, very still. But it was getting hard to hold my breath. My lungs felt like they were about to burst. "Hey Donnie, wanna see something cool?" He waited until he had Adonis's attention, and then looked to me. "Drop dead."

"No!" Adonis's face contorted with fear. His fingers bit into my shoulders, yanking me into his arms. Then everything went black.

Chapter XXXI

"COME ON!" A familiar voice cried, hands pushing down on my sternum with bruising force. His mouth covered mine, and he exhaled. My hands twitched in a pathetic attempt to grab his shoulders and push him away. There was something about that voice, something important.

"Look, she moved!" Another voice came from my right side.

Elise?

"Can you hear us, Aphrodite?"

I managed to pry my eyes open, squinting against the harsh fluorescent light. Elise's gold eyes flicked over me, so full of concern, I opened my mouth to reassure her. But opening my mouth brought on a whole new world of pain. Oh, gods, every bit of me hurt.

Another face entered my field of vision.

Tantalus! I clamped my eyes shut and tried to scramble back but only managed some weak twitching.

"Is she seizing?" Elise demanded.

"Aphrodite?" Tantalus demanded. "Aphrodite? Look at me."

"N-no," I whimpered, panic flooding my chest as his hands closed on my shoulders. "No!" I batted weakly at his arms. He would control me, remake me, hollow out my insides and turn me to a living doll. There'd be nothing left of me, nothing left. "Please, no!" A hysterical sob caught in my throat. I wouldn't go through that again.

Elise sounded truly panicked now. "Is she—?"

"No, she has"—he sounded distracted as he gathered me to him—"nightmares, sometimes. It can take her a minute to come out of it." He made soothing noises and stroked my hair, warmth radiating from his fingers. "I've got you, love."

"Ares?" I whispered, not daring to open my eyes.

His arms tightened around me. "I've got you."

"Oh, gods," I gasped, clinging to him for all I was worth.

He held me just as tight. "I thought you were dead. I thought—"

"You *were* dead." The voice belonged to Elise, but the tone was all Artemis. "I've never seen anything like it. You had almost no power baseline, without CPR, you wouldn't heal. Every time we stopped—"

"Your heart stopped."

"How long?" I managed to ask.

Ares shook his head, but couldn't seem to manage a response.

"Hours," Artemis replied. "Glad you pulled through." She gave my shoulder a gentle squeeze before she stood. I felt her move away from us, but couldn't manage to turn my head to see where she went.

Hours. They'd kept me alive for hours. I drew in a deep shuddering breath. "Thank you."

Ares grinned. "Anytime."

With effort, I raised my head from his shoulder, taking in the metal walls and the barred doors of what appeared to be a prison cell. The entire cell looked maybe as long as two queen-sized beds from base to headboard, and wasn't much wider. Three of the walls were solid metal, and the fourth was made up of actual prison bars. Through the bars was a small hallway, empty except for a wooden desk shoved up against a cell identical to ours on the other side.

"I can't heal him." Artemis's whisper drew my attention to the corner opposite mine where she knelt over a blood-soaked Adonis. "Are we shielded? I'm not sensing anything."

Adonis. Blood matted his gold hair to his head. The skin splitting along his cheek, temple, and jaw seemed more the result of the swollen tissue bursting free than blows. I remembered the look of horror on Adonis's face when Tantalus told me to drop dead. Based on his injuries, I could guess what happened next.

The pressure of Ares's arms around me eased as he pushed to his feet. "I don't sense anything either." He knelt down and placed his hand on Adonis's forehead, then frowned. "That's weird."

I stayed cemented to my corner, unable to tear my eyes off the demigod. He'd drugged me, betrayed my trust, lied to me, and gods knew what else. But this? I never wanted this.

I must have made a sound, because Ares glanced over and flashed me a reassuring grin. "He looks worse off than he is. Demigods heal, too. It just takes longer. We can speed that up—" He glanced around the cell furtively. "He's not as bad off as you were. Once we get out of here, he'll be good as new."

Artemis paced the cell, running her hand along the metal wall. "Last thing I remember before waking up here, was settling into the room. Someone must have 'ported in behind me, but—" She pitched her voice so low, I almost couldn't make out what she said. "I thought the rooms were shielded against teleportation."

"They were," Ares confirmed, dropping down to sit beside me. "Same thing happened to me. Whatever this is, shields don't stop them."

"Well, it definitely got a lot more up close and personal with you two." Artemis looked at me, her eyebrows arched in question. "You guys must have put up one hell of a fight."

They didn't know. Panic flooded my chest as I realized why they were still in their glamours, why they were whispering. They thought the plan had worked. They'd impersonated their demigods and been captured. Now they were waiting to see what information they could glean before calling in the cavalry or 'porting out. They didn't realize they were trapped.

Adonis groaned, and I jumped. Ares followed my gaze to Adonis and his eyes narrowed. "Aphrodite?" Ares tilted my chin up, wincing at the blood and bruising on my face. "What happened?"

"He—" I struggled to form words to explain that Adonis had betrayed me. But he'd tried to save me, too. There were two conflicting images of him in my mind—one reaching out an arm to embrace me, the other offering me poison—and I couldn't reconcile that they were both true.

Taking a deep shuddering breath, I adjusted Ares's jacket and recounted everything that happened since I got on the boat. *Everything.* The clues and warnings seemed glaringly obvious to me now, but I'd missed them before, so I didn't dare leave anything out.

"Well, crap." Artemis rocked to her feet. "*That* changes things. Drop your glamour, Ares. If we don't make it out of this, we don't need them using our bodies to justify their war."

Ares dropped his glamour, but didn't say anything. He hadn't said a word through my entire story, though his arm around me went rigid about midway through.

"This is still Poseidon's realm," she continued, circuiting the cell, searching for any weakness in the structure. "So we can't teleport out. If Poseidon could trace us, he'd be here by now."

Realm rulers could typically sense an unauthorized deity in their realm. Given how sparsely populated Poseidon's realm was, and our general need to breathe, finding us shouldn't be hard.

"They're not responding to casual summons, so either the others are preoccupied," Artemis continued, "or we're off the map. I guess the only way to call in the cavalry"—she stopped in front of Adonis and knelt down—"is to use a summons they can't ignore."

A divine cause of death. "Don't," I protested.

Artemis looked up in surprise. "Are you kidding? He completely took advantage of you. He *drugged* you. He lied and—"

"I know," I managed to whisper. Gods, moving hurt so bad. "But . . . look what they did to him. They aren't treating him like an ally. If he's really against them, we need to know what he does."

"For all we know, they can heal," Artemis argued. "I know it looks like he tried to help you in the end, Aphrodite. I get that. But he didn't tell you about the poison until after you found it. He didn't make it to Tantalus's room until *after* you were under his control. They. Can. Lie." She met my eyes. "I know you want to believe in him, but we can't risk it."

"Let him live." There was no inflection in Ares's voice. No emotion at all.

"But—"

"He could be a trap either way, Artemis. We can't summon Persephone into this until we know what we're dealing with."

"She can teleport right back out," Artemis protested. "*With* us."

"Not with all of us."

With a twist of my stomach, I realized he was right. The last time Poseidon had teleported with me, I'd stopped breathing. And at that point, I hadn't consumed a fraction of the poison I had in my system now. Every time I used my powers, I got worse, and anytime anyone else used their powers on me, worse didn't even begin to describe it.

But Persephone would never leave without me.

Artemis narrowed her eyes as she thought over everything I'd just told her, letting out a string of curses when she realized Ares was right. "Okay, new plan. I'm going to try to dreamwalk, see if I can reach anyone. If anything here changes . . ."

"I'll wake you," Ares promised.

Chapter XXXII

ARES FLEXED HIS arm behind my back, groaning as he stretched. We sat in the corner, angled so we could see the whole cell and the hall outside. A few feet to our right, Artemis slumbered, trying to dreamwalk.

I winced, scooting forward so Ares could shift positions, but he stopped me, his hand falling back over my shoulder. "You don't have to keep—" I paused, trying to find a way to say the right words without implying I didn't want him touching me. "I mean—"

"Sorry." Ares dropped his hand from my shoulder. "It's just . . . my token."

"*Oh.*" I slipped my arms free of the jacket with a pained hiss, but Ares's hands shot out to stop me.

"No." A thinly veiled undercurrent of panic laced his tone. Ares tugged the jacket back over my arms. "For all we know, it's the only thing—" He started to move away from me, but I stopped him.

"Don't. Please? I didn't—I didn't mind. I just thought . . ." Bracing myself against the pain, I turned my back to him, angling myself into the corner so the entire length of the jacket pressed against him, then wrapped his arms around me. "Is that comfortable?"

I felt the smile in Ares's voice. "Yeah. It is. Thank you."

I closed my eyes. He was thanking me for sharing his token with him. "This is all my fault."

"Hey. No, it's not." Ares moved in front of me so he could see my face. "I'm going to do everything I can to get us out of this, okay?"

"I keep *hurting* people. Gods, no wonder—" I swallowed hard.

"No wonder what?"

I couldn't stop shaking my head. Every word I said to him tore out of me from some deep, painful place I didn't want to acknowledge. I didn't want to care this much. I didn't want to *be* this needy. But I couldn't seem to pull myself together.

"No wonder what, Aphrodite?"

"You left," I whispered, hating how broken and pathetic my voice sounded. "What I am—What I did—I told you everything, Ares. *Everything* Zeus did to me. Everything he made me do and—"

"*No.*" Ares shook his head. "You were a tool, Aphrodite. You had about as much agency as a loaded gun in the hands of a killer. *Nothing* he made you do was your fault. I don't blame you."

"—and you left."

"It wasn't you." The heat of his hands burned through the jacket. "I promise, it wasn't you."

"I know. It was him. But it's like you said, I can't—It's not something I can fix. And it hasn't stopped with his death. I keep—People keep using me to hurt my friends. You're stuck here because of me. If I'd figured this out faster, if I'd let Poseidon—"

"None of us saw the demigods coming. Hey, hey. Look at me." He waited until I made eye contact before continuing. "What Adonis did to you, what Tantalus did . . ." A muscle twitched in his jaw. "That's on us. You took a risk, and walked into a situation none of us understood, to protect *us*. You could have left when things got scary, but you didn't. For *us*. You've done your part. Now it's our turn. And if we fail, if this ends badly, that's on us."

He touched my chin to stop me from shaking my head, careful to avoid the worst of the bruising. "You got to the bottom of this, something none of the rest of us managed, at *great* personal cost. And as for Zeus . . . you keep focusing on what he made you do, not what you *chose* to. You turned on him, knowing he could kill you with a word. You resisted him, knowing he would retaliate." Ares's throat bobbed when he swallowed. "You are bold, and beautiful, and *brave*. And leaving you that night was the stupidest thing I've ever done. But it wasn't because of you."

"Then why?" My voice sounded hoarse.

"I left because—" He broke off, his hands falling away from me, and when he spoke again, I heard centuries' worth of pain and baggage weighing down his voice. "Zeus destroyed us, Aphrodite. The way he used us, the things he made us do. They weren't our fault. But if you let them haunt you, if you can't make them stop, then eventually, they change you. Make you someone you'd never recognize. But you're new." He pulled away from me. "You had a chance, Aphrodite. To heal. You were just starting to piece yourself back together again."

"Ares . . . ," I breathed.

"I couldn't do that to you. I couldn't hurt you. Because, when I look at you, I see everything he did to me. And I can't make that worse for you. It feels like I—" He drew in a deep breath. "I break everything I touch. I couldn't—I didn't want to hurt you."

I closed my eyes, remembering all the myths that said how disgusted Zeus was with Ares. I remembered all the horrible visions I'd seen when Ares first introduced himself. The battles, the bloodshed, the screaming people with melting faces. Zeus made him War. He took his kindest, gentlest son, and he made him War. "Gods," I whispered, horrified.

Persephone and I had been at Zeus's mercy for what? A year? Two, between the both of us? Ares and the others had suffered at his hands for millennia; thought Zeus was dead for centuries. Then, all of a sudden, he came back again to terrorize the gods. Killing his children left and right, and forcing them to bow down to him. I'd been so focused on what Persephone and I had gone through, so focused on what we'd survived, I'd never considered what a nightmare Zeus's return was for the others. What his death brought back to the surface.

I think, Persephone's voice echoed through my mind, *maybe he doesn't feel like he has a right to be . . . upset, or whatever, because what I went through was worse. Only it doesn't work like that.*

Gods, I was such an idiot. Such a selfish idiot. I leaned into Ares, tucking my arms around him, and tilted my chin up so I could whisper in his ear. "You could never break me." I was done giving anyone that kind of power. "But it's okay if you're not ready for this. For us." I kissed his cheek.

He turned his face toward me, his lips brushing against mine. He kissed me gently, his motions featherlight to let me know I could draw back at any time. And I did what he'd done so many times for me—held him until he could pull himself together enough to stand on his own feet.

Chapter XXXIII

SOMETIME LATER, Artemis opened her eyes. "I found them," she announced. "They're looking for us. But Poseidon thinks we must be shielded, because he can't sense us."

"We need to get out of here. Signal them somehow." I stood, then realized what a *bad* idea that was.

Ares jumped to his feet, reaching out stabilize me. "Easy."

Artemis gave me a level look. "I mean, we haven't *not* tried that in the hours we've been here."

"Fair enough." I winced as Ares lowered me to the ground.

"How are we going to do this?" Artemis asked in an undertone.

Ares shushed her, but not before I figured out what she meant. Even if they did escape, they couldn't get far with me. I drew my knees to my chest, wincing at the pain, and did my best to not pass out or throw up all over the cell.

Adonis groaned, drawing all of our attention like a magnet.

"Told you he'd heal," Ares murmured, shifting in front of me.

"What happened?" Adonis's voice sounded thick. "Aphrodite—Is she—"

"Dead?" Artemis crossed her arms. "She was, technically."

Ares's fist clenched and unclenched. "Near as I can figure, when Tantalus told her to drop dead, she wasn't strong enough to swear over her powers, so she went for the more mundane death of stopping her heart. Lucky for you, he never said how long she had to stay dead and she had enough power left to heal the damage once we brought her back."

Why would that be lucky for Adonis? I glanced up and caught the murderous glare in Ares's eyes. *Oh.*

Adonis coughed, a wet hacking sound that left me wondering if Tantalus had done more damage than I'd thought. He looked over at me, waiting until I met his eyes. "Glad you're okay."

"You don't get to look at her," Artemis explained, kneeling in front of the demigod. "Look at me. And if you try to charm me, Ares will snap your neck. We clear?"

"Clear," Adonis agreed.

"Aphrodite said you were going to tell us everything? Now would be a good time."

Adonis swallowed hard and recounted his side of events. "No one was supposed to get hurt," he said, wrapping up. He pushed up into a sitting position. "But Tantalus has completely lost it. It's the curse. He's been babbling about furies and—"

"Wait, the Cursed House of Atreus?" I interrupted. "I thought that was ancient history."

"It is. That story *ended* with Orestes," Artemis said, referring to the last cursed descendent in the House of Atreus, and Tantalus' distant descendent.

"It did," Adonis agreed. "For Tantalus' descendants."

Ares froze. "Wait, are you saying he's *the* Tantalus?"

Adonis nodded. "And here I thought you guys knew everything?"

"There are limits," Artemis said distractedly. "If another god withholds the information, it doesn't travel down the bloodlines. And we're not omniscient. I can't tell you what you had for breakfast yesterday, what you're thinking, or whether you'll be alive in an hour. But if you invented something, I'd know how to use it."

Adonis considered that for a moment, then continued. "Tantalus was cursed with immortality with a sadistic twist. Drinking makes him thirstier, eating makes him hungrier. And every now and then, it all kind of drives him insane. His mind heals eventually. For a while, at least."

I knew that curse. It was one of Demeter's favorite standbys. "He doesn't look particularly starved."

"Zeus countered the curse," Adonis explained. "It doesn't change the way Tantalus feels, but his body can process food and drinks."

"Why would Zeus counter the curse?" Artemis asked.

"In exchange for his daughter."

"His daughter?" I interrupted.

"Niobe. She and Zeus had fourteen children. Seven sons, and seven daughters. And each of those daughters—"

"Had more daughters with Zeus," I said, realizing where this was going.

Adonis nodded. "For generations. But then a couple of years ago, Zeus decided we were strong enough to steal our powers back through fealty. He started murdering us. Tantalus, Jason, and Narcissus banded together and started DAMNED to find the descendants, and protect as many of them as they could find."

"Where are they based?" Ares demanded. "What—"

"This trip was all about recruiting me and Elise," Adonis interrupted. "I got the sales pitch, but not much else in the way of details. Especially since I made it pretty clear I wasn't interested in joining any group Tantalus was a part of. I met him a couple of years ago when he just got into modeling. I didn't get the whole backstory then. We didn't exactly didn't get along."

My mind flashed to Tantalus's comment about Adonis's little sister being a great lay and auditioning for a role on *Teen Mom*. Not getting along seemed like a pretty massive understatement.

"Jason asked me to hear them out, and in terms of gigs, the cruise didn't suck. I didn't actually plan on joining them. The only reason I even knew about the weapons is because she showed up." He motioned to me.

"Back up." I rubbed my forehead, trying to keep all the names straight. "You've mentioned Jason a few times now. Who is he?"

"He's—"

Down the hall, a door slammed. Artemis stepped between me and the bars, Adonis pushed himself to his feet and more or less shambled to the front of the cell, and Ares pulled me off the ground and placed me in front of him so I faced away from the bars.

I collapsed against him. "If they dosed you, you might not be immune to his charm, either of you." I lifted my head, intending to look to Artemis to make sure she heard my warning, but Ares stopped me.

"We know." He tilted my chin up and met my gaze.

"Now that you're all up."

I glanced over my shoulder as Tantalus came into view, carrying an ancient-looking spear in one hand.

Ares jerked my chin back to him.

"We can get started."

All up? How would he know?

Ares read the confusion in my face and glanced up, casting a significant look at a small black dome hanging from the ceiling. I'd mistook the camera for a burnt-out light. He'd been watching us. Did he have audio, too?

"Recognize this, Ares?" Tantalus asked. "Agamemnon ripped it from your hands at the fall of Troy. He was strong, so strong. But it wasn't enough to save him."

"You," Ares said to Tantalus, keeping his eyes locked on mine, "are either the bravest, or the stupidest demigod I've yet to encounter."

"And that's saying a lot," Artemis added. "We knew Hercules."

Tantalus ignored them. "Adonis. You're looking better. So either the compound doesn't work on demigods, or we need to up your dosage. Interesting implications, either way."

"What dosage?" Adonis's voice became wary.

"You betrayed our cause. So we're using you to test the chemical compound's effectiveness on demigods who prove unworthy of their powers."

"You're doing *what?*" Adonis demanded.

I resisted the urge to comment on Adonis's apparent shock and horror at the prospect of being drugged.

"Compound?" Ares's dark eyes flickered, and I yanked on the neck of his shirt to keep his gaze down. "What sort of compound?"

"Oh, it's quite remarkable." As Tantalus spoke, I winced at the distinct sound of metal scraping against the floor. "Our scientist broke down some of the more unusual properties of adamantine. It takes power to invoke, but we have that, so it was just a matter of isolating the isotopes that acted as a catalyst for the severe reaction your kind experiences upon contact." He sounded so smug, I itched to punch him. "I'm sure you've all noticed the effects by now. We developed a highly effective lipid soluble solution for the perfect desired outcome."

I snorted in disgust. "Do you actually understand any of that, or are you just parroting what you've been told?"

"Was my explanation too complex?" Tantalus asked, his tone snarky. "Sorry, I forgot I was talking to Goddess Barbie."

"Desired outcome?" Ares interjected before I could come up with a witty response. "Which was . . . ?"

"To leave you powerless, of course." Tantalus seemed surprised we hadn't put that together, as if the answer should be obvious. "There are some in our number who don't want to resort to anything as drastic as murder, but you've proven you can't be trusted with your powers."

"Not the recruitment pitch," Ares snapped. "You have to know we die without powers; you've been around too long not to have picked up on that. But you've got Steele, which is a much easier way to kill us. So, why all the rigmarole?"

"Oh, we couldn't actually remove your powers," Tantalus explained. "We divert them. The compound works to break you down from the inside out, and your powers work to heal you. Our scientists discovered your powers *always* prioritize keeping you alive, whether you wish to use them for something else or not."

And how did their scientists do that? Maybe Zeus wasn't the sole reason so many gods had gone missing last year.

Oblivious to my thoughts, Tantalus continued. "It's involuntary, like a heartbeat. The process is certainly not painless, but it is temporary."

Not entirely. Lipid soluble meant the drugs dissolved in fat, so while the brunt of the impact would be felt right away, the compound could take months, possibly even years, to get completely out of our systems. But none of that changed the fact that if the compound was based in Steele, I should have been dead ten times over. *Unless the Steele they make isn't deadly.* When a *god* imbued Steele with powers, all hell broke loose. But demigods had never made the weapons before.

When Ares tensed, I realized that focusing on how they could or couldn't kill us was thinking too small. *Why* bother with temporary measures when their concern seemed to be that we couldn't handle power at all? The demigods didn't want us dead, and they didn't want us powerless. They wanted us controlled. We could be charmed if we were powerless, and forced to make promises we'd be bound to keep when our powers returned.

"Well . . ." Tantalus dragged the word out as if a thought had just occurred to him. Maybe he wasn't familiar with the sensation. "There is a caveat. We have to be very careful how much of the compound we administer. Otherwise, you might not have enough power to heal. But over the last few days, we've gotten a much better idea how much you guys can take. Thanks for nearly overdosing, Aphrodite. You provided some very valuable data. Or should I be thanking you for that, Adonis?"

"Go to hell," Adonis barked.

"Been there, didn't take. Jason will be along soon with some of our scientists to take you all to another facility. In the meantime, there is one more test I'd like to run. You see, I promised the scientists a cadaver, and you went and brought it back to life. But I'm not picky."

A loud popping sound filled the cell, paired with a white-hot flash of lights and the scent of sulfur. Ares's gaze jerked toward the source of the commotion.

"Don't look," I yelled, grabbing his chin and trying to get his gaze back on me. But Tantalus's distraction had already done its job.

Tantalus laughed as Ares went still, his pupils widening. "Kill whichever one of them you want to live the most." He passed the spear through the bars.

Chapter XXXIV

"APHRODITE, RUN!" Artemis yanked me away from Ares so fast, I lost my balance and fell to the ground, landing eye level with the spent firecrackers near Tantalus's feet. *So that's what that noise was.*

The short goddess shoved her way between Ares and the bars in a desperate attempt to break Tantalus's eye contact before the charm took hold.

Run? Run where? I tried to get up. Oh, gods, I couldn't—I couldn't do this. My entire body sang with pain. I slouched against the wall, breathing in gasps as my vision clouded over.

Ares stood stock still, teeth clenched together, hand wrapped around the spear so tight his knuckles turned white. Every muscle in his body looked tense as he fought Tantalus's influence. His eyes darted to me, filled with panic.

I couldn't defend myself under normal circumstances, much less when I was half-dead from fever, beaten to a pulp, sore from CPR, and locked in a cage with nowhere to go. But then, I was a goddess. Even poisoned, we were a good bit more resilient than the average person. Maybe I could—

The average person would be dead five times over by now, the annoying side of my brain pointed out. I ignored my irritating logic. Acknowledging I wasn't just screwed, I was *super screwed* wouldn't help anything right now.

Never had I felt so keenly aware of the lack of space between four walls. I saw nothing to hide behind. Nothing to slow Ares down. Just a small stretch of empty space, illuminated by a harsh, flickering fluorescent light.

"Tantalus, why are you doing this?" Adonis's bruised and swollen face contorted in confusion as he glared Tantalus down. His might have been intimidating, if it hadn't been so obvious that his death grip on the cell bars was all that kept him on his feet.

"I told you, I needed a cadaver. But I'm pleased it worked out this way. Your girlfriend nearly broke the charm on the passengers we armed," Tantalus explained, passing something shiny and stake-like from one hand to the other. Olympian Steele. Great. If Ares failed to kill me, Tantalus would. "We need to see if breaking charm is possible with the right motivation. Also, we need a divine cause of death."

"Ares!" Artemis poked the war god in his eyes. "Snap out of it."

He winced, jerking backward and out of her reach, but the order had already been given, the charm already taken. Ares grabbed Artemis by the shoulders and moved her out of the way with a rough shove. His shaking hands filled me with hope.

"You don't want to hurt me." Conviction filled my voice. "I *know* you don't want to hurt me. Fight it, Ares. I know you can."

"Run," he managed to say between gritted teeth before he threw me across the cell. I slammed into the wall opposite Ares and slid to the floor, stars exploding across my vision.

Oh, gods. I pushed myself up on my arms, then collapsed. There was nowhere to go.

"Hey!" Artemis snapped her fingers in front of Ares's face. "You know who you should want to live the most?" She waited a beat. "You."

"Artemis!" I managed to rise to a crouch. "No!"

She ignored me. "You are the most egotistical deity I've ever met, and that's saying something. Admit it, Ares. You think you're our only hope of getting out of this. You can't be the hero if you're dead. If you die, you can't save us."

"Stop it!" My pulse pounded in my throat. If Artemis convinced Ares *he* wanted to live the most, Ares would kill himself. Ares couldn't die. None of us could die. We'd lived through Zeus. I wasn't going to sit here and let us get killed by some psychotic demigod.

Ares lunged forward, pushing Artemis out of the way with enough force to send her sprawling to the floor. In a matter of seconds, he cornered me.

"Yeah, kind of figured that was a long shot," Artemis muttered, brushing herself off.

"Stop this," Adonis demanded, turning to Tantalus in appeal. "If he could break the charm, he would have. Experiment over, okay?"

"Not necessarily." Beads of sweat shimmered on Tantalus's forehead with the strain of holding the charm, and I realized something.

He wasn't like Adonis. Zeus's "special" demigods grew stronger with every generation. Tantalus predated the whole experiment. He might have lived long enough to learn to control and perfect his charm, but he couldn't be strong enough to hold it for long.

"He could be faking." Tantalus continued. "The only way to know for sure is if he does something that can't be reversed. If he kills her, then—"

"Do you hear yourself?" Adonis yelled. "This is insane! Drugging people, knocking them out, throwing them in cages, *murder?* You can't—"

"They are not *people.*" Tantalus's eyes flared with indignation. "They are gods. *They* are wrong. Their very existence. The things they've done. *Everything* about them is wrong. How can you side with them?"

Ares came at me, his hand gripped tight on his spear. When Artemis threw herself at him, he slammed her into the wall with so much force, I knew he'd completely lost against the charm.

"Stop," I begged. "Ares, *please.*" I twisted out of the way with a scream and the spear struck the wall, jabbing deep within the metal and sticking there.

Adonis met my eyes. *Do something,* he seemed to say. He stood wheezing as he huddled against the bars, mere feet from me. But he might as well have been in another realm for all the help he was. I saw no hope in his expression, no strength. He just looked frightened and hurt. Tearing my gaze away from him, I looked across the cell to Artemis. She lay in an unconscious heap against the cell wall.

No help there. Only me.

My mind raced in a desperate attempt to find some way out of this. *Think, Aphrodite.* I watched Ares struggle to pull the spear free from the metal wall. The spear could cut through metal? Well . . . that opened up my options a bit. Turning so the bars were at my back, I watched as Ares ripped the spear free and ran toward me.

I waited until the last possible second then pushed myself out of the way. The tip of the spear slashed the iron of the bars like they weren't even there, creating a gash in the metal. Not a promising escape route. But if I could get him to hit the bars enough times . . .

Then the pain from rolling out of the way hit. Tantalus had done quite a number on me. When I moved, I felt things shift inside of me that shouldn't be able to shift. Slumping against the bars of the cell, I took deep breaths in a desperate bid to stop the room from spinning. I couldn't move anymore. "Ares, please. This isn't you."

To my left, Artemis groaned and sat up, cradling her head in her hands. Then she seemed to remember where she was and jerked toward Ares.

He held up the spear. The metal glittered in the fluorescent lights as the weapon thrust through the air. I closed my eyes.

"Aphrodite!" Adonis threw himself between Ares and me.

My eyes flew open in time to see the spear drive through Adonis's middle and into my side.

A scream bubbled up within me, but I couldn't seem to unlock my lips to let the sound out. I gasped as Ares wrenched the spear free. The pain felt so intense, I could see red bursts of anguish behind my eyelids. I sank to the floor, but somehow Adonis managed to stay on his feet.

"Stop." Adonis met Ares's gaze. "Don't—" He faltered, knees folding beneath him as he collapsed in a heap on the floor before me.

The charm snapped. Ares twisted, throwing the spear through the bars and into Tantalus's chest with eerie precision. Tantalus coughed, then fell forward.

"Artemis?" Ares called, rushing forward. He reached through the bars of the cell and grabbed the spear.

"Got it." Artemis grabbed the spear from him. "Help them!"

She didn't have to tell Ares twice. He rushed back to my side, dropping to his knees. "Aphrodite! I—I—" He looked more distraught than I'd ever seen him. He pulled his shirt off and moved to press it to my side, but I blocked his hand.

"Divine death," I managed to say, clutching Adonis closer to me. "Persephone." If Adonis died, she'd port in. Just because Tantalus was down for the moment, that didn't mean this place was safe. Ares and Artemis needed to wipe out any chance of a threat before she came here. "Havoc," I cried.

Chapter XXXV

ARES NODDED IN understanding, a grim expression on his face. "Pressure," he reminded me, pressing the shirt to my side and putting my hand over it. His voice sounded hollow as his words echoed through the metal cell, and my heart wrenched for him. For the guilt written across his face.

I break everything I touch, his voice whispered in my memory.

That's not fair, I wanted to tell him. *This wasn't your fault.* But I knew better than most how empty those words rang.

He glanced at Adonis one more time, then seemed to realize there was nothing he could do for him. He joined Artemis at the bars of the cell, took the spear, then

threw himself at the bars, sliding his spear against them. Artemis kicked the Olympian Steele from Tantalus's hand and worked on keeping him down while Ares broke down the door. The sound of metal slamming into metal filled the cell, and my chance to reassure him was lost.

My thoughts slowed and I knew I was in shock. Everything around me occurred in stop motion, like gruesome snapshots that came complete with scent and sound.

Warm liquid pumping from my side.

Ares breaking through the bars, blind with rage.

Adonis's blood soaking through my dress, plastering the fabric against me and the cold metal floor.

The copper scent overwhelming in this small space.

"Don't." Adonis lifted his hand to touch my cheek, and his fingers came away wet with my tears.

I hadn't realized I was crying. Hadn't realized the low, keening wail permeating through the room came from me. Hadn't realized I was capable. No, I couldn't trust him, and yes, I still felt furious with him, but not a single bit of that rage felt strong enough for me to want him dead. There's a league of difference between being angry at someone and hating someone enough to do nothing while they bled out. And that difference had nothing to do with the other person. "I should be able to heal you," I sobbed, clutching him tighter.

Adonis shrugged, the movement costing him. "Kind of fitting." He coughed, blood so bright it didn't look real bubbling from his lips. "After what I—" His eyes closed as he lost the battle with consciousness.

"You don't get to do this," I said, hating how my voice warbled. "Do you hear me? You don't get to *do* this." I'd spent a third of my life feeling indebted to him for saving me, and less than twenty-four hours hating him for poisoning me. I wasn't done being angry yet. I couldn't add guilt into the mix. Not on this level. I wouldn't be able to survive it.

He couldn't die. Not for me. He couldn't die.

A cell door slammed and I glanced up, surprised to find Tantalus slumped over in the cage across the hall. Given the lack of death deities or Reapers, Tantalus wasn't dead yet. "What are you doing? Why haven't you—?"

Ares slammed the door of the other cell and pocketed the key. "He's immortal," he reminded me. "And we can't break the immortality curse on Tantalus while the drugs are in our system. Persephone or one of the others will have to lift the curse. I need to make sure no one else is here. The demigods are armed, remember?"

He had a point. If they snuck up on us, it could be fatal.

"Artemis, go left?" Ares called.

"Yell if you need us," Artemis called over her shoulder, dashing down the hall.

"I'll be right back. Keep pressure on that," Ares motioned to my side as he headed down the hall in the opposite direction as Artemis.

The pain in my side when I did just that intensified beyond belief. I stared down at the streams of blood mingled together. The stuttering fluorescent light illuminated a warped reflection of the macabre scene in the growing pool of viscous fluid.

Blood.

I was a goddess. A drug *couldn't* change that. And now, thanks to Tantalus's bragging, I knew how the compound worked.

My powers weren't gone, just diverted, an involuntary reflex linked to healing. But gods didn't have truly involuntary reflexes. Powers weren't the only difference between god and man. We differed on a physiological level. We were fundamentally different beings.

And so were demigods.

My breath caught as I realized what I could do. Apotheosis had only been accomplished once before, and at great cost. But the process was possible. Even without my powers, because I didn't have mortal blood flowing through my veins. I had ichor.

And so did he. I just needed to activate the ichor in his blood and imbue it with divinity. He'd heal on his own because ichor was the frickin' blood of the gods.

Adonis shuddered in my arms, reminding me I didn't have much time.

Taking a deep breath, I called my powers up from deep within myself. With a grimace against the pain, I diverted my power away from keeping me healed. I dipped my fingers in my blood, then flicked droplets into his wound. My blood flowed into his, indistinguishable despite all our differences.

Now came the hard part. Focusing, I connected the ichor in our blood back to the Before. To a time of darkness and chaos and power. That void, that insanity, was my birthright because I was more than a daughter of Zeus. The blood of Chaos ran through my veins. The raw power of the primordial deities. And no one could take that from me.

Adonis's blood glittered, red flickering to molten gold. Bright light blazed from his wound, enveloping both of us. My hair floated in the light, and, for a moment, time seemed to suspend. Then the gold light sucked into his wound. The pigment leached from his skin, drawn inward to heal the damage within him, completing the transformation. I watched with a stunned fascination as his torn muscle tissue reconnected to his bone, and a sliced artery zipped closed with a golden shimmer. The light moved outward, healing everything in its wake until finally his skin knit together. His skin and hair turned sheet white. When his eyes fluttered open, they were pale silver.

"What?" he gasped, sitting up. "How?"

"You're a god," I managed to say, my vision wavering as I slumped over him, consciousness fleeing my body yet again. "I saved you." Now we were even.

Chapter XXXVI

I SHOULDN'T BE able to see my body, sagging against the wall or the blood, red and gleaming against the silver floor. As a rule, unconscious people don't see much, and I'd know, given the inordinate amount of time I'd spent unconscious lately.

But I saw it all through pale, silver eyes.

Aphrodite? Adonis thought, panic saturating his thoughts. He reached out, pale hands trembling as he shook my shoulder, as if he could just shake me back into my own head.

It's temporary, I assured him, curiously devoid of feeling. I felt relaxed. Untethered. *The "being in each other's heads" part only lasts a few minutes. Or at least, it had with Hercules. Then the connection will be reduced to powers flowing back and forth, and after that?* I gave the mental impression of a shrug. *You'll have yours and I'll have mine.*

You made me a god. His mind flashed back to our conversation about apotheosis. *You saved me. Why? I mean, I'm not complaining, but after what I did to you . . .*

I could feel the explanation he hoped for. The idea that saving him had been part of some grand romantic gesture, filled with forgiveness, love, trust, redemption, gratitude, and a thousand other meanings too loaded for one action to contain, glimmered in the corner of his mind. *I could love you.* His mind seemed to bleed the thought.

But then he untangled my thoughts from his own and saw the truth. There was a difference between being angry with someone and being spiteful enough to let them die. And the difference had nothing to do with what he'd done and everything to do with what I could live with.

I could feel the regret and pain swirling through his mind. The truth behind his intentions. His desperate need to make this right. I'd been there, and knew the feeling all too well. Maybe I could forgive him, but I couldn't trust him. And that meant I'd never be able to love him.

I had no choice, the thought looped through his mind, along with a million other justifications.

So I opened my mind and for one second let him feel exactly what it was like to have no choice. There was a world of difference between being conflicted and forced.

He pushed to his feet, staggering back from me, as though putting physical distance between us would somehow lessen the impact.

Don't talk to me about choices. I slammed a mental door on the memory.

Footsteps rounded the corner. Ares came running in, carrying a first-aid kit. He came to a full stop, staring at Adonis for a solid minute.

Artemis, coming from the opposite side, skidded to a halt beside him. "Did she—?" she asked.

Adonis held up his hands. "I didn't—"

"Brilliant," Ares said, sounding as though he meant it. He rushed into the cell, knelt beside my body, dropped the spear on the ground, and pulled bandages and gauze out of the first-aid kit.

Adonis slumped to the floor, relief flooding his mind.

What did you think was going to happen when they saw you? I asked.

More like when they saw you, he explained. Sudden death? I'm not an idiot, Aphrodite. If you die, somehow I doubt I'll be far behind you.

Artemis regarded him carefully for a moment, then seemed to decide he was surprised but not otherwise injured, and moved to Ares's side. "Brilliant? You're going to have to walk me through that one."

Ares tore a bandage. "The stuff he gave her—"

"That we really need a name for," Artemis added, taking the bandage from Ares and passing it beneath me to hand back to him.

"That we really need a name for," Ares agreed, unrolling more gauze from the first-aid kit. "Attacks her powers. If hers are in him . . ."

"They've got nothing to attack," Artemis finished, moving on to my face with an assortment of alcohol swabs and bandages.

"So long as he stays alive, anyway."

Adonis took a moment to digest that.

Can you look anywhere else? Watching them mop away my blood was a bit much.

Gladly. He glanced up at the ceiling, his gaze snagging on the camera. We're going to have to do something about that.

"Oh my gods!" Persephone's voice echoed through the cell.

Adonis jerked in surprise to find her standing at the entrance with Poseidon.

Where's Hades? I asked.

I don't see him.

Kind of my point.

"Ship approaching," Poseidon reminded Persephone.

That snapped her out of her shock. Persephone rushed to my side. "Let me—"

"Don't," Artemis and Ares exclaimed at the same time.

"You can't heal her," Ares continued. He caught her up, his eyes never once leaving me.

"Okay." Persephone stood, chin tilted up with determination. "So we can't heal her, and we can't teleport. We're going to need another way out of here."

"There's a ship approaching," Poseidon reminded her. "For all we know, it's full of armed demigods immune to everything we can throw at them. They"—his outswept hand took in Adonis, Artemis, and Ares— "aren't in any shape to make a stand. We have to get them out of here."

"So I should just leave her?" Persephone's green eyes narrowed. "Yeah, that's not gonna—"

"Yes." Ares glanced up. "You're going to leave both of us."

"What?" The word burst from Adonis, but I couldn't tell which one of us had spoken.

"She needs help. If they can get her to a hospital, then—"

"Why would they take her to a hospital?" Persephone demanded.

"They wouldn't. But Elise is a different story." As Ares spoke, his features shifted, his dark hair lightening to gold. Within seconds, he looked just like Adonis, pre-apotheosis. "I can't keep this up for long." He locked gazes with Persephone. "So I'm going to need your help. Can you make her look like Elise?"

No, I thought, realizing where Ares was going with this. Adonis didn't seem to hear me. Adonis, don't let them—

My—no, his—vision blurred for a moment, then went black.

"I thought using powers would hurt her," Persephone's voice objected. "I thought—"

My hearing cut out, but then all my senses kicked back in, like a television clicking back on after a power failure. Given Adonis's lack of concern, I realized this wasn't happening to him. The connection, this phase of it anyway, was fading.

"Internally," Ares explained. "External stuff like shields and glamours shouldn't affect her at all. Artemis, can you deal with the camera?"

"On it. Come with me." Artemis rushed out of the room, pulling Poseidon with her. "Just in case Ares missed someone."

Persephone knelt to the ground beside me.

"Perception only," Ares cautioned. "Not a full glamour. She's the right height and close enough in build. Given what she's been through, no one will expect her to carry herself the same way." A thought occurred to him and he turned to Adonis. "Can any of the demigods see through glamours?"

"No." Adonis struggled for words to explain. "Your powers don't work on us, erm, them. We can walk through a shield unharmed and any power you throw at us don't affect us, but we still don't see anything through shields or glamour until we pass through, or hear, or whatever. Perception-wise, we don't differ."

When Persephone touched me, I felt the glamour settle over me through a fog of unconsciousness.

No, I wanted to object, but the word wouldn't form.

"I'll make sure she gets help," Ares promised Persephone. "And I'll collect as much information as I safely can. But you have to keep up the glamours for both of us. Can you do that?"

"Yes. I mean—" Persephone hesitated. "For her, yes. She's still connected to me through the bond, but you . . . distance is going to—"

Ares didn't hesitate. "I swear fealty to you."

"They're coming." Poseidon's voice rang through the room, and I could hear Artemis just behind him. "We need to go."

"You up to teleporting?" Ares asked Artemis.

"It'll hurt like hell, but I'm pretty sure I'll survive it."

"Take her some place safe, one trip only. Oh, and Poseidon—" I felt Ares pick up the spear beside me. "I'm gonna need you to stab me."

The End

It's not easy being a goddess . . . and Aphrodite has it rougher than most.
Don't miss her upcoming adventures, amorous and otherwise.
Available in the fall of 2016, only from ImaJinn Books.

Acknowledgements

First, as always, thank you to my family—my daughter for the long hours playing quietly in her room pretending to train dragons, my husband for stepping in when that got boring, my mother for cheering me on and providing pizza when I forgot to cook dinner, my brother for taking the time to edit the audio book. It cannot be easy to listen to your little sister read romance. Thank you. Seriously.

Thank you to every member of the Robot Unicorn Cult (long story). You guys are the best writers' group. Thank you newest members for reading the entirety of my last draft and providing feedback: Kathryn Pagan, for worshipping at the altar of Hades and providing all the pertinent medical information, Alexa Roney, for your amazing research, Anderson Pope, for your insane attention to detail, and Jara Lane, for asking the questions that matter.

Thank you older members and members who have since moved far and wide who saw this story take shape in five thousand word increments: Dallas Bono, for shouting FIX IT! Angela Powell, for your insight, Michael Rupured for teaching me that "it is a missed opportunity", Misty Hawkins for bringing in reams of information when I most needed it, Amy Adams for your amazing copy editing, and Stephan Morgan for helping me in literally every way and for helping me make the most awesome query letter ever. There were many more Robot Unicorn Cultists who passed through our little group. You all helped this story come to be. Thank you.

Susan Sipal and Coreen Montagna, thank you for taking a last look at my content and copy before I took the plunge and sent it to BelleBooks. Kelly Johnson thank you for your beautiful illustrations. Amber Floyd and Jessica Jones, thank you for beta reading and providing awesome feedback about Adonis.

To the amazing staff at Bell Bridge, thank you for giving my books a new home when Musa closed its doors. Thank you even more for taking a risk on this expansion of the universe. Debra Dixon, thank you for Ares and for making my beginning and my plot a thousand times stronger. Deborah Smith, thank you for making Aphrodite more likeable. Brenda Chin, thank you for your patience with my endless questions and my infatuation with the word like and my many other flaws. Pam McCutcheon, thank you for being so amazingly thorough and for being so patient explaining all those little things I got hung up on.

Thank you Danielle Childers for the amazing social media art, Jenny McKnatt, Nikki Flowers, and Jeanna Paden for taking the time to answer every marketing question I ever sent.

Thank you, thank you, thank you. Aphrodite wouldn't be the amazing book it is without your help.

About the Author

Kaitlin Bevis spent her childhood curled up with a book and a pen. If the ending didn't agree with her, she rewrote it. Because she's always wanted to be a writer, she spent high school and college learning everything she could to achieve that goal. After graduating college with Masters in English, Kaitlin went on to write The Daughters of Zeus series. kaitlinbevis.com

Milton Keynes UK
Ingram Content Group UK Ltd.
UKHW010159061223
433783UK00003B/163